CITY IN
A FOREST

GINGER PINHOLSTER

Black Rose Writing | Texas

ISBN: 978-1-68433-318-9
PUBLISHED BY BLACK ROSE WRITING
www.blackrosewriting.com

Printed in the United States of America
Suggested Retail Price (SRP) $18.95

City in a Forest is printed in Plantagenet Cherokee

For Caroline, with love always.

Praise for *City in a Forest*

"I completed the reading of Ginger Pinholster's *City in a Forest* with the sense of gladness that always comes with discovering a new and talented writer ... Her use of language often begs for the awe of a re-reading. The plotting stays in focus. The tease of turning another page never falters. Recommended? Absolutely." —**Terry Kay**, *To Dance with the White Dog* and *The Book of Marie*

"*City in a Forest* engages us in the myriad ways that our ideas of home can keep us down, and lift us higher. An observant, compassionate debut." —**Jessica Handler**, *The Magnetic Girl*

"A laudable story with robust female characters and skillfully woven themes of race and gender." —*Kirkus Reviews*

"Ginger Pinholster, a master of significant detail, weaves her struggling characters' pasts, present, and futures into a breathtaking, beautiful novel ... *City in a Forest* is a lush, poignant, layered novel about the power of the past, and freeing oneself to build a better future." —*IndieReader (Approved Book)*

"Ginger Pinholster's first novel, with her insightful knowledge of downtown Atlanta, and of time and history passing, and of life itself, will make you proud of her effort and her talent." —**John Logue**, *Boats Against the Current*

"*City in a Forest* is a compelling novel addressing the complexities of racial inequities, friendship, child sexual abuse, and privilege intertwined with differing desires for a piece of land in Atlanta. Pinholster's lush descriptions and artful imagery enhance her skills in weaving distinct multiple narratives." —**Libby Ware**, *Lum: A Novel*

"This is a character-driven novel with a delightful, descriptive understanding of specific individuals ... While the plot of the novel twists like a kudzu vine and keeps the reader guessing, the heart of the novel is its memorable characters, characters that will tug at the readers' memories, good or bad, of real people in their own lives." —*Authors Reading*

CITY IN
A FOREST

1.
ARDEN COLLIER

On her breezy aquamarine porch, Arden ran a thumb over the letter's sinister return address, which featured an amateurish sketch of two crossed nails, reminding her of the county's plan to crucify her. Above her head, a wind chime trembled. A rooster-shaped weathervane turned in creaky circles on the roof. In the side yard, a glass menagerie hummed. The mangy lawn, surrounded by forest, sat lifeless. Her grandfather's half-bald chickens were long gone.

She opened red double doors and moved into her house, through a narrow maze of cardboard boxes. Plastic bags stuffed with clothes, furniture piled high with crushed paint tubes, broken picture frames, and half-finished charcoal drawings blocked her path. In the room she had at one point used as an office, she stepped over more boxes to reach a desk buried by paper.

After speed-reading the county's latest citation—this one demanding five-hundred dollars in fines—she placed it on top of the others, next to Jared Astor's letter asking to visit her studio.

For a moment, she rested her hands on the letters, pressing down as if they might fly off.

She picked up Jared's message again, typed and with his handwritten signature in looping black ink. She liked reading it, although she hadn't answered it—couldn't possibly invite a famous art dealer like Jared Astor to visit until she decided where to put everything she had been saving. The elegant cursive letters of his name made her think of his famous, mahogany-colored face above the tightly knotted purple tie he was always wearing on TV.

"An opening in the gallery schedule," the note said. "Curating a retrospective on Atlanta artists ... Impressed by your feminist take on African *dikenga* figures ... bold color choices ... call me at ... would like to visit your studio."

As she read his last line, her hands felt chilled where they were touching the thick paper with its distinctive watermark. No one had been inside her house since her husband Joel left. She returned Jared Astor's letter to the stack, climbed over a chair, and squeezed through a side door she couldn't fully open because of a rolled carpet that was pressed against it, too heavy to be moved out of the way.

She loved how the east wall of her house seemed to stretch on forever as she walked beside it: overlapping ivory planks, stained glass, and gingerbread trim in shades of rose and lilac. She stopped to remove her sneakers at the halfway point, near a basement door where her toes sank into a soggy patch of strawberries. The ground was wet because of an overflowing septic tank—the county's latest cause for concern. Below the back deck, she unlatched a purple gate, stepped into her sculpture garden, and blinked. Like kudzu vines, the menagerie had grown thick and tangled, impenetrable in spots.

My home, she thought.

Silver Park.

Atlanta.

Light sparkled through hundreds of antique blue, green, and red bottles arranged like delicate soldiers on shelves built into the garden's narrow brick entryway. Popping through it, she ducked under strings of sea glass and multicolored Christmas lights to survey her frozen ballet: bronze women on pedestals with outstretched arms and gaping mouths—dancing, giving birth, fighting, weaving—each separated from the next by waist-high walls painted orange and red, yellow and blue.

These were the *dikenga* figures she both loved and hated. They were her one claim to fame, completed many years earlier. Each wooden base told a story, intricately carved, about the bronze figure's history so that the top and bottom made up then and now, a complicated past segregated from the striving present. The life cycle, cut off from a future. On the surrounding walls, wobbly black brush strokes formed words too small to decipher from a distance.

"Racism," one said.

"Chasm."

"Prism."

A cloud flickered overhead. The garden dimmed. Wind rippled across the glass bottles, making them hum—a cascade of discordant notes that nonetheless fit together, like M.C. Escher's crazy upside-down staircases. She stepped into a gazebo, pulled open a blue curtain, and lashed it with her ex-husband's necktie.

Inside, wrinkled paint tubes, brushes, and strips of gauze were heaped onto a butcher's block along with a bucket of milky water, scissors, and an open jar of Vaseline. She perched on a stool, greased her face, and covered it with wet gauze. When she picked up the mirror, she was hidden, as usual, except for her eyes. Behind the mask, her pupils contracted to pinpoints surrounded by faint reddish-brown halos. Her long braids fell forward, sticking to the gauze. She inspected her teeth and flared her nostrils, momentarily happy with the effect until she looked at all the other plaster copies of her face, arranged in rows across the floor, one after another.

It had been a year since Joel moved away. Still, she couldn't seem to come up with new work. She had been stuck looking at her own face every morning, unable to decide what should happen next in her life, or with her art. Her last show had been badly reviewed. The critic's words still triggered a withering inside of her.

"Self-indulgent … It's like she's obsessively turning the same jewel over and over, refusing to let it go."

Idiot, Arden thought. *Stupid self-important narcissist.*

"She seems pinched."

Really? What the hell's that even supposed to mean? Misogynistic bastard. God forbid if she should try anything new, or ambitious, and fail to pull it off perfectly.

Each mask took at least an hour to dry, and longer than that before she could paint it. Arden lowered herself onto a damp armchair, careful to avoid the spots where rusty springs were erupting through the upholstery. Reaching into her satchel, she pulled a scarred scrapbook onto her lap. The words, "Our Family" were stamped across the cover under a faded pink ribbon that had come untied on one side. Leather crackled when she opened the book. She had thought of the scrapbook

3

last night, a second after her eyelids fluttered shut. Usually, she looked to history books for inspiration: the movement of Africans to America, the Trail of Tears, or Jim Crow.

Maybe it was time to look at her own history, finally, to learn what she had lost, and what was holding her back.

2.

PARKER GOZER

Parker's throat clenched, and in her mind, she was transported back to Atlanta, her hometown, the place that had tangled itself around her heart like flowering kudzu vines, achingly sweet as a beloved child, lost but never forgotten.

A paved road crumbled into gravel and dirt. She pictured Silver Park, vivid and noisy with birds all around the waterfall that was technically open to the public, but still mostly a secret. She imagined herself in another world and time, bright green with moss-covered trees, algae shining on wet rocks, and leaves crackling underfoot. She smelled smoke from a fire. Nearby, her childhood friend Arden's Great Aunt Wilma stirred a pot with a boat paddle. Sheets and shirts and underwear snapped on lines strung between trees.

In reality, she was stuck in her fishbowl office, twelve stories above street level in Washington, D.C. Sirens blared and protestors shouted below the windows while her boss, Dr. Tinley, explained why she would have to work late again. Parker sank deeper into her chair. She had promised to chauffeur her daughter's lacrosse team to a game.

"The deadline's tomorrow," Dr. Tinley said, clutching yet another research grant application—twenty-three pages of essay questions, boxes to be checked and long sections for filling in facts. His quiet, dignified tone almost made the demand sound reasonable. "The thing is, dear, the funder's going to stop by at four-thirty. I wish we could postpone it, but we need the support and we've been personally invited to submit this one. It's a wonderful opportunity for a nonprofit like ours."

The paper whispered in his sweet, wrinkled hands. A four-thirty meeting meant she would be trapped at work until five-thirty, after which she would be caged in D.C. rush-hour traffic. She might make it to Northern Virginia by seven-thirty, tops, if she got lucky. "I can't write anything else today," Parker said. "I need to take my daughter and her friends to a game. I'll be back bright and early tomorrow."

Below his caramel-colored eyes, a brittle smile formed. "I remember when my children were young, how hard it was to juggle everything."

Parker took the application and set it face-down in her to-do box. "Thanks for understanding. I'll get it done first thing tomorrow."

At street level, the protests intensified. She could hear the questions but not the answers. "What do we want?—*garble, garble!* When do we want it?—*garble!*" It had been going on all day. It was driving her crazy. What *did* they want? She knew what she wanted—more time with her daughter and an occasional whiff of fresh air. In all the years she had been working in D.C., she hadn't heard a single birdsong from her office, where the windows were sealed shut.

Dr. Tinley shifted his weight without turning to leave. The ultra-thin wool of his pearl-colored suit rustled. "I need you here to meet this funder," he said, mournful but resolute. "You're part of what we're selling. Nobody makes it rain like you do. That's well-known."

Parker's mind raced. If she couldn't reach her husband, she would have to call her best friend and self-appointed "Life Coach" Jolene. Maybe Jolene could pick up the girls. *Once again.* How many more favors could she ask of Jolene? Parker's mouth opened and closed, but no words emerged. She spread her fingers lightly across the application without touching it, as if it might be diseased and her job was to heal it. "I—I just can't do it. I'm sorry. It's my turn to chauffeur. I skipped my last turn. I promised the other parents I'd be there. The girls will be waiting for me."

Dr. Tinley stopped smiling. "Phone a friend. Ask your husband to leave work early."

"I could call into the meeting. You could put me on speaker phone." Parker imagined herself in the bleachers by Joie's sports field, struggling to hear the conversation through her earbuds, shouting into the phone while other parents glared.

"We both need to be here in person. This is a two-million dollar invited grant application we're talking about. Your ability to generate publicity is a big part of why they're interested in working with us. You know as well as I do that we're three months from closing our doors if we don't find more funding."

Parker sat up straighter. "What? No. I didn't know it was that dire, actually."

"I didn't want you to worry, dear, but yes, it is that dire, and if we go under, we'll all lose our paychecks. We also wouldn't be able to help people all over the world. I know you love your daughter, but think of that little girl we met in Nigeria, the one who was drinking water poisoned by oil flares. She needs you, too. You could tell your daughter what you're doing to help children like that. You would be her role model."

His liver-spotted hands and sing-song voice reminded Parker of her father before he died. She picked up the application and turned it right-side up, feeling defeated. She needed her paycheck, and his mention of Oba, the tiny girl with enormous brown eyes, made her chest ache. "I understand."

"That's my Parky," Dr. Tinley said, mangling her name, as usual. He either couldn't pronounce the second R, or he thought of "Parky" as an affectionate nickname, or maybe he had once owned an obedient dog by that name. "You're the best public relations director I've ever met. Everybody says so. I mean it. I'm lucky to have you."

From Parker, a rogue laugh escaped, half-snorted. "I'd say so." *Which is why you need to pay me a lot more than you do,* she thought.

"Come to my office a few minutes early. Don't be late."

"No sir. Never."

When he was out of earshot, Parker lowered her head onto her desk, tapped it lightly against the glossy wood, and groaned. She tried calling her husband Beamer, but he almost never turned on his silly Radio Shack flip-phone—it was an issue—and she got voicemail at his work number. With construction jobs in a slump, he hadn't been spending much time in his office lately. Jolene also didn't pick up or answer a text message. Parker left messages for three other parents, but after fifteen minutes of agonized waiting, she hadn't heard from anyone. Probably they were all ignoring her, given her track record as a no-show for carpool duty.

She fished two twenty-dollar bills out of her wallet and walked down the hall to see her work friend, Liam.

He was watering one of his many pink and white orchids, which lined the windowsill of his corner office, with its stained-glass table lamp and red shag rug. When she waved the cash at him, he stopped, set down the pitcher and parked his knuckles on his hips. He was wearing vintage purple corduroy slacks with a matching blazer and a rose-colored tie. "Oh, my," he said. "Are we going to the casino?"

"I know it's a lot to ask," Parker began.

"Then the answer's no. I mean, if it's a lot to ask." Liam sat down, deadpan, and he crossed his legs, exposing royal blue socks dotted with stylized green sea turtles.

Parker folded the twenty-dollar bills over three times. She pictured Joie's heart-shaped face, contorted with worry while she looked and looked for Parker, who wouldn't be there. She hoped Liam didn't notice the slight tremor in her chin. "Okay."

"Ha," Liam said. "Girl, stop it. You know I'm kidding. What's going on?"

"I'm stuck here until dinnertime. I have to be in a meeting with this new funder, and after that, I have to write a whole grant application. The boss wouldn't let me off the hook."

"So, a typical Tuesday at the office," Liam said, smiling while he plucked lint off his socks. "What's different this time?"

"I'm supposed to pick up Joie and her team at three-thirty and get them to the lacrosse field. I've begged off carpool duty for a solid month. I can't reach Beamer or any of the other parents. The girls are going to be sitting there, waiting for me."

Liam made a *tsk-tsk* sound, rubbing one pointer finger over the other one like he was trying to start a fire. "You're a bad, bad working mommy. You're probably going straight to hell."

"That's definitely how I feel, like I can't win."

Clapping his hands, Liam stood up and kissed her cheek with a flourish. "Leave it with me. I love that little princess more than rainbow sprinkles on chocolate ice cream."

Her shoulders collapsed with relief. She shoved money into his hand. "I'm compensating you for this. I insist."

Liam shoved back. "Oh, good grief, no. What do you think I am, a stripper? Put your money away. Seriously, this is what friends are for."

"I feel badly. It's such an inconvenience for you."

Liam took hold of Parker's fingertips. "Let me ask you a hypothetical question—if I came to you and said I needed your help—let's say, I needed surgery and there was nobody to drive me home, or maybe I needed somebody to check on my Dad while I was out of town. How would that make you feel?"

"I would feel honored. Like you trusted me."

"Exactly." He gave her fingers a squeeze and let go. "So stop it. I'm honored you asked me to pick up Joie. You know I adore her. Plus, now I have a perfectly good excuse to leave work early. By the way, have you ever thought about eating something? I know thin is in, but you don't have to work yourself to the actual bone."

"I sure do love you."

"Who doesn't? I mean, look at me. I'm fabulous."

Parker laughed. "Three-thirty. You know where I live. Joie can give you directions after that. Thank you. Really, thank you."

Checking his watch, Liam said he should skedaddle. He shouldered his satchel, offered a military salute, and he was off.

More than she could explain, Parker was grateful for Liam.

She had time to kill before the meeting at four-thirty. She should have worked on the grant application, but after skimming it once, the Internet unleashed its strange siren's song. Facebook and Twitter were no fun—nothing but laughing babies and cats shredding toilet paper to trance music. She opened her feed of Atlanta news and started scrolling. It made her feel closer to home, to read about what was going on there. Coca-Cola had released a new flavor that reminded Parker of a Starbucks Halloween offering. A driver who'd been stuck in gridlock for four hours because of a six-car pile-up on the downtown connector had ripped off his clothes before streaking north on I-75, screaming. A meth lab had exploded inside a Cherokee County trailer home; metal fragments and chicken feathers were found a quarter-mile away. Trees Atlanta was planting blight-resistant hybrid chestnut trees because all the real chestnut trees had gone extinct before Parker was born.

At the next headline, Parker took her hands off the keyboard and sat back.

"Caldwell Developers Announces $5 Million Silver Park Deal," the headline said.

Parker's breathing sounded amplified, as if she might be underwater, snorkeling. Her father had left her a fifty-acre parcel of land in Silver Park, which he had bought from her friend Arden's grandfather, Mr.

John Roberts Collier. The property had been set up as a nature preserve. It was designated as historic—legally protected until the end of time from any and all development. Parker couldn't build on the land. She couldn't sell it or even give it away. She could only have the trees pruned and the grass trimmed now and then.

The headline made no sense.

She began reading:

"William 'Buddy' Caldwell, president of Caldwell Developers, LLC, today announced a $5 million agreement with an unnamed partner to build a six-story luxury condominium complex in Atlanta's Silver Park, overlooking a protected area designated as historic due to its significance to the African-American community."

Funny, she thought, how the letters in his name, a word, or a smell could take her back so quickly. She pictured the papery creases around Buddy's eyes, above his scraggly beard where the light tugged at his skin when he smiled, tight-lipped. A trace of cigarette smoke could summon his gamy scent, which wrapped itself around her all over again, as if the decades had never flown by. She was sitting in her office, fifty-two years old, but she might as well have been shivering in the smoky cocoon of Buddy's car at fourteen, scooching across the seat, as instructed—smoke and leather and the heat from his skin.

In one of the high-rise windows across the street, a man pulled his blinds shut. On the street below, the so-called Barking Man said, "Hoo! Hoo!" He was jogging backwards below her window, as he did at the same time every day. With shaking hands, Parker closed her door and kept reading.

"County officials last month approved a grading plan for the project on the condition that Caldwell must secure access for water and sewer services to the new development. Caldwell, 62, has served as project manager on various Atlanta initiatives, working with many developers over the years, including powerhouse builders Wilson Banks Corp. and Kenneth Hawthorne Properties, Inc. The Falls at Silver Park venture marks the first time he has assumed a leading role on a major development."

The story went on. Well-known developers were quoted as saying Buddy was a "remarkably efficient project manager" and "clever about finding a way to make things happen, no matter what."

Parker closed her web browser, leaned over her plastic-lined trashcan, and involuntarily disgorged the remains of her lunch into it. Sitting up, she smoothed her hair, tied the plastic bag shut, and stuffed the whole mess into a paper sack. Again, she tried to reach her husband. Beamer wasn't answering his mobile or work numbers. After pulling a small mirror out of her desk drawer, Parker freshened her lipstick. Clicking a ballpoint pen, she eyeballed the research grant application, ready to make it rain.

3.
ARDEN COLLIER

In her family's crumbling scrapbook, the first picture showed Arden's grandfather, *Mr. John Roberts Collier,* with his sister Wilma, who was perched on a stool wearing an oversized gingham dress with lace around the collar.

Wilma was a girl, in the photo, balanced on a stool with her bare feet dangling above the floor. Standing behind her, a man in a white shirt and suspenders looked old enough to be her father. His hand was wrapped so tightly around the back of her neck, the tips of his thumb and middle finger were visible on either side of it. Sadness hovered, tight-lipped, in the corners of Wilma's smile. Arden fingered the scalloped white edge of the photograph, which was faded and cracked down the middle.

With a grunt, she smacked the picture of Wilma's disgusting husband George.

She knew by heart the story of Wilma's premature betrothal, having heard her mother tell it many times before she died. Wilma was barely out of grade school when she married George. Her father had left the family, and her mother had four other kids to feed. Old George had a car and a way to make money by selling moonshine. It must have seemed like a pretty good deal, letting him have Wilma. He fed her crappy booze he had cooked up in old car parts. Soon after drinking the poison, George collapsed, gripped by a seizure. He died with his eyes rolled up in their sockets. Wilma lived, but milky blue clouds bloomed in her eyes, leaving her mostly blind.

Arden pictured herself as a girl, headed to school with her textbooks and a small brown Bible in a pink fabric bag—a gift from her Aunt Wilma. After Arden's mother died, Wilma took over. She fed Arden homemade bread, warm from the oven and slathered with butter, and sweet rice pudding spiked with raisins. The old woman's cloudy eyes were constantly red from washing, starching, and folding white people's laundry every day.

The scrapbook smelled like cobwebs and lavender potpourri. On the next page, Wilma was all grown up, dressed in her housekeeper uniform, a blindingly white dress with a matching headscarf. Her brother John was smiling beside her. This was the way Arden remembered her grandfather, with his perpetually wrinkled smile, his luminous eyes, and the steady certainty of his fingertips around the tattered brim of a brown felt hat. She recognized the magnolia tree behind them, remembered hiding under it as a child, on summer days when Wilma went to work for the Gozer family and Arden tagged along, to play with her friend Parker.

Arden shuddered at the next photo of the old patriarch Foster Gozer and his creepy sidekick Buddy, smiling in front of a yellow bulldozer and a small forest of scrub pines. Her grandfather was barely in the frame— more of an afterthought or a shadow—leaning against the handle of a wooden shovel nearly as big as he was. Staked into the ground to his left, a red and white sign said, "Coming Soon! Another Beautiful Kudzu Castle from Gozer Homes!" Beside her grandfather, Parker Gozer held the hem of her skirt like a basket, at seven or eight years old, frowning as if she wanted to hide inside the fabric.

Arden pressed the tip of her finger over Buddy's eyes so he would stop staring up at her from the photo. The orange, bushy beard covered his whole neck. He was a good two inches taller than Foster and the color of cooked ham, from working outdoors.

"You were such a redneck," she said, remembering how Aunt Wilma had never allowed Arden anywhere near Buddy. "Literally."

The gauzy strips on Arden's face had hardened into a mask. They pulled at the edges of her cheeks, tightening around her eyes and lips. She slapped the scrapbook shut, cradled it briefly against her chest, and shoved it back into the burlap satchel. She wasn't ready to think about what had brought her grandfather to Georgia. She definitely didn't want to see her old photos of her ruined marriage to Joel.

She made her way across the backyard instead. Under a circle of pines, her grandfather's wood-plank workshop leaned hard to the right. Inside, sunlight shot through gaping holes in the walls. The room smelled strongly of damp soil and oiled tools arranged in tidy lines across his old worktable.

She laughed, thinking about her grandfather's disgruntled mule and all of the old man's comical tales of farming efforts gone wrong. His stories were mostly funny. He had told her a sad story only once—a long yarn about loss, the cotton thorns that cut his fingers to shreds, and the house he built from scratch. Arden ran her hands over the rough slats of his table, picturing his face, animated by kindness, deeply lined around the eyes as he broke into a huge grin, waving the tattered hat, back and forth, whenever he saw her.

Why he had decided to sell most of his land for a pittance to Foster Gozer so it could be turned into a nature preserve, Arden couldn't imagine. "Keep your peace and know your place." That was one of her grandfather's favorite sayings that drove her insane. "The Lord rewards the meek." Foster had shined the penny by saying it would be the Collier family's "legacy." Maybe Arden's grandfather, like Foster, wanted to make sure nobody could ever mow down his trees or dump sewage in his lake, after he was gone. Maybe he needed the money or felt a debt to Old Man Gozer, who had kept him employed for many years.

Whatever the case, Arden felt robbed of what should have been hers.

She leaned over the table, pushing her fingertips under the mask until it started to peel off her skin. Blood surged back into her temples. Had she made a terrible mistake, dredging up the past? Maybe she needed a change of venue—a trip—new surroundings to get the ideas flowing. She loped across the yard, into the gazebo. After strangling water from a rag, she swiped it across her cheeks in quick, brutal strokes.

The phone was ringing as she pushed her way back into the house. It was her grandfather's old rotary model, a massive green relic that rang in a series of rapid burps. She was breathing hard by the time she picked up the receiver, having climbed over a stack of dishes and a dry cleaner's box containing her mummified wedding dress. She didn't say hello. She waited, catching her breath, ready to hang up if it was a telemarketer or a county official wanting to know when she would pay her fines.

The man repeated her name in a thick drawl that made his words sound like they were dripping with something. Sarcasm, thick as molasses. Condescension like pinesap. Entitlement, heavy as spent oil from a rusty motor. She recognized the tone right away and stood staring at the grimy receiver, not sure whether she wanted to reply.

"I heard about your troubles with the county and I think it's just terrible," Buddy Caldwell was saying. "I might be able to help you out with that. You mind if I pay you a little visit? I think you'll want to hear my plan. Things could get a lot easier for you, Arden."

When she finally used it, Arden could barely hear her voice, it was so maddeningly quiet. "Okay," she said. The syllables had rushed out on autopilot, against her will. Why did she feel compelled to be polite to everyone—even Foster Gozer's greasy hired hand?

She set the receiver back onto the phone without saying goodbye, picked up Jared Astor's letter, and pressed it against her heart. She wanted to lie down, but the bed was covered with clothes and children's games she had found at yard sales: Candy Land, Hungry Hungry Hippos, Operation, and all the others she remembered playing before her family disappeared, one by one, dying or divorcing her, leaving her alone. She put Jared's letter back onto the stack and picked a path into the basement, where she sifted through her bagged and boxed treasures until she found what she needed.

Finally, her hands closed around the small box containing her grandfather's hat. The cardboard, marked with his initials, was frayed at the corners where she had tried in the past to duct-tape it, to keep it from splitting apart completely.

This, she carried back up the wooden stairs that had long ago lost their railing, over an uneven heap of her mother's flowery dresses, still on their hangers, into her bedroom. She squeezed through a narrow opening between two rows of stacked magazines and climbed onto the bed. Positioning her grandfather's hat in the exact spot where his head used to hit the pillow, she curled beside it, safe.

4.

BUDDY CALDWELL

The smell hit Buddy first. After all the construction jobs he had done, he knew right away Arden Collier had a leaky septic tank that she probably never got pumped out. He tugged a point-and-shoot camera from his pocket, walked around a pile of wet, termite-infested lumber and started clicking off frame after frame. Squatting painfully over his ankles, he zoomed in for extreme close-ups of shredded car tires, rusty tin cans, broken bottles and pipe fittings—all the teetering stacks of what Arden probably called art. He would make huge color copies to show how the periphery of her garden looked like a junkyard. He hoped she might have a few dozen feral cats crapping inside the house, too. That would surely clinch the deal with the county.

Hope you've had fun in your second childhood, Arden. Get ready to grow up fast.

Buddy couldn't wait to stick a road straight through the middle of her stinky, run-down old property. His mouth watered at the thought of it.

He wandered, snapping pictures, through her collection of dust-encrusted bottles, keeping his head raised in case she might be somewhere nearby. He didn't want to risk scaring her. Buying her property was his first choice, much easier than getting the county to seize it under eminent domain laws. A string of broken glass brushed the top of his head, making him flinch. Buddy moved as quickly as he could through her weird sculptures. All the female figures gave him the creeps. One time, he had made it with a black chick. No big deal. Pretty much the same deal as with all the others.

He bent to squint, grimacing, over a miniature wall covered with what looked like graffiti. "Who buys this kind of crap?" He said it out loud, and it made him laugh because he knew the answer. "Nobody. Not a single person wants to buy this crap. That's why your yard stinks."

All the windows of her house were dark. Several were shot through with cracks. Near an overflowing trashcan, he pressed his face against the glass, cupping his hands to get a better look. What he saw caused him to swear under his breath. Furniture was buried under mounds of magazines, newspapers, clothing, cardboard boxes, and children's toys. When he stepped back, his reflection startled him. For a split-second, he thought his dead father was alive and walking around inside the house, staring at him through the window. His face looked scarred—leaner now than it used to be, and hollow under the cheekbones. The bloodless yellow patches on his cheeks made him feel like he was already gone, or a zombie. Deep lines crisscrossed his skin. Too damned many cigarettes, he knew, but at sixty-two, he wasn't about to quit in the middle of the biggest business deal of his life.

He shoved the camera back into his jacket and adjusted his tie with both hands. The knot was a darker burgundy than the rest of the thing. It was flimsy and threadbare, ready for recycling. His back throbbed from all the bending to take photos. Every few minutes, a sudden knife-stab of pain radiated from his spine to his fingertips, turning them numb. He wished like hell he had popped another pain pill before driving to Arden's house. Oh, those pills and the joy they gave him, in an instant. He worried the doctor might cut him off, but it hadn't happened yet.

The back door squeaked. By the time he walked the full length of the house, Arden was standing on the bottom step. She stopped in her tracks when she saw him. Looking down, she adjusted her floppy hat and braids.

Buddy offered his hand. "My, my, Miss Arden, you look the same as always," he said. In fact, she looked nothing like the little girl who used to glom onto crazy Parker. Whenever he tickled Parker until she wet herself, Arden would run and tattle to her aunt, who swung a mean broom. That was way back when Wilma and Arden's grandfather worked for Foster—practically the Stone Ages. "It's great to see you again."

She stared at his outstretched palm for a second before letting him shake her fingers, which were damp and limp as willow leaves. "Hello," she said.

By waiting a beat, Buddy let the awkward silence swell between them. She started pulling a piece of her floral dress through a closed fist without taking her eyes off him. The dress looked like a nightgown or a blanket, shapeless and huge. "Thanks for meeting with me," he said. "Could we go in the house?"

Her eyes zoomed back and forth, expanding. She pulled in a breath with her mouth open. The veins in her neck rose to the surface of her skin. "I'd rather visit outside." He was surprised by the sudden strength of her voice. "There's a nice spot in my garden, right over there."

"That's fine," he said, working to keep his tone soft. He wanted her to feel safe, to let her guard down.

Back he went into the spooky maze of her sculptures, following her to a rickety-looking gazebo. The hem of her big dress whipped behind her in amber and mocha waves. Arden sank into an armchair that might have been red before it turned black from mildew. Pointing, she directed him to a dirty plastic milk crate. He tried to act casual while he hunkered over it. His knees poked up like he was a big kid, or a frog. Pain rocketed through his spine. He stifled a grimace. "Hey, I read about your show at the High Museum," he said. "I was really impressed. I meant to send you a card. You've really made a name for yourself."

"That was a while ago," she said. Her words sounded tight, like in the old days when Buddy would try to carry on a conversation while pot smoke scorched his lungs. He hadn't done that kind of thing in years. Too much fun had eventually taken its toll on him.

He nodded toward all the masks on the floor. "Oh, come on now, looks to me like you're staying busy."

Her pointer finger twitched against her leg. It was strange how she stared at him without talking. Maybe she was autistic or something. "I guess you read about my troubles with the county," she said.

Buddy shook his head. "It's awful how they're treating you, Miss Arden. All those fines they want you to pay on top of repairs you'd have to make? I don't think they understand how hard it is for an artist like you."

Arden stood up and tossed a mask onto the butcher block in the middle of the gazebo. "It's not like I want to live this way," she said dunking a paintbrush into a bucket. "I'd like to get everything all fixed up. I'm here by myself nowadays."

Buddy struggled to his feet, groaning. "Sorry about your Aunt Wilma." He was standing across the table from her. "I saw the obituary in the paper back when it happened. Did you ever marry? Any kids?" He needed to know if there were any relatives who might help her hire a lawyer.

Her tapping paintbrush sounded like feet, running away from him. She was bent over the mask, squinting, with red paint all over her hand. "No." She plunged the dirty brush repeatedly into a blob of green paint. "What did you want to talk to me about?"

He slipped his hands into his pockets and looked across the yard at a crooked wooden shed he knew he could bring down with a single hammer blow. At least his back felt better when he was standing. "I know you love this place. I do, too. I've got fond memories of your grandpa, good old Junebug."

Arden slapped the paintbrush onto the table, closed her eyes, and whispered at him. Her face shook. "Don't call him that. You might as well call him Uncle Tom." The way she whispered made him feel like she was screaming. "Nobody called my grandfather Junebug except you people—white folks who had him cleaning toilets and shoveling trash for thirty-five fucking years. His name was John Roberts Collier. *Mr.* John Collier."

Buddy's hands were raised as if she had shot him. Heat ricocheted through the fleshy parts of his face, intensifying until his eye sockets felt like they were vibrating with electrical current. "Gosh, I'm sorry," he said. "Nobody ever told me not to call him that. He was a great man. I mean it. A brilliant, genuinely good man. The way he helped Foster Gozer set up that park down the road from here? That showed real vision, you know?"

Arden started BB-gunning the red and green mask with pellets of black paint. "Sure, what a wonderful idea, giving away our land, letting all kinds of people take over my family's estate. Now all I've got is this lot and my falling-down house. But here's the thing—it's mine, my home. I plan to stay here until I die. So you know."

"Yeah, and that might happen sooner rather than later, from what I saw. How'd your house get to be such a mess?"

"I'm by myself," she said again, breathing hard. "I'm doing the best I can. I don't care what the county says."

He pondered his next move, tapping his fingers against his lips. They felt dry and cracked in the corners, as usual. He mashed a lip balm over them. "What if you could keep living in Silver Park but without all these county fines and septic tank headaches? I'm building some luxury condos by the waterfall. It's going to be beautiful. A huge, huge improvement. I'd like to give you a corner unit, as a gift."

"What are you even talking about? You can't build over there. That's all been designated historic. It's protected. Parker Gozer owns all that land now." In her eyes, the fiery coronas flashed.

Buddy smiled. "I own the lot right next to the park. Foster gave it to me before he died."

"Why? You're not even related."

"I worked for him a long time. My parcel's unencumbered. That means—"

"I know what it means. I've got a college degree. Who said you could do that?"

"The county. My grading plan's been approved. But it's contingent on access for services—water and sewer lines and a road to get folks in and out. I can't cut a path through the park without a special variance."

Arden gripped the edge of the butcher block so hard her fingernails seemed to be digging into the wood. "That's too bad for you. You're definitely not cutting a path through my property instead, if that's what you're thinking."

"I'm prepared to offer you an amount much higher than market value for your land," he said, pinning her with his eyes. "I just told you I'd throw in a free luxury condo, too."

She started talking before he had finished his sentence. "I'm not interested. My grandfather built this place with his own hands. I'm staying right here. I'm not chopping it up to help you cut down my trees, either. I want you to leave now."

He closed his eyes and shook his head. He wasn't smiling anymore when he looked at her again. His fingers slid inside his jacket. When they reappeared, he was holding an envelope. He dropped it on the table between them. "You need to read this and think about it." He used his deepest voice so she would know he meant business. "You can either accept my offer, which is more than fair, or you can wait for the county to seize your property out from under you. Your choice."

Arden's cheek twitched below one eye. "You're not scaring me. I've got friends, too. Friends high up the food chain, a lot higher than you."

"Oh, yeah?" he said. "Like who?"

Her bottom lip jerked. "Like Jared Astor. I'm getting ready to do a show for him." Buddy could see from the way her eyes shot back and forth that her mind was leaping ahead of her mouth, racing. "He's giving me a cash advance and a publicity tour and a wardrobe allowance."

"Interesting. A minute ago, you said you can't afford to get this place fixed up because you're all by yourself."

"I'm doing a show for Jared Astor." She sounded like a damaged music disk, repeating the same lyric over and over again. "He's a good friend of mine. We're very close. I'm not somebody people can push around."

"Is that right?"

"It's the truth. Anyway, this is America. The county can't kick people off their own land."

"Sometimes they can." He smiled down his nose so that he felt slightly cross-eyed. "Sometimes they do."

"Get off my property," she said again. She threw a bucket of dirty paint water against the base of a tree. Beads of water rolled down the bumpy tree trunk, dropping like pennies from a broken piggy bank.

He pushed the envelope closer to her, postponing his exit to make her even more nervous. "Do yourself a favor. Read what I'm offering you. There's a hearing on Friday. You're going to get summoned."

"I'm not going to any hearings."

"Once you get summoned," he said, ignoring her, "it's not going to be good for you. I don't want it to be like that. It's not my best option, believe me. But you'd better believe the county can and will seize this place. Then you'd get next to nothing for it."

"If you don't leave, I'm calling the police."

He was glad to see her shoulders crumble. He felt relieved, watching the tears roll down her face. He knew he had won. Now she was scared. Now she understood why she had to play nicely in the sandbox. She had no other choice. He spun a business card onto the butcher block, Frisbee-style. "Call me," he said. "Get in touch by Thursday morning. After that, the wheels will be in motion."

Her chin tipped sideways and the corners of her mouth puckered. She pulled the black paintbrush through a white rag. "Please leave."

The last teasing winks of daylight pierced the canopy and her garden wasn't cool but it was damp. A slow breeze was snaking through the gazebo. Her gauzy blouse fluttered while her chest heaved up and down. The tree trunk gleamed, shiny as her paintbrush, where she had hurled the water at it.

Buddy's temples were pounding and his back felt like a steel rod being smelted down. The high stakes involved in putting together big projects—the hunt and the take-down—no longer excited him the way it had when he was younger. He turned on his heels without saying goodbye.

He needed a pain pill.

5.

PARKER GOZER

Twenty miles west of D.C., Parker found Beamer strapped to a ladder behind their townhouse. He was pounding wood planks into the cherry tree he had planted in the middle of the ground-floor courtyard. She wanted to be mad at him. It had been a pain for her to call and call all afternoon, needing to ask for his help with the carpool, wanting to tell him what she had seen on the Internet. Why he wouldn't actually turn on his cellphone except to make a call, Parker could never understand.

His shoulders flexed while he worked, though, and with a voice like a trade wind, he sang an old song she knew well: "Trouble, oh trouble, set me free, I have seen your face and it's too much, too much for me." *Cat Stevens.* Her high school crush.

Instantly, his singing took her back, as it always did, to Silver Park in Atlanta and the waterfall where the trees annually turned red, purple, and yellow, shaking in the spray. She didn't have to crane her neck backwards or stand on her toes to meet him halfway. He bent down for her and his lips were soft, barely pressing, not mashed against her teeth. She could kiss him and breathe at the same time. Watching him from their top deck, she wanted to run down the stairs. She wanted to sit with him the way they did when they were kids, making out in the park or in Atlanta's many abandoned warehouses. That was before all those old buildings turned into glitzy, expensive condominiums.

Grief rolled through her in icy waves. So many years had passed since then. With all the long hours at work and in the car, commuting, they had grown apart lately.

She trudged down the steps leading to their tiny garden, positioned herself under the tree where he could see her, and briefly yanked her blouse over her head, bra and all. The hammer stopped, along with his singing. Beamer stared at her with a nail tucked in one corner of his mouth.

"Nice tree house," she said.

"Nice farmer's tan." He spit the nail onto the partially finished platform. "Get this. I'm stringing a zip line so we can zoom straight from our bedroom window into this tree. Cool, huh?"

"Very." For once, it was an invention she could get behind—not a footbridge he wanted to whittle from a tree trunk or a toaster oven playing music in sync with a rotating display of colored lights. Ever since his construction business hit a dry spell, Beamer had been building an assortment of odd contraptions around their home. She remembered climbing a sweet gum tree outside his parent's ornate gingerbread house in Atlanta's Inman Park neighborhood, the week she met him. He was parked by a red-shaded lamp in his boxer shorts, bent over a guitar like he wanted to play it with his mouth. His voice was so sweet, it made her teeth hurt. "You are the reason I've been waiting so long. Somebody holds the key." *Blind Faith.* She had peppered his window with botanical shrapnel—dried-up monkey balls, brown and spiky—until he let her in.

"Glad you approve," he said. "I live for your approval, my goddess."

"I assume Liam picked Joie up on time?"

"Liam? Why would Liam be picking her up?"

"I had to work late."

"Ha. News flash."

"You weren't here when Joie got home from school?"

He holstered the hammer. "Nope. I had to meet a guy about a job. She's got a key."

A giant hosta plant was shaking, in a corner where their brick wall ran into a neighbor's courtyard. "I'll pick her up after lacrosse."

"Oh." Beamer started climbing down the ladder. "I almost forgot to tell you. You don't have to pick her up. She's got a ride lined up. She's got late practice and then there's something about dinner with the girls. I didn't catch the whole thing."

A fat squirrel popped its head through the leaves, cheeks bulging. Parker braided her arms across her chest. She was trying to remember any emails or flyers or text messages from Jolene about a late practice. But no—Beamer's report was the first she had heard of it. The president of the athletic boosters association, a jowly man named Howie whose daughter was still prone to wearing pink princess skirts when she wasn't in lacrosse shorts, had accosted Parker at the last scrimmage about hosting a team dinner. His striped golf sweater reminded her of Charlie Brown and it struck her as odd, generally, considering the warm weather and the way he was constantly fingering his oversized belt buckle. He had never mentioned late practices. "Something smells," she said.

"My manly aroma?"

"No, I mean, about Joie being late." Parker glared at the squirrel, which was always eating her pink azaleas, in the spring. "Nobody said anything to me about a change in the schedule."

"Oh, goodie." Beamer's big shoulders deflated. "Here we go again."

"Seriously, honey, who told you lacrosse ends late tonight?"

He unlocked the ladder and let it collapse with a bang. "Our child."

She was sure that Beamer, being a big kid himself, hadn't talked to a grown-up. She didn't even bother to ask. "She called you? What did she say, exactly?"

He turned away from her, hauled the ladder across the courtyard and tossed it onto the back wall of their house. "Let's see." He smeared dirty handprints across his new black jeans, which she had finally convinced him to wear instead of his droopy antique painter pants. "She said, 'Dad, tell Mom not to freak out but I'll be with the team until after dark and tell her not to worry because I've got a ride and we're all eating dinner together.'"

"But what I'm wondering is, how did she even reach you? I mean, your phone's been turned off all day. I kept trying to call you. I had to send Liam all the way out here because I couldn't reach you or Jolene or anybody else."

He stared at Parker with his hands on his hips. Feathery yellow clumps of hair were stuck to his glasses—round wire frames that made him look like a 1960s folk singer. "I turned it on when I got home. I needed to make a call. She said she's got a ride with friends."

"But, I mean, which friends?"

"I don't know." The words came fast and dark as a warning clap of thunder.

"So, she's got lacrosse until late and we don't need to pick her up." She ignored his tone of voice. "We don't know where she's eating dinner. Is that right?"

Beamer didn't budge. He was starting to remind her of a statue in the town square. "That's what she said."

"This isn't making sense to me."

His head dropped to his chest. He shifted his weight, rubbing the back of his neck. "I'm only the messenger."

Parker wanted to bite her tongue into ribbons. "I'm going over to the field. I don't like not knowing who's giving her a ride. What if it's somebody we don't know? What if that weirdo Howie's driving? He gives me the creeps."

"Are you insane?" He asked the question in a way that let her know it wasn't a hypothetical one. "You're worried about Howie now?"

"She's fourteen," Parker said.

"That's right." He was clenching his fists in front of his shoulders like he wanted to shake her, although Parker knew he would never do any such thing. "She's *fourteen.*"

Before she could say anything else, the squirrel darted up a tree, squealing. Parker pretended to rub her eyes, not wanting to give the tears a chance to gather and spill. He had been so cross lately. Parker had chalked it up to the lack of construction work. "I'm sorry, honey," she said, forcing her voice to sound softer. "Something happened today that's got me pretty upset. Something I read online. It was about a new company in Atlanta."

Beamer tugged his shirt out of his pants and he cleaned his glasses. "A new company." He positioned the frames, newly smeared with dust, back over his ears. Through the cloudy lenses, he watched her, waiting. "Is there more?"

Between them, a spot of sunlight flickered on the brick patio. "The Dirtbag's set up his own company," she said, using their code name for her father's long-ago handyman. "He's buying up property down there, building on any little scrap of forest he can find. Like Atlanta needs to lose even more of its trees for another crappy development—and get this—it's in Silver Park, right next to my property."

Beamer exhaled at length, forcing all the air from his lungs. She could tell he was sneaking cigarettes again. He needed to find work, and fast. "Buddy Caldwell's a developer now?"

"The story gave this whole trumped up history of him as a businessman. What a joke."

Beamer didn't say anything for a minute and he didn't move toward her, either. "That's it? That was the news, he's got a real-estate company?"

"My Dad taught Buddy everything he knows. Now he's using what he learned to bulldoze what's left of my hometown. Oh, Beamer, Atlanta was so green and quiet and beautiful when we were kids. Sometimes when I visit the neighborhood where we grew up, I can't believe what's happened to it. Now it turns out Buddy's going to help ruin any spots that somehow didn't get paved over yet."

"Shake it off, sweetheart," Beamer said after a minute. "Let it go."

She stretched her eyes open as wide as they would go, determined to keep them dry. She felt lost and hollow. Her husband couldn't see it. "Yeah, that's definitely what I'd like to do," she said. "Maybe I should smile, damn it. Ha ha."

He turned his head to watch the squirrel creep back down the tree. "I guess I don't understand what's been going on lately. You've been fine for a long time. All of a sudden, he's on your mind every other day for one reason or another."

The skin on her arms, as she hugged herself, felt refrigerated and chicken-bumpy, right there in her sunny garden. "Joie's the same age now—same as I was back then."

He puffed up his cheeks, squirrel-like, and let them pop. "I know, but it's been, what, nearly forty years? I don't want to go through this all over again. It was bad enough when we were first married."

Parker's locked knees began to vibrate. She moved for the back door, slipped into the darkened ground-floor room where she and Beamer and Joie usually ate alone, one at a time, parked in front of the TV set because Parker worked past dinnertime to make ends meet and her daily commute into D.C. was hell on Earth. "There's shish kebab on the counter," she said. "You'll probably have to nuke it."

In the computer room, Joie's seat felt warm and the swirling screensaver hadn't gone to sleep yet. Parker moved a half-eaten bag of popcorn out of the way and tapped the greasy keyboard, making the Web browser spring to life. Joie had never logged off her Facebook page. Two more clicks and Parker was scrolling through the full text of her daughter's most recent online chat.

She zoomed to the bottom of the string and started reading an exchange between Joie—disguised as "Treehugger007," whose thumbnail photo showed a magnolia leaf under a magnifying glass—

and somebody named James P. Wentworth Sr. Parker had never heard the name before. Instead of a photo, the guy had used the default image, a menacing blue silhouette of a man's head. She tried to steady her breathing. "What the heck?"

Vaguely, she recalled Joie talking about a new kid in her AP Government class. His name escaped Parker. It might have been Jimbo—a boy noteworthy because of his skateboarding skills, his long Rastafarian braids, and his interest in rock-climbing with Joie. As she started to read, Parker immediately decided to hate the boy.

James P. Wentworth Sr.: Hey, there's a party at 114 Shagbark on Fri nite.
Treehugger007: Kewell.
James P. Wentworth Sr.: B there.
Treehugger007: R U hitting on me, Mr. Skanksworth?
James P. Wentworth Sr.: ROFLMAO. Fo sho, if U want me 2. U dress like such a ho, I bet U want me 2 slip U da sausage. U like bratwurst, shawtie?
Treehugger007: Ha. More like a Vienna sausage. Stick a toothpick in that thang. See U soon, Mister.

Parker shoved a few sheets into the printer and hit the green "go" button. She was blinking back tears by the time Joie's chat rolled through the chute, one line at a time. She ripped the paper free. The last sheet wound up saying:

M i s t e r.

Folding the paper on the fly, she headed for the stairs, shoved the message under her bra strap, and grabbed her bag. She bolted from the house and hopped into the car. She didn't stop to tell Beamer where she was going.

Shagbark Court was in the part of town where all the streets were named after trees or rodents, but she wound around Marmot Circle and back across Lemming Creek three times and still couldn't find the address. Pulling hard on the steering wheel, she rolled onto a curb and tapped new coordinates into her GPS. By driving two more blocks, she somehow hit Shagbark. The house at 114 was dark—a split-level that might have looked like the set for the Brady Bunch TV show, except for the rusty Maverick parked on cinder blocks by a stack of tires.

Parker wondered if she was right about Wentworth being the new boy in AP Government class. What kind of little boy would write messages like that? She also didn't know where Joie had learned to reply like a raunchy hip-hop rapper. It didn't really matter. Joie wouldn't have access to computers after being grounded for the rest of her natural life in Camp Hell. *But wait—how could a kid be named James Senior? He couldn't be a Senior anything unless there was also a Junior somebody.* Wentworth must be a man, maybe even Howie fiddling with his zipper under the horrible musty golf sweater, or someone else with the blue silhouette of a man's head, trolling the Internet in search of underaged girls.

The image was too ridiculous to entertain. Again and again, she elbowed it out of her brain. It kept coming back.

Nobody answered the doorbell. Banging with the side of her fist didn't trigger any noise or light inside the house, either. The front door was situated on top of concrete steps and she couldn't lean far enough over the black iron railing to see through the windows on the main floor. They were covered with Venetian blinds, all of them louvered shut. Below the railing, giant boxwoods blocked a series of grimy ground-floor windows. They reminded her of Buddy's basement room. His lone window had been partially buried in dirt where worms struggled behind the glass. Black fingers of mold had reached across the walls, all around the sill that leaked every time it rained.

She moved down the steps two at a time and slipped behind the bushes. She was rapping on the windows when headlights shot through the glass, giving her a glimpse of an empty room with a huge flat-screen TV on one wall, a saggy brown couch and a battered air-hockey table. No Joie. A blue SUV rumbled into the driveway by the bushes.

It stopped, the lights clicked off, and a door popped open. A familiar voice rang out. Parker stepped out of the bushes with bits of leaves and spider webs stuck to her face.

"Hello?" Jolene said. "Good grief, is that you?" She was standing at the bottom of the steps, clutching a casserole dish between oven mitts shaped like two charred lobster claws.

"I need your help," Parker said. "Joie's missing. Have you seen her?"

Cradling the casserole against a sparkly rhinestone belt, Jolene slipped one hand free and plucked a twig from Parker's collar. "What happened to you?" Her eyes roamed Parker's face. "Are you drunk?"

"No, unfortunately not." Suddenly, Parker craved the mother of all cocktails. She shook her head, trying to get her bearings. "Why are you here? Do you know this guy Wentworth?"

Jolene laughed, cocking her head to the side. She was watching Parker with one squinty eye. "What are we talking about?"

Parker pulled Joie's online conversation out of her bra, unfolded it for Jolene, and set it on top of the casserole. "Look, Joie's meeting this guy Wentworth." She hated the sound of her voice, thin and winding down, like a toy airplane about to crash. "I don't know who he is, but how could a kid be named Senior anything? I'm really worried."

When Jolene opened her mouth again, she laughed so hard, she had to stagger to the porch with her dish. The tin foil slipped as she set it on the concrete steps and Parker got a strong whiff of meat and potatoes. "No, no," Jolene said, forcing her head between her knees as if she might pass out. "Wait—no, not again, no, wait."

Parker blinked hard, not yet sure whether Jolene was laughing at her or with her. "What's so funny?" she whispered. "Have you seen Joie?"

"Listen to me carefully, psycho lady," Jolene said when she came up for air. "Remember, I'm a professional life coach. I do this for a living. Yes, I've seen her. She's fine. She's at lacrosse practice. This is Martha's house. There's a team dinner here at seven-thirty—didn't you get the email?"

"No." Parker shook her head, face stinging as it began to dawn on her that she had made a terrible mistake and now she was standing on Martha's lawn with a spider web glued to her neck. She would owe Beamer an apology later—a big one—if he let her back in the house. "But where's Martha?"

"She's working the concession stand over on the athletics field." Jolene gasped to keep from laughing again. "She sent me over to set everything up."

"I didn't get any email. Who's Wentworth?"

"That's Anne Marie," Jolene said, meaning her daughter. "I don't let her chat online unless she's using a pseudonym and she came up with that one."

Parker bent over, suddenly exhausted, and she braced herself against her thighs. "Nobody told me." Her brain felt like a hundred-year-old tortoise, slow on the uptake.

Jolene stood up and rubbed Parker's back like she meant to exfoliate it. "You poor neurotic weirdo. Did you go all Freaky Jason? Hey, I might join you. I've already had three other complaints from parents who didn't know about this party, and here I am with a giant vat of bratwurst. I knew it was a bad idea, letting Howie handle that email list. He's such a wanker."

"I'm feeling pretty stupid right about now."

Rhinestones dug into Parker's ribcage when Jolene hugged her.

"You work too hard at that job of yours." She kissed Parker's earlobe before letting her go. "Look, you've got a couple of free hours. The party won't end until nine o'clock. Why don't you let me drive Joie home so you and Beamer can chill out?"

Jolene's eyebrows pulsed up and down.

Parker returned the kiss, jumped into her car, and tried not to let her tires squeal as she peeled away. When she pulled into her driveway, Freddy the ancient psycho tomcat strolled under a gardenia bush. Upstairs, Beamer was stretched across their waterbed with his eyes closed, listening to African jazz. He tensed up at first when she curled beside him, rocking their waterbed. After a minute, he wrapped an arm around her.

"Sorry," she whispered into his chest.

"Where'd you go?" The music disk changed tracks. "You didn't eat."

"I'm not hungry." His chest moved up and down, broad and warm, in time with the little waves inside their mattress. Her eyelids kept fluttering.

"I'm really going to finish that zip line," he mumbled, sounding on the verge of sleep. She thought the project must have worn him out because it wasn't even eight o' clock, his usual bedtime, yet he was nearly gone already. "It's going to be so great."

"*You're* great," she said and she made a half-hearted attempt at seduction, heaving one leg over him. She was so tired, it felt like chunking a pumpkin—dead weight. Briefly, she knocked the wind out of him. "I love you, honey. I really am sorry I got so wound up."

"I love you, too, my weird, beautiful wife." He gave her back a couple of pats. "Can I take a rain check, sweetie? Pretty tired now."

He was snoring by the time she said, "No worries."

Parker was also fading into a zombie-like form of half-sleep when her phone buzzed across the room, rattling coins at the bottom of her pocketbook. She could have let it ring, but it might be Joie or Jolene. She took the phone into the hallway, clicking the bedroom door shut.

"Sorry to disturb you." It was her boss, Dr. Tinley. His voice echoed through the line as if he might be inside a tiled restroom. "You won't believe this. I'm here at the club, having dinner with your reporter friend Bart."

"Oh yes, how's that going?" Instantly, Parker was alert again. She had completely forgotten about her plan for Dr. Tinley to wine and dine a journalist interested in their human rights research. They needed more publicity if they were ever going to find new funding to keep the program alive for another year. She had made a reservation for Dr. Tinley and Bart the reporter at an old-school downtown D.C. club with tin ceilings, dangling chandeliers and a locally famous piano player who wore a long tuxedo coat.

"Just listen to this." He sounded happy enough to burst. "We ran into the Healing Voices Foundation president, Charles Van der Griff. Remember him? Turns out he's up here from Atlanta, doing some business in D.C. One thing led to another, he started talking to Bart, and before I knew it, Van der Griff was offering me money for the project. I mean, *real* money. Bart asked him, 'Is that on the record?' He said, 'You bet. You can quote me.'"

Parker slid down the wall onto her ankles, relieved and thrilled and not quite believing their good luck. The program's future was at stake. As Dr. Tinley had explained earlier in the day, without a quick infusion of cash, there would be no more do-gooder work for his nonprofit, and no more salary for Parker, which she needed to pay for their house, car insurance, groceries, Joie's dental bills, and heat in the winter. "Congratulations," she said, imagining how Dr. Tinley's cheeks must be bright red with excitement. She pictured dear funny Bart the reporter, too, pointing his chewed-up pencil at the foundation president. "That's great news."

"There's one catch." Dr. Tinley paused just long enough for a bolus of adrenaline to flood Parker's arteries. "Van der Griff wants you to put together a press event right away. He wants it to happen at his facility in Atlanta. His research director would be the featured speaker. You don't mind spending a few days in Atlanta, do you?"

Parker's head felt like a massive tumor.

"It's Joie's last week of school before the summer break." Her argument came out squeaky and pointless. "I need to be here for her."

"This is important." His voice had dropped an octave. "This isn't optional for us. It's a make or break deal."

"I know."

"I wouldn't ask you, otherwise. I remember how much you hate to travel."

Parker crumbled. She couldn't let Dr. Tinley down. He had been so good to her, almost like a father, and anyway, it wasn't as if she had much of a choice. She and Beamer couldn't make ends meet without her salary. Propping her head against the wall, she thought of Joie's wide blue eyes inside the little Valentine frame of her face and their puny college savings fund. "I understand," she said, breathless and beyond tired. "I'll book a flight."

By morning, Parker was elbowing her way through the packed Atlanta airport, where everyone seemed to be running around as crazy as sprayed roaches. She boarded a train that zoomed over the treetops, to Rental Car City. On her car's radio, familiar-sounding voices reminded her of music from a metal saw, which made her laugh out loud. Instantly, her Southern accent came back. "Hey, y'all," she said, trying it on for size. "I'm home, bitches."

Rounding a curve on the downtown connector, all at once, there it was, springing into view—the city's gold-domed capitol building, a giant spinning peach, and a whole world of glittering skyscrapers surrounded by a vast sea of green. Her lungs expanded. She breathed more deeply, being home at last, back in Atlanta, her City in a Forest.

6.

JARED ASTOR

When the driver opened his door, the famous Jared Astor popped out, mumbled a dignified word of thanks, and began striding toward the massive white cube of his gallery. As always, he admired the shape of his name across the building. The gold leaf caught the sun, making the big letters glint. He smiled and kept moving. His stomach felt hollow, aching with hunger after a dull series of morning meetings. He could already taste his favorite lunch: salad niçoise, extra feta cheese, heavy on the olives. He needed to get inside quickly. He didn't want some starving artist to accost him in the parking lot. This happened on a surprisingly regular basis to Jared Astor. The very idea made him shudder.

The numerical keypad clicked under his fingers, turning from red to green, and the door hummed open for him. A surge of cool, filtered air instantly formed a cocoon around him. The door locked back into place and he exhaled, tipping his chin at the guard, a sinewy ex-boxer with a buzz cut.

"Sir," the guard said.

Jared nodded again, wishing he could remember the man's name, not because he would ever want to use it, but just to prove to himself he wasn't getting Alzheimer's yet. Along the walls, precise circles of light looked like white shawls tossed over his framed pieces. Two small spotlights cloaked a large metal sculpture with starkly folded, origami-like shadows. In the east corner, a trio of well-manicured women whispered, hands cupped around their waxed chins. Jared climbed the back stairs, breathing hard, through a foyer of gleaming golden wood leading to his office, where he hoped his lunch would be waiting for him.

To calm his breathing, he stopped on the landing and pretended to check his tie in an antique mirror. Squinting through the spider-veined glass, Jared inspected his jowls. He was certain they had been shrinking, and he flashed his best movie-star smile at himself, happy his latest diet seemed to be working. *Resplendent.* Yes, that was the word for it. He was resplendent in a double-breasted dark blue suit with small gold buttons, a sapphire-colored tie and matching pocket scarf.

A woman's voice, too loud against the muted whistling of an overhead fan, made Jared turn, frowning, into the atrium where his assistant Sarah usually sat behind a small white desk with a navy-blue telephone, a matching pen, and a pink notepad. He cringed to find Sarah on her feet, face to face with an unkempt woman Jared didn't immediately recognize. The woman's braids, threaded with gray, brushed the top of a large belt that looked like a monk's rope, and she was wearing green socks under hiking boots caked with red dirt. He wondered if she might be homeless or mentally ill, or both.

"He doesn't meet artists in his office," Sarah said, eyes bulging over the woman's large shoulder where it bloomed from a sleeveless purple blouse. "I'm sorry."

"He sent me this letter." The woman brandished a sheet of paper at Sarah, who looked like a kid, craning her neck to make eye contact with the visitor.

"He prefers to visit artists in their studios," Sarah said, sidestepping her desk. Jared knew she was trying to make the woman turn, to clear a path for him.

He ducked his head, charging forward like a bull, but he was too slow. The woman had seen him. She touched his arm. Her voice rose, loud enough to be heard by the trio of wealthy clients with hairless chins.

"There you are," she said. Her eyes were a lighter brown than her face and—interestingly—shot through with a red velvety color at the center, around her pupils. "I'm answering your letter. I was hoping to tell you more about my *dikenga* figures and my current work, too."

Oh, God, he thought. *It's Arden Collier, in the flesh.*

He took the letter from her without comment, staring at his signature and the gallery's imprint on heavy, cream-colored paper. Silently, he cursed the former recruitment manager who had talked him into sending a series of missives to marginally viable candidates for exhibition. Jared had agreed to sign Arden's letter after being reminded of her earlier work. The staff member disappeared soon thereafter, having fled to Miami Beach with a lover, leaving Jared to deal with a dozen wannabes he never would have pursued on his own. Making matters worse in Arden's case, he had seen the newspaper article about her tumbling-down house and her problems with county inspectors. In the commercial gallery business, negative publicity was the kiss of death. There was no way he was going to touch her work with a ten-foot pole.

He pushed the letter back into her hands, planting his multi-colored leather shoes farther apart. "As Sarah said, I never meet artists here."

Sarah gestured toward the exit, pointing with her whole body, rigid arms outstretched like a member of the ground crew at Hartsfield-Jackson Atlanta International Airport. "Please," she said. "May I show you the rest of the gallery? It's truly delightful. We have some wonderful pieces. I could give you a personal tour."

"I called." Arden's voice boomeranged off the tin ceiling, tossing an echo over the office loft where they were standing. "I had an appointment."

"It's not on his calendar," Sarah whispered, "and as I've told you, he doesn't discuss representation here, so I'm sure I would never have—"

"You wrote to me." Arden's chin began to shake through a smile. She wouldn't take her eyes off Jared. "You remembered my figures. It's very important. I wouldn't have come here unannounced, otherwise."

Downstairs, someone coughed. Arden was bearing down on him. He didn't want a scene. God forbid one of his customers should post a Twitter message about the crazy woman bellowing in Jared Astor's gallery. His chest expanded and collapsed completely when he sighed, resigned to his fate: the inevitable postponement of his lunch. He turned toward Sarah. "Has my lunch arrived?"

She shook her head, disturbing the precise symmetry of her glossy, black bangs. "No, sir. Not yet."

"All I need is a minute or two," Arden said, practically yelling.

Jared's finger flew to his lips. He turned quickly, waved his hand like a magician, and ushered Arden into his glass-walled sanctuary. "See what's taking them so long," he told Sarah. Behind Arden's back, Jared tapped his wristwatch, letting Sarah know she should rescue him in exactly five minutes. It was their code.

He couldn't decide whether Arden smelled more like mint or olive oil. Patchouli, perhaps, not a bad aroma, and yet her fingernails were caked with dried paint that was the same color as the mud on her boots. The edge of her collar sagged, frayed in spots and discolored with sweat. A shudder made him tremble, nostrils flaring, as she sank unapologetically onto his favorite sunset-colored pigskin couch. He eased onto a red leather chair positioned a safe distance away from her. "I've got a conference call in a few minutes," he said, lying. "I haven't had my lunch."

She was perched on the edge of the couch, leaning over his coffee table. The tips of her beaded braids tapped the glass. The beads were yellow and orange, stuck onto tinfoil balls she had wrapped around the end of each braid. He wondered if the tinfoil might scratch his table, which had cost him six-thousand, five-hundred dollars and had to be shipped to Atlanta from Norway. "I was glad to know you saw my exhibit at the High Museum."

He had seen the show, in fact, some years earlier. It had been stunning for its time—female figures sculpted from bronze, twisted into complex shapes and painted. *Emotive.* He had bought and resold a pair of the figures, at a huge markup, to the owner of a marble-encrusted mansion on West Paces Ferry Road, a collector of African-American art.

As he watched Arden's expectant face, Jared tried to fish the collector's name from the murkiest pool of his memory. He had met her once, years earlier. After that, to his chagrin, she rebuffed his various overtures for a subsequent meeting. The letters of her name bobbed like soggy corks in his mind, mercifully drowned by the many paper-thin crystal flutes of champagne he had consumed at her cocktail party. *Virginia?* No. *Vivian?* Wrong. *Veronica?* No—*Vera.* Yes, that was it. A skillfully preserved middle-aged woman of color. Shellacked helmet of chemically relaxed, light brown hair shot through with gingery highlights. Rich as Midas. *Vera Van der Griff.* Her story floated back to him, buoyant as flecks of pepper in a Bloody Mary. She had made her money in an unsavory way—selling bangles on television, the home-shopping network. Overstated beadwork rotating on gray velvet pedestals.

Running his tongue over his teeth, Jared thought about the sourdough bread they usually brought along with his salad. He wasn't supposed to have butter with his bread, but perhaps he could make an exception. It had been such a stressful day. "That was what," he said in a flat voice while he lasered Arden with a sharp gaze, "ten, fifteen years ago?"

Her eyes filled and cleared, and she seemed to shrivel like a geriatric turtle into her enormous blouse. "I've got new work."

"Do you, now?"

"Yes, a series of masks." Her head dropped toward the floor for a moment. When it popped up again, she was holding a cheap canvas-covered portfolio.

Jared stifled a groan as she flipped it open to show him several photographs of her face, replicated in plaster and painted. "Oh, yes." He leaned back, covering the slope of his belly with his hands. "I read about your little show last year. Where was that?"

Arden froze with one hand on the photos. Her fingers were shaking. "Vista Gallery."

"Vista Gallery." Jared pronounced the syllables as slowly as possible. "Vista. Gallery. That's located—where is that? Somewhere in a suburban area, I believe?"

"Sandy Springs."

"Oh, yes, yes. Of course." Jared brushed his lapels with his pointer finger while staring out the window at a massive magnolia tree. "A thriving art community there."

"I've got another project in mind at the moment. I'm developing a new body of work based on memory."

"Memory." Where the hell was Sarah with his lunch? Surely it had been more than five minutes. "Trust me," he said, "it's been done. It's called confessionalism. The exploitation of one's tragic childhood as creative fodder. The result, in my opinion, is almost always autobiographical drivel, rarely art."

She slid the portfolio onto her lap and doubled over her knees, staring at her own angular face, reflected by his polished table. For a second, he wondered whether she was going to be ill, there in his executive suite. When she recovered, exhaling, her blouse made a popping sound. A button whizzed onto the smallest of his Persian carpets. Her pendulous breasts, straining inside a dingy-looking brassiere, peered at him through a newly formed gap in her blouse. He was glad his recruitment manager had moved to Florida. Thrilled, actually. He might have killed the man, otherwise. Talk about bad publicity. *Murder at the Jared Astor Gallery.*

"I'm thinking of a multimedia presentation," she said finally, fumbling with her top. "Not just sculpture or paintings, but music and found objects and visual poetry. My family's history would be a metaphor for the human condition, for our memories of shared experiences."

He was tapping an unused pencil eraser against his chair, over and over again, when he realized she had stopped talking. "Like Radcliffe Bailey's Memory as Medicine show?" The association sprang forth unbidden, in an automatic fashion. He admired Radcliffe Bailey. He generally liked visual poetry. He didn't like this minty-smelling woman who was coming between him and his lunch, but so long as he was stuck with her and his lunch was still missing, he might as well try to introduce some mildly interesting conversation.

A smile gradually took over her jaw and her whole face, lifting her prominent cheekbones even higher. "He's been an inspiration, yes, but I don't want to capture big historical events like Hurricane Katrina or colonial American slavery. I want to share a more intimate, personal story about my family's memories."

Stretching forward, Jared placed his pencil on the table between them so that the tip pointed at her. "I'd need to visit your studio and see some results. That's how it works, Arden. You know that."

"I'd need an advance."

She belched it out so suddenly, it took him by surprise and he laughed with such force that he had to retrieve a silk handkerchief from his pocket. "I don't do that. No commercial gallery owner in the world would do that for you. I mean, get real, sweetheart, all right? Look, my lunch should be here by—"

"Please." Her eyes wobbled. She pulled a photo out of the canvas binder while her pupils began to swim and she slid it across the table until it was touching the pencil. "I'm asking for a leg up, not a handout. My grandfather made his own way, built his house and just about our whole neighborhood from scratch. I want to tell his story."

The photo was old, brown and faded with a ruffled white edge. In it, an old man was gripping the brim of a bedraggled felt hat. Jared thought suddenly of a favorite uncle on his mother's side who had constantly clutched a similar hat, turning it in slow, maddening circles while pressing its brim with his calloused fingers. The hat had always struck Jared as a wretched symbol of subservience, of back-breaking work and racism and raw hunger. When the old man died, he left Jared an unexpectedly large inheritance—all the coins and dollar bills he had earned over many years in service to The Man. Jared had opened his gallery a year later.

A spasm rocketed through Jared's empty stomach. He was genuinely afraid Arden was going to cry, in the middle of his glittering office. Also, Jared had loved his uncle. "Look, dear," he said, wincing at his slight show of affection, "if you can show me some real work—not sketches, not mockups, but at least three real, new pieces by Tuesday, then we can talk again."

It took her a few seconds before she remembered to close her mouth. "Yes," she said at last. "I'm sure I can do that."

Jared was positive he would never see her again. *Thank God.* She hadn't produced any new work in ages, and she wouldn't be able to come up with anything so quickly. Then again, if by some miracle she managed to pull it off, perhaps he might even be able to arrange a second meeting with Vera Van der Griff. So really, he thought, he couldn't lose by making the offer, taking the high road, having mercy on her. The idea made him feel good about himself. *Magnanimous.* Yes, that was the word that sprang to mind. He deserved to have butter on his bread. "If I like it, and only if I like it, I'll give you a modest advance to tide you over. I'm not talking about a large figure. Okay? It seems as though you've hit upon some hard times. I try to support my local artists."

"Yes," she said again. She seemed too stunned to speak. "Thank you. Yes."

The door opened and Sarah appeared, carrying a glass bowl on a silver tray.

"Bring some work back on Tuesday," Jared said as his assistant placed the food in front of him. "I'll expect to hear from you."

Arden stood, still shaking. "Tuesday," she said. "I'll be here."

Sarah, smiling and silent, took Arden's elbow. They drifted into the hallway while Jared unbuttoned his jacket, leering sideways at his meal. Six olives, three generous scoops of feta cheese, dressing on the side. Desire pooled on his tongue. He picked up his fork but quickly slammed it back down onto the table. *Damn it.* No sourdough roll. No butter, either.

7.

PARKER GOZER

Inside the Healing Voices Foundation, Parker jogged in her high heels, clutching a work binder to keep up with Dr. Tinley's benefactor, Charles Van der Griff, who seemed hell-bent on staging a press conference as soon as possible in his musty warehouse outside Atlanta. Parker needed to talk him out of it, and fast—ideally, before three o'clock. That was when Joie would be at home in Virginia, briefly available for a phone call before lacrosse practice. Parker would have a half-hour window to hear Joie's sweet voice.

Van der Griff had billed his facility as a "state-of-the-art" video laboratory, yet all Parker saw were hulking, ancient computers sitting idle in a dark, empty room—an embarrassing setting for a press conference that would draw too few reporters and potentially tarnish Dr. Tinley's stellar reputation. The machines' yellowing plastic heads with their tiny screens and massive keyboards made Parker think of her first-ever word processor, which had hummed like a Concorde jet and got so hot after a few minutes, she was always afraid it might spontaneously burst into flames. In the room's far corner, an overhead projector sat glumly beneath a wrinkled pull-down screen. It looked like the sheet her father used to drape over one wall of their living room, back in the early 1970s, whenever he wanted to show his vacation slides to the neighbors. Those had been good times—before her mother's condition grew worse, before he moved out of the home where Parker grew up.

Stealing a peek at the time, Parker calculated how long it would take to drive to her favorite place, Silver Park—forty-five minutes, if she got lucky with Atlanta traffic. This seemed improbable, especially since it had rained earlier. Atlanta drivers were well known for losing their minds at the first sign of precipitation. It was Parker's ritual, every time she visited her hometown, to call Joie from Silver Park, but she needed to get there no later than three o'clock. It was already one o'clock, and she couldn't leave the Healing Voices Foundation until she talked Charles Van der Griff out of his ill-advised plan.

Hosting a press conference at his creaky facility, miles beyond the city limits, next to a check-cashing service and a furniture rental store, was a bad idea. The worst. She had to find a tactful way to explain the problem to him.

"I received the background information," she said, flipping her binder to a page on the Healing Voices Foundation. "If I understand, your idea is to—"

"Expand your human rights research by orders of magnitude." His voice was deep, tightly curled around a Southern accent and loud enough to rattle her eardrum. "With my funding, you won't have to rely on basic before-and-after satellite images to confirm human rights violations. You can buy more images at much higher resolutions."

He was a tall man, standing close enough for her to smell the milky, sweet granola stuck between his teeth. His small, amber-colored eyes were round and active—propelled perhaps by his many grandiose ideas. She thought about Dr. Tinley's eyes, which were caramel-brown, nearly green around the edges, and the time they had toured oil-slicked villages in the Niger Delta. Children had chattered, playing tag by a black river while an orange oil flare roared behind them. Black smoke had burned Parker's eyes. Dr. Tinley's image analysis had revealed the children's lives, before and after the devastation, raising awareness of their plight.

The memory made her think of standing over a campfire with Arden, by Mr. Collier's house in Silver Park, the year they both started first grade. Arden's Aunt Wilma always seemed to be boiling water to cook a chicken caught and plucked from their side yard. For some years, Arden's friendship, now lost, had been a constant. Blinking back a wayward piece of mascara, she willed herself to focus on the task at hand.

"We're excited about this partnership," she said, careful not to sound like she might be groveling. Part of her job was to make sure sponsors knew Dr. Tinley had to be in charge if he was going to be involved at all. "As you know, our algorithms let us tally hundreds of damaged buildings, abandoned crop fields, burn marks, artillery craters, burial sites, prison camps, stockpiled weapons—many types of evidence—based on satellite images."

"But you're limited by the images you can afford to buy." Van der Griff pried open a metal door, leading her down a stairwell. On one side of it, midday sun burned through a wall of windows. Outside, the woods were thick and green—mostly pines and dogwoods and a few sycamores with peeling white trunks. In a tiny clearing by the building's back door, wild honeysuckle vines curled around the legs of a small wooden bench, dotting it with orange flowers.

Her heels, clicking down the rickety steps, echoed in the cinder-block enclosure. "You're exactly right." She kept a death grip on the railing. She couldn't afford to take a wrong step—literally, or in her conversation with Van der Griff. "The goal would be to pinpoint recurring patterns of change to landscapes and structures."

He smiled, waving Parker through another door. "Eyes in the sky."

"That's the idea." They entered a dingy hallway that smelled sharply of Pine Sol. Naked tubes of greenish fluorescent light hummed from the ceiling. Parker thought about the young girl she had met in Nigeria. She had eyes as brown and deep as the river where Parker's Dad had grown up in Piney Tangle, Florida, swimming with alligators that never bit him and mosquitoes that bit him all to pieces. The girl's name was Oba. Her whole family had been killed and she was living with strangers, drinking oil-polluted water. "Of course, the goal would be to protect villages and families, or maybe even individual children, if we can actually turn our assessment algorithm into a predictive system."

"Our main lab," Van der Griff said, sweeping his hand across another empty room stocked with what appeared to be slightly newer-model computers and a real display screen. He squinted at his enormous wristwatch, frowning as Parker slid past him, into the cool silence of the darkened room. "Our research director should be here by now."

She flashed her teeth at Van der Griff, trying to look as though she had all the time in the world. "Our plan is to someday predict human rights attacks before they happen," she said again, easing onto a plastic chair. As she said it, her mind drifted. She imagined a software program that could have predicted what Buddy did to her, or the effect that being a child bride had on Arden's Aunt Wilma, who went half-blind after drinking her husband's poisoned moonshine.

Van der Griff parked himself behind a desk, planting his elbows on either side of a stack of papers, and he stared over his hairy knuckles. On one corner of the desk, a boy and a girl grinned at Parker from a series of gold picture frames. They looked like Van der Griff, although slightly more tanned, with the same expansive forehead and piercing eyes. She could imagine, by looking at the children, how he must have been exceptionally handsome at an earlier point in his life. "One thing I don't understand," he said. "Why Nigeria? There are so many other regions at risk. Why not Tibet or Myanmar—somewhere in Asia? For many Americans, Africa's a less compelling choice."

Parker's mouth went dry. She thought of Rocky, Joie's pet hermit crab that had shriveled up and died when they forgot to give it any water for three days. *Less compelling?* It sounded like code, a racist dog whistle. With an escalating sensation of certainty, Parker knew she would always hate Charles Van der Griff. She licked her lips and launched into her talking points. "Since 2003, hundreds of thousands of Nigerians have been killed in Janjaweed and Sudanese military attacks. Many more are at risk of being raped. Gas flaring by oil companies has poisoned whole villages, contaminating the air and water. The violence and destruction continues even now, in 2014."

Van der Griff shrugged. "Tibetans can't even wave their flag or sing their national anthem. Trouble happens in many places. Think about all the U.S. cities with dirty water."

Heat surged through Parker's cheeks. She pictured Buddy, leaning over to pop open his car door for her when she was a kid, and Arden, trying to hide, wide-eyed, behind her aunt's starched skirt.

Parker took a breath, held it an extra second, and released it as slowly as possible. Dr. Tinley's research was already underway in Nigeria. He needed support to complete it. "That's true. I'm sure Dr. Tinley would be happy to consider another region after we finalize the Nigerian report. You may be right about most Americans feeling disconnected from anything that happens in Africa. What most of us don't realize is that more oil gets spilled in the Niger Delta every year than the Deepwater Horizon disaster in the Gulf of Mexico."

His eyebrows shot up, making his vast, pale forehead look like carefully draped silk. "That can't be right."

"It is."

Van der Griff let out a heaving sigh. "Of course, it doesn't matter whether I think Africa is the best location for this research. My wife has a special interest in the region." He leaned forward, whispering, and he winked at Parker. "We have a mixed marriage."

Parker cringed at the awful, outdated term, which sounded obscenely racist, conjuring an image of naked people with frightened eyes—pasty legs intertwined with dark ones. How could he say such a thing about his wife, or his marriage? Did he think it was funny? "Her family was originally from Africa?"

"Generations ago, yes," he said, "and her vote is the one that counts."

For a moment, Parker watched him with her mouth slightly ajar. She wasn't sure what his wife had to do with the project. Her name wasn't anywhere on the hastily written contract. "Dr. Tinley does excellent work," she said.

"When will you plan my press conference?" His eyes kept shifting back and forth. "I've given the first check to your boss. He'll get the second half of the money after you get reporters here. This week works best for me."

Thinking of Joie and the minutes ticking away, Parker turned her attention to his family photos, hoping to soften the tone of their conversation. "Are these your children?"

"Yes, when they were little," Van der Griff said, repositioning the photo frames, one at a time. "They're grown now. The auditorium should work nicely, don't you think?"

Squaring her shoulders, Parker locked eyes with him. "We need to talk about the staging question. Atlanta's not a huge media market, and with all the downsizing in newsrooms, getting reporters to travel this far from the city would be—"

"That's why they pay you the big bucks, right?" He pursed his lips and blew dust off one of his family photos. Most of the particles flew horizontally off the desk, swirling in a circle before floating down onto Parker's lap. "To get reporters here?"

She resisted the urge to brush the dust off her cream-colored skirt. "I want the press announcement to be as effective as possible for you. It's important to pick the right venue. Generally, it's best to stage these sorts of things in major media markets in a building that's centrally located. You're pretty far outside the city here. You'd be lucky to get a handful of reporters. We'd have to patch everyone else in by videoconference."

"So there you go." He tried to stifle a yawn, which made his upper lip and his nostrils wiggle when it escaped. "Do that. I'm trying to build some name recognition. I want to bring reporters here, show them what we're doing."

"We could stage something downtown and play a video to introduce your foundation. That would be better choreography and you'd get much better turnout."

"I didn't attach many strings to this funding." Again, he looked at his watch and stood up. "The event needs to stay here."

Parker kept her seat. "In that case, I'd need a couple more weeks to build some buzz for your event."

Van der Griff slid his hands into his pockets so that his jacket flared out like a cape on either side of him. "It's got to happen this week. Friday gives you three days to plan."

"Friday's not a good day for press events." She said it before he had finished talking. "You wouldn't want to hold a press conference on a Monday, either. Tuesday is usually the best day of the week for generating news."

He stared at her, not blinking. "This Friday. That's a deal breaker for me. I'm in the running for a major defense contract that's being decided next week. I need the visibility now."

A shiver ran up the back of Parker's neck, under her hair. He had an angle. Van der Griff was using Dr. Tinley to get a big federal contract. "I see."

"I don't know where the hell my research director went. I'm going to go find him. Make yourself comfortable."

As soon as Van der Griff disappeared, she shook the dust off her skirt and looked around, without success, for a water cooler. Time kept passing, taking her further away from any hope of catching up with Joie, the magical baby who had appeared so late in Parker's life, lighting it up. She palmed her smartphone and read all of her emails twice. Finally, she picked up one of Van der Griff's photos—an old shot of him posing with a baby and an elegant-looking woman of color. Parker couldn't tell if the baby was a girl or a boy, or whether Van der Griff looked happy about whatever he had gotten in the childbirth lottery.

The short version of her father's story—whispered on several occasions while he turned the pages of a blurry brown scrapbook—hummed in her ears. She knew the words by heart, like a poem:

The grasshoppers screamed—loud, soft, loud.
He walked off through cotton the day I turned four.
The punch-drunk sun and the soft, faraway sound of my breath
pinned me down, held me there, and we were alone—my mother, my
brother and me.

Foster Gozer had been born on a sandy road in a rural Florida community, several years before electrical lines were brought to his town. His family ate what they could grow or raise. When his father walked out, times were hard. For the rest of his life, the old man's abandonment lurched like a ghost behind Foster's eyes, haunting him.

Parker heard the complete version of her father's story only once, near the end of his life:

"The top half of the morning sun was still a pale pink across the field, as weak as my Dad had been the night before, stumbling home. I eased onto my elbow—I remember because my arm had a scab on it, so it hurt—and I set my chin on the peeled paint of our windowsill.

What woke me up was the screen door, creak-popping on its hinges. The grasshoppers were kind of rattle-screaming, you know how they do: loud, then softer, then loud again. I watched my Dad lumber off toward that old horizon. Later, I found out he was heading back to the city where they had a pool hall.

In my mind, I was yelling after him, 'Wait, don't go.' I thought about running barefoot over the yard, but what really happened was, I stayed put. I can't explain why, exactly. I was feeling something like a weight, pulling me down. When I was grown, I realized it was just a child's fear, but I still feel it sometimes, even now. I blame myself because I didn't do anything to stop him. The feeling gets bigger or smaller, but it's always with me.

Watching my father shuffle off across that field, the weight came on me like an alligator, closing its jaws, tight enough to snap my neck if I so much as moved my eyes. I really wanted to run and catch my Dad, but the grasshoppers and that old punch-drunk Florida sun and the sound of my brother breathing in the bed next to me felt like a heavy weight, pinning me there. I turned four years old that day."

Parker knew this loss probably explained her father's irrational soft spot for Buddy, whose old man had also disappeared.

At thirteen, Parker hid her father's scrapbook under her bed—drop-kicked it through the dust ruffle when her parents divorced. He moved out of the house, leaving Parker alone with her mother, who wandered around with a tumbler full of bourbon most of the time. She gave the scrapbook back to him, hoping for a smile, before he died. He had wanted a son, she knew that, although he never said it. Parker was what he got.

She lowered Van der Griff's snapshot back onto the desk, careful not to knock over the whole row of family photos like a dysfunctional set of dominoes.

Closing her eyes, Parker meditated on the persistent whirring of the air-conditioner and the ringing in her ears. She would have to call Dr. Tinley later, to get his advice on managing this guy Van der Griff, who clearly thought money could buy him love. She never heard any footsteps, only the familiar voice hovering close above her head. "Good grief," he said. "Are they letting just anyone in here?"

Her eyes flew open. "Are you kidding me?" She couldn't stop laughing. She had seen him on TV a few times over the years, talking about his work. One time, she found his TED Talk on the Internet. She hadn't dared to keep in touch. "You're the research director?"

Dylan turned his palms to the ceiling, clowning. "Crazy, huh? Bet you never thought I'd get a straight job."

On her feet, Parker opened her arms for his hug, which was as warm as ever. Her cheek got pressed against his chest. His Trees Atlanta T-shirt, under a dark blue jacket, smelled of a flowery detergent. "Last I heard, you were going for a graduate degree at Georgia Tech. Let's see, you were majoring in pottery or macramé or—"

"Mechanical engineering."

"Ah, yes, and your undergraduate degree was in geography, I think." She couldn't help it. She sneaked a peek at his left hand. No ring.

"Yep." Lifting his chin, he waved an arm through the air with an exaggerated flourish. "And now, as you can plainly see, I'm the king of this entire fabulous research center with its massive staff and cutting-edge equipment."

He was making fun of Van der Griff's facility. Parker knew better than to agree with him. She had a job to do. "I thought you were working for *National Geographic.* I saw you on TV as an explorer-in-residence or something."

Dylan winced, rolling his eyes. "Yeah, well. That fell through a few years back. Philosophical differences, *blah, blah, blah.*"

She stared at him with her mouth slightly ajar. His face was still chiseled but softer at the jaw line, and she realized, when he started talking about his work, that his voice hadn't changed a bit. His words, warm as liqueur, seeped into every corner of the room, silencing it, rolling up Parker's spine. "Hey, Dyl," she said. "It's good to see you after all these years."

"I couldn't believe it when Charles told me your name." His laugh lines, stretching all the way across his temples, made her want to cry. When had they both gotten so old? "I've never met anyone else named Parker Gozer."

"I didn't change my name when I got married."

"Oh, yes. What was his name? Boomer?"

"Beamer."

"Well," he said, "I'm glad we're doing this job with Tinley."

"We're glad, too, believe me. Talk about the nick of time. I shouldn't tell you that, but we needed the funding, man. Not exactly sure I understand why you needed us. I guess your boss hopes to score some federal money."

"That's true. Also, I don't have the math power in-house to handle the algorithms with these higher-resolution images." Dylan straddled a chair and clicked his computer to life. "That's where you guys come in. Van der Griff means well, but he doesn't know jack-shit about setting up a lab—or math, as it turns out."

"Dr. Tinley's brilliant with math. We've also got the supercomputer."

"Plus, let's face it, nobody knows who we are. We're just getting started here. Everybody knows The Tinley Institute, especially Mrs. Van der Griff, and frankly, she calls all the shots around here."

A spinning rainbow appeared on his computer screen. "Your boss mentioned that. He said she's interested in Africa. Is that her heritage?"

Dylan nodded. "Yeah, I'm sure that's part of it, and she's a smart businesswoman with eclectic interests. A big advocate for science, art, history, literacy—all that good stuff. Very interesting person. Self-made and all that."

"What's her business?"

"Ever seen QVC, the home-shopping network?"

"Sure, flipping through the TV stations," Parker said, lying. She didn't want to admit she had watched the shopping channel.

"She's the founder of VMS Designs."

Before she thought better of it, Parker punched Dylan in the chest with both hands. "No way! Mrs. Van der Griff makes Vera Mae Smith jewelry?"

"Yep," he said, rubbing his chest where she had hit him. "She seems to have other people running the company now, for the most part."

"Oh man, I love her stuff. All the department stores have it on display. It's way too rich for my blood, but I always stop and look at it."

"I see her name in the news pretty regularly, supporting some cause or other. She's got a bunch of volunteer titles with the historical society and so forth. Charles is clearly in a supporting role, in that marriage."

"He's the arm candy."

"Ha! I'm not sure how she sees it, but she definitely holds the purse strings."

"Good for her."

"Yeah, honestly, I wish I could work for her instead of Charles. She seems genuinely tough, but nice, you know? She basically insisted he should hire me after the *National Geographic*—"

Dylan went silent.

"What?" Parker said. "What happened?"

A series of square icons appeared on his computer screen. "Hey, sit with me by the screen here," he said. "You're going to like this."

Parker resisted the urge to check the time.

"You look strangely youthful, by the way. I assume work was done?"

"Ha ha. Like I could afford a nip and tuck."

A few keyboard clicks later, an aerial view of a city street came into view. He pushed a lever that looked to Parker like an old joystick from an arcade game. She gripped her chair as the image rushed toward her until she could see people—monks in orange robes, women in billowing trousers, two children carrying a bucket between them. "Is this real-time satellite video? I've heard about it, never actually seen it."

"Incredible resolution, isn't it? This is Myanmar. We're using a new generation of cameras, much better lenses, and we can precisely manipulate the angle of the shot, too."

"I'm never sunbathing nude on my balcony again."

He let out a laugh that cracked her up. "Where did you say you live?"

Memories from her senior year in college, when Beamer decided to sow his nonexistent wild oats and Parker wound up doing the same with Dylan, kept popping like giant intoxicating bubbles in front of her face. Dylan had been a great kisser, the best, never in a hurry, with a kind of electrical warmth to his lips. When Beamer had finally asked her to marry him, she was ambivalent, to say the least, about dumping Dylan. She had dreamed of Joie's face, though, and Dylan would never commit.

Sweet baby Joie. She would be waiting for Parker's call at three o'clock. "Listen, I'm pretty worried about holding a press conference out here," she said with more urgency than she had intended. "I don't want your boss to be embarrassed. It would be much better if we could talk him into a nice venue downtown, or better yet, we could host an event in D.C. or Manhattan, where there are more reporters."

Dylan swiveled on his seat, unleashing a shrill, metallic squeal from the chair. "I know this building's crappy, but he's determined to have you bring the mountain to Muhammad. I don't recommend trying to talk Charles out of anything once he's got it in his head."

"I could use your help on this."

"What if I made a glitzy multimedia presentation for you? The auditorium has screens on three sides, believe it or not, behind the green curtains."

"I noticed those," she said. "I guess the moths are a real problem."

"I could put together a video that would be like taking a wicked acid trip." He pressed the back of his fist against Parker's arm and reeled his head in a circle, pretending to be tripping. "Lucy in the Sky with Diamonds."

"Like the old Chevy Show at Six Flags or something?"

"Way better." He flashed two thumbs up at her. "Their minds would be blown."

Shuttle buses might work, Parker thought, *if I could convince enough reporters to get onboard.* "I've got some great field video and photos from the Niger Delta."

"Excellent. A little video, a couple of heart-wrenching photos and a real-time satellite tour. Voilà. They'll laugh. They'll cry. They'll become a part of it."

She had forgotten about the size of Dylan's hands. Her fingers disappeared under his palm when he set his hand on top of hers. "I'd have to get a script and all the raw files to you by tonight, and I need to check in with Dr. Tinley." She slid her fingers free. "He's very particular about how our brand gets presented to the public. Everything has to look good. If you thought your boss was stubborn, believe me, he's met his match."

Dylan scribbled a phone number on a business card, shoved it into Parker's hand. "That's me. What are you doing for dinner?"

"Oh," she said, looking down at her pocketbook while she tucked the card into it. She pressed her left hand against her collarbone, leaving it there long enough for him to see the ring, to remember Beamer. "Thanks, but I've got a lot to get done. I'll give you a buzz tonight to see how it's going. I'll come back tomorrow."

He stood up and squeezed her so hard, her feet briefly left the floor. For a second, Parker's face got mashed against his sternum and she worried her ribs might crack. "You know," he said, setting her back down, "my heart's still broken. I think it's just a wad of shredded ribbons in there by now. See you tomorrow, little one."

Parker couldn't get back to her rental car fast enough. She went through six antibacterial wipes, disinfecting her hands, her throat, the steering wheel, the car handles, and the dashboard. She wondered what his condescending signoff was supposed to mean. Buddy had always said the same thing to her—"little one"—shriveling her right down to size until she felt mute and helpless as a newborn, but she really was a kid then, literally small. It made some warped kind of sense for Buddy to constantly remind Parker of his power over her. Why Dylan would use the same expression when they were both cruising past fifty, she had no idea.

What the hell?

Her stomach kept quivering from too much coffee, an occupational hazard anytime she had to catch an early-morning flight, or in moments when she remembered every line and shadow of Buddy's hands, no matter how hard she tried to forget him. In earlier years, Parker had imagined she could drown him, once and for all, in her subconscious, but he was lodged in the primitive base of her brain like an eel wrapped around her spinal cord, leaking poison. A metallic taste flooded her mouth, deadly and sweet as a quivering bead of mercury.

She cranked the car and wheeled back down the highway until it finally became Ponce de Leon Avenue. She turned onto Clifton and parked by a red brick bungalow so she could speed-dial Dr. Tinley. The car was rumbling softly and she kept the electric windows cracked. When she checked her phone, it was only two o'clock, after all. Still plenty of time to talk to Dr. Tinley, visit Silver Park and call Joie. She took her time retrieving a notepad and a pen.

Near the curb, a vine heavy with wild scuppernong grapes telegraphed a tangy aroma across the front seat, taking her back to the field where she had picked blackberries, as a girl. The field had stretched farther than Parker could see, dotted here and there by oak trees and surrounded on three sides by pine forest, smelling like a huge jar of jelly. She remembered hearing the bees before she saw them, hovering above the bushes. It got paved over, of course. No more quilt of blackberries and bees and white umbrella-shaped flowers her father had called Queen Anne's lace.

Dr. Tinley's cellphone rang four times before he answered it, calling Parker by the wrong name as usual. "Parky," he said over the unmistakable electronic ping of a computer game, "good thing you called."

His calm, happy voice always pulled her heart rate out of the stratosphere, back down to Earth. "Oh, Dr. Tinley." To Parker, he was like the Dalai Lama, or Santa Claus. "I'm glad you're there."

Through the phone line, his game pinged again. Psycho Beavers, his favorite. "Wait," he said. "I'm up to Level Twelve."

She breathed deeply, enjoying the scuppernong-scented breeze. It reminded her of the gritty wine her grandmother had strained through old pantyhose in the freezing basement of her terrifying house. "I just left Van der Griff's lab."

"No, no," Dr. Tinley said over the sound of a cartoon beaver exploding. "Oh, for Pete's sake. Why can't I ever get all the way with these things?"

"Listen, boss, I need your advice." She didn't mean to raise her voice.

It just came out that way. "I've got a couple of problems down here."

When his computer game went silent, Parker was surprised to hear the sharp edge of sarcasm in his voice. "So I heard. Charles called me. He was pretty cranked up. He said you don't want to do this press event at his place and you don't want to do it this week. We have two-million dollars in the bank right now. We'll get another two after you give him what he wants. I guess I don't understand what kind of problem could be bigger than money like that?"

A white moving van roared by her door, rocking the tiny rental car. "His facility is way out in the boondocks and the neighborhood's seedy. Used car dealerships, adult video stores—that type of thing. The building itself looks old and it's not even clean. I'm concerned it wouldn't make the right impression. I'm not sure I can get enough reporters there. There are plenty of options downtown."

"I hear you, but look, he's dead set. So dress up the room to look pretty, call in some favors with your reporter friends. That's your job, right?"

How many times in one day would older men tell her how to do her job? Leaning forward, Parker pressed her forehead against the steering wheel, which smelled strongly of disinfectant. She closed her eyes, listening to his fingers as they moved over the keyboard. *Yes, Dr. Tinley, that is my shit-eating job.* In the decade they had worked together, she had heard him use a strong tone only a few times, never directed at her, always when funding was at stake. "My job is also about protecting your brand," she said. She could usually win him over by talking about the value of his name. "Your brand is pristine. That's why Van der Griff came to us. I don't want your image to be compromised."

"I appreciate that, but we can't afford to be quite so high-minded this time. Look, don't be anxious about this. You're the best, Parky. I know you can pull it off."

Again with the nickname.

"I don't think I can stand it." Her mouth was hovering over the middle of the steering wheel. Briefly, she wanted to ram her head against the car horn. Sleep could have kidnapped her right there in the car. She wasn't sure which worried her more: the risk of public failure, or the prospect of having to scramble like a madwoman all week while being away from her daughter. She had been in the same sort of situation many times before. Parker's job exhausted her. "This isn't how we roll," she said.

His computer pinged. "Just rip it off, kid. Like a Band-Aid."

She hung up and slid the car into gear, pulled a U-turn, and merged back onto Ponce to Leon. Turning right, she weaved through the overhanging trees and tidy brick houses of Virginia-Highlands until she popped onto a seedy patch of Piedmont Avenue. Neon signs flashed outside X-rated dance clubs and liquor stores. Her car climbed the hill toward a shopping center where the Great Southeast Music Hall used to be. Hanging a right onto Peachtree, Parker cruised by Lenox Square and the MARTA station in Brookhaven.

Finally, she hit a familiar four-way stop. A hand-lettered sign by a small white church said, "Welcome to Silver Park, established 1933."

8.

PARKER GOZER

Music drifted across the car's front seat, carrying Parker into another world. Distant voices, tambourines, and stomping feet reverberated through the walls of Mount Zion Baptist Church. A man in paint-speckled pants nodded under a purple hat. She lifted one finger in greeting and rolled through the intersection. Pastel bed sheets fluttered from a line stretched between two oak trees—faded pink and green and yellow. Smoke snaked through her open car windows. An old woman trimmed hedges while Parker's car bounced off the last of the paved road, crunching onto gravel. Wind whistled through her windows. When the woman arched her back and smiled, Parker waved, exhaling. She was home, her real home.

She missed Joie so much, she had to keep reminding herself to slow down on the dirt road. *Just enough time left to park and make the call.* Turning the car left, she rolled under tree branches that stretched from one side of the lane to the other. All around her, the forest was tightly packed, sweet with pinesap and bright, mossy patches amid the shadows. Her car rumbled by a familiar house with a weathervane and piles of car tires on the lawn. Blinking to ward off the memories, she wondered if Arden might be home, and if they would ever be friends again.

When the road came to an end, Parker tucked the car's front bumper under a cluster of scrub pines, next to a small "Public Park" sign that was partially obscured by tree branches. She abandoned her high-heels, grabbed her laptop and pushed through mountain laurel to reach a pine-needle path. Winding left and right, her legs tensed as the path pitched downhill and she heard the waterfall tumbling over rocks on the far side of the lake. From a distance, the spray looked like a cloud, lifting in slow motion, shot through with sunlight. The trees were full and green, no shaky leaves ready to drop like the first time she had dragged Beamer there and he kissed her. Blue and green triangles of light shifted across the water. The tiny pointed heads of turtles dotted the lake's smooth surface, here and there.

She tiptoed toward a bench, sat down and eased back against a gold plaque with her Dad's name on it. She had it installed under an oak tree when he died. *Stupid cancer.* His death had come as a surprise only because her mother hadn't died first, despite years of hard living. Inheriting most of Silver Lake had been the real shocker. He must have known, after all, how much she loved it. He left her little else, which was strange, given that everyone said he had built half of Atlanta, in his heyday. Where the rest of his money had gone, Parker couldn't guess. She had no siblings. He wasn't keeping any women, so far as Parker knew. She couldn't sell any of her land, either, because it had all been designated as historic—a protected area. Life might have been a little easier for Parker and Beamer if she had been given land she could sell, yet every time she visited the park, she was grateful.

A hummingbird buzzed through a dogwood tree. Farther off, the soft soprano whistling of a Carolina wren floated toward her. It was officially a public park, but usually deserted because of its location, hidden at the end of a dirt road. She released every breath as slowly as she could, reluctant to move too quickly, happy to sit still and wait another ten minutes until the alarm on her phone chimed.

God lives here, she thought.

"Hey, Sid," she said.

Picturing her high school teacher's snaggle-toothed smile and long beard, Parker remembered, once again, the day he had saved her. They had been sitting by the lake. The morning had a bite to it, that last week of autumn. A cool mist rolled over the water, clinging to her jacket and the faded green nylon of her funky old tent. Beamer was already gone, off to college. Parker was floating through her final year of high school with no idea what might come next. Sid had brought a group of students to camp overnight, as part of his class. She knew he was aching to launch into one of his endless, droning lectures that would start with phase transitions and shift to the value of banjo music and its relationship to sine functions and trigonometry—his approach to *paideia,* the ancient Greeks' concept of an ideal education.

It was the 1970s.

They were sitting on pointy rocks by the waterfall, staring at the sky, waiting to see murmuration—a sudden swarm of starlings. Parker's friend Mindy was bored and freezing, a half-hour before sunset. She stretched, winking, and headed back around the lake with the other kids. Some of them had smuggled beer into their backpacks.

Parker stayed behind, with Sid. "You know, you're going to be okay," he said, out of the blue, and at that moment, a monstrous *whooshing* sound cracked like an enormous whip over their heads. Thousands of birds converged simultaneously, rolling across the tops of the trees, their thunderous, whispering dance shifting one way, then the other. Parker sucked in a breath and held it as the birds tightened themselves into an undulating black knot, loosening as they rose, turning as one, wings spread, spiraling into the next air-sculpted pattern, and the next, and the next.

She sat with Sid, her favorite teacher, the responsible adult in her life, not talking as the magical exhalation of rustling wings and beaks and feathers rolled across the sky, over and over. He didn't have to tell her a second time, and if he secretly felt the urge to lecture her on Newton's Third Law of physics, he restrained himself, letting his last words dance in the twisting sky instead. *You're going to be okay.* When Parker remembered to exhale, the small space separating her from Sid seemed to be expanding and contracting, and she felt herself catapulted into the place where God lives, in the constantly shifting human synapse, the connection between two people when time stands still.

That, she had carried with her.

The alarm on her phone went off. Parker snapped to attention, tugged her computer onto her lap, and fired it up. Leaning close to the screen, she smiled as a series of colored pixels turned into jagged geometric shapes that softened and dissolved into the familiar silhouette of Joie's sweet, round head.

"Hi, Mom, I can see you. Can you see me?"

Immediately, Parker knew from the slow rhythm of every syllable and the slight tremor of Joie's chin that something was wrong. "You're gorgeous," she said, standing up so she could move toward the lake with the laptop. Joie's long, pale hair looked practically white, caught in the glare of a lamp shaped like a lacrosse stick. She was wearing a red and white jersey with her team's logo on the front. Nothing had ever been more fun for Parker than watching the back of that jersey—"Hatfield 1"—Beamer's last name, which he had given to their daughter—blasting down the field like a miniature rocket. "Do you know where I am?"

Joie pulled both knees onto her chair and hugged them, letting her head fall against one shoulder. "Silver Park. Our favorite place."

"Can you hear the birds?" Parker turned the computer away from her to show Joie the waterfall and the woods behind it, moving in a slow circle until she was back at the bench. When she sat down again, Joie was smiling sadly into the distance. "I wish you were here."

"Grandpa must have loved you so much, or else he would've made a bunch of money selling that place instead of giving it to you," she said. Typical Joie, always coming up with something kind to say, even when it was clear she was upset.

"He was a pretty smart old Grandpa." Parker had explained to Joie how the land had been locked down, designated as historic because of her father's plan to protect it. She could never turn it into a parking lot or a big-box store even if she suddenly lost all her marbles and morphed into a greedy real-estate developer. After her father died, she had used the park's trust fund to make sure the trees got pruned and the path stayed clear enough for neighborhood fishermen. She tried to visit the property once every season.

Whenever she spoke with Joie, Parker tended to skip the part about her father talking Arden's grandfather out of his land.

"I wish you didn't have to work this week," Joie said.

To Parker, the words sounded like a lacrosse ball whistling straight into the net at warp speed. Her heart thrashed inside her ribcage. "Tell me what's wrong," she said. "What happened? Don't leave anything out."

Still hugging her knees, Joie laid her chin against her arms and stared at Parker through a pair of blue puddles. "I got out of class at noon today," she said. "The seniors had an exam, so I went straight to practice after lunch. The boys came onto the field around two o' clock."

"The boys' lacrosse team." Parker had completed a parenting class once where the instructor explained the importance of "passive listening" as a way to keep your child talking to you. A neat trick, especially if Joie was telling Parker, for example, about certain kids who liked to have sex in the school stairwell, or how she wanted to convince a depressed friend to stop smoking weed and guzzling cough syrup.

Through the magic of passive listening, Parker had learned to avoid screaming, *"Oh, my God, that's terrible!"* or, *"He did what?"*

Joie nodded and sniffed. "Yeah, I guess a pipe broke or something? I'm not sure. Their field got all flooded so they had to run drills on the same field with us."

"That must have been crowded," Parker said, measuring every word. She couldn't believe the idiot boys' lacrosse coach would have done that to the little girls. How predictably stupid. He should have gone into the gym with his boys instead of squeezing onto the girls' turf.

"Coach Billie had me catching pop-ups with Irene and you know how Irene throws the ball really high sometimes," Joie said.

She was too sweet to say Irene had never been able to throw for shit. That was probably why the coach had them working on it. "That was nice of you to help Irene practice her aim." Parker brushed an ant off her arm. Across the pine-straw clearing, one turtle sank under the water. Two more popped through the surface.

When Joie frowned, her chin quivered again. "I was trying my best, but I kept missing my catches and Coach Billie only gave us two balls. I had to keep running over to the boys' side to pick up our balls."

Parker's arm started itching like mad where the ant had bitten her. She couldn't scratch it without making the laptop wobble. She wanted to ask why the coach didn't give Joie a whole basket of balls, the way she usually did, or why the girls didn't simply turn in another direction so Irene's crazy pop-ups wouldn't fly into the boys' space. "How annoying," she said instead.

"A couple of the boys were being real jerks," Joie said it through her teeth. Her neck and face flashed red as a spanking. "They started being really juvenile when I ran by. A few other guys joined in, and after about the fifth ball, they were all doing it."

The late-afternoon sun was weak but shining directly on Parker's face. Her forehead and cheeks felt like they were on the verge of crispy. "What were they doing, exactly?"

"Oh, at first this guy Julian—he's a junior—he was saying stuff like, you know, 'Nice balls you got there,' and, 'Hey, stop grabbing your balls, kid.' Then creepy Steve and Beau started calling me names."

"Why didn't one of the coaches tell them to stop?" Parker had forgotten to bring her water bottle from the car. Her throat was parched.

She sounded hoarse.

Joie looked at her lap with her eyebrows bunched together and she shook her head. "Coach Billie was way down the field, talking to the boys' coach. I think she was mad because our drills got screwed up. Anyhow, the boys weren't being loud. They were kind of whispering at me, every time I ran by."

The wind shifted. A stench rolled across Parker, gamy and thick, as she sat on her father's bench. She thought it might be a dead opossum, decomposing on the other side of the lake. The ends of her hair fluttered briefly. She shuddered as she inhaled and asked, "Then what happened?"

"Julian started saying, 'You're such a BILF, Hatfield,' and like, 'I love me a little redneck BILF.' Stuff like that. The other guys were sort of chanting, you know, 'BILF, BILF, BILF, BILF,' whispering it. They're such assholes, Mom. I hate their guts."

Parker sucked in a mouthful of the rotten wind. "What does 'BILF' mean?"

Joie latched onto her mother's gaze, staring without blinking as a watery film tumbled down her cheeks. "Barbie I'd Like to Fuck," she said, hitting the last word hard.

It was real work for Parker, that passive listening. A few times, she had been called a "MILF," most recently by a girlfriend who meant it as a joke that fell flat. The M of course stood for "Mother," in her case. Her breath sounded supernaturally loud through her nose all of a sudden, like the snorting of a bull ready to charge. "I'm sorry that happened to you," she said in a voice she no longer recognized, a crazy Mama Bear Ready to Bite Their Heads Off voice. "You know what the boys did was sexual harassment, right? They were bullying you and being totally inappropriate. I hope you gave them a piece of your mind and told Coach Billie right away."

Joie started crying for real then, lips shaking, nose running—the whole nine yards. "That's the worst part," she said, squeaky and loud at the same time. "I didn't do *anything*. Now, I keep thinking of all kinds of stuff I should have said to that jerk-off Julian, but when I was on the field, I wanted to be cool, you know? They never pay any attention to me. I didn't want them to think I'm some stupid baby. I didn't tell them to shut up. That made me feel worse than what the boys did because I let them get away with it. It was my fault for letting them go too far."

Forget passive listening, Parker thought. "Don't say that," she said, level and low. She was pinching the inside of her arm to keep from yelling. "Don't you ever say you caused some morons to harass you. They had no business doing what they did. It was not your fault, and your coaches ought to be ashamed of themselves, too."

"But Dr. Martin Luther King Junior said if somebody says something bad and we don't speak up, it's like we agree with it."

"No—what Dr. King meant was, 'Don't laugh at racist jokes,'" she said, quick as a bee sting. "This is different. You're fourteen. You shouldn't have to fend off future date rapists on the sports field. Look, I'm going to fly straight home tonight. We'll meet with Coach Billie in the morning. I'll make sure this never happens again."

"No," Joie shrieked, dragging out the vowel for a good thirty seconds until it was an all-out scream. "Don't talk to anybody. Don't come up here. I'd die of embarrassment. It's the last week of school. I don't want it to end on a bad note. Please. Please, please, please. Don't do it."

"Okay, take it easy, take it easy." Parker couldn't stand to see her daughter so upset. "Try to breathe, sweetheart. Let's talk this through. Can you calm down so we can talk some more?"

Joie was huffing wind so fast, Parker worried she might get dizzy, pass out and hit her head against the computer. "I'm calm, I'm calm, I'm calm, I'm calm," Joie said. "Please don't tell Coach Billie I complained. She'll think I'm not tough enough to keep playing midi-attack and everybody would know and the boys would make even more fun of me. I'd never get a date after that."

The sun, lower in the sky than when Joie and Parker first started talking, slid sideways through the trees, near the waterfall. The last of the day's sunshine seemed to be heating up whatever had died over there, making it stink. Parker wasn't sure what to say next. She wanted to call Jolene and ask for more Life Coach advice. Maybe Jolene would know how to put in a quiet word at school without turning Joie into a freakish outcast. She wanted to call Beamer, too, to hear his voice, although his phone was no doubt turned off, and anyway, he would only tell her to let Joie fight her own fights. He had told Parker the same thing many times. "Maybe you and Daddy can come down here," she told Joie, "for a little vacation."

"Yes," Joie yelled, punching a fist into the air. "I love Atlanta and we haven't been down there together in, like, a million years."

"Exactly a million years, or approximately a million years?" Parker was teasing Joie. Excessive use of the word "like" was one of her pet peeves.

"I haven't been there in one-point-two million years." The silver wires in Joie's braces were gleaming.

"I'll talk to Daddy. Meanwhile, would you do me a favor and stay away from those nasty little boys?"

Joie's smile disappeared and she squared her shoulders. "I won't pick any fights, don't worry. But if they say one word to me again, I'm getting right up in their grills. I'll tell them to shut their stupid fucking pie holes because I'm not putting up with their bullshit again, ever."

"Wow. Okay, fair enough. Will you do me another favor? Remember you're a smart, beautiful, talented young woman. Don't let mean words make you feel any less than what you are, which is amazing."

"Oh, and can we go to that big Lenox Square shopping mall when I'm down there?" Joie said, immediately breezy again. "You said last time I could get those jeans I want, and I have to get my nails done. They're totally gross. No wonder I don't get asked out."

"I'll take that under advisement," Parker said. "Let's talk again tomorrow. I love you."

Joie pressed her lips against the computer and gave it a hug, said, "Love you," and she was gone, sucked into the swirling vortex of cyberspace.

Parker snapped the laptop shut and sat listening to the birds. A white glare like a bullet boomeranged off something to the left of the waterfall. Shielding her eyes, she left the computer on the bench, picked up her phone, and headed around the lake to investigate. She had to take the long way, picking a path over green slime-covered rocks in one spot. Slippery red clay squirted between her bare toes. An orange butterfly kept pace with her part of the way, flapping a ragged pattern between the trees. By the halfway point, five minutes later, the white glare had turned into a rectangular sign, staked into the ground. She could only see the back of it, so she kept going.

The phone, clipped to a decorative belt on her skirt, vibrated once, then twice. She was about to look at it when she spotted the dead deer, marooned on the far shore with one hoof dangling in the water and its tongue draped over a rock. At first, it seemed to be glistening in the sun. Moving closer, she saw maggots swarming over a bloody coil of intestines. She wondered what could have killed it, so far from the road. Poor thing was still tiny, just a fawn. Maybe a coyote had gotten to it. Parker made a mental note to have the groundskeeper dispose of the carcass and she plowed on toward the white sign, eager to see what it said.

Another buzz from her phone hit the exact point on Parker's hip where her arthritis usually kicked up. She stopped and unclipped the phone, annoyed. Her hands went numb, seemingly detached from her arms when she saw what was typed across the tiny screen. "Hey, give me a call," the message said. "It's important. Here's my number. Buddy."

Parker walked a few more yards, past the boundary of the park, into a thicket of wild brambles where nobody had been mowing. She circled the sign until she was standing in front of it, staring. "For Sale," it said. "Caldwell Developers, LLC." The phone number on the sign was the same one Buddy had just texted to her.

Lowering herself on a log, she hawked a wad of metallic spit into a fern, took a deep breath and hit the number. She dreaded talking to him, but she needed to know what was going on right next to her father's park. The newspaper article hadn't provided much detail. Two rings later, he answered. His voice was like the growl of a junkyard dog, snarling with sarcasm. "Well, well," he said. "She lives and breathes. Thanks for calling me back as soon as I asked you to, little one."

"Don't call me that." Parker stood up to steady herself over both feet. She couldn't stop shaking. "How'd you get this number?"

"A little thing called the Interwebs. You're pretty easy to find. I was impressed to read about all your awards for communication stuff."

"Listen, I don't know what you want, but let's get it over with. Spit it out."

He laughed through his nose. "I'm trying to be nice here. I need to talk to you. It's important."

"So go ahead."

"Couldn't we meet face to face? This seems so impersonal, over the phone. I could fly you to Atlanta, if that would help. I could have you on a plane tomorrow."

Parker stifled the urge to scream. The idea of seeing him in person made her stomach flip. Accepting a free plane ticket from him was unthinkable. "Just tell me now."

"No, I—I want to say some things to your face. It's too complicated to explain over the phone like this. Please."

A blue jay screeched, dive-bombing a bug at the water's edge.

"Hello?" he said. "Are you still there?"

"I'm in Atlanta this week." She blew it out like a rotten seed. "I can be at your office at nine o' clock tomorrow."

"Okay, that sounds great, but the thing is, I have a meeting at nine. I could see you in the afternoon, if you swing by at— "

"I'll be there at nine tomorrow. I have work to do after that. Whatever you have to say to me, be ready to say it. I won't come back."

When she clicked off the call, the waterfall crashed louder for a second, then softer over rocks and moss and wiry tufts of grass. Near the shore, a turtle lifted its head.

9.

BUDDY CALDWELL

Thirty-six stories above Piedmont Park, the cherry wood of the conference table felt slick as a snake under Buddy's fingers. Ken, his partner on the Silver Park deal, was pacing in a deliberate way, head down, in front of the floor-length windows. As Ken walked across the hardwood floor, onto the plush, rose-colored carpet and back again, his loafers tapped out an odd rhythm—*loud, soft, loud.* Through the glass, construction cranes wheeled over steel girders where a new high-rise had erupted like another giant concrete pimple on Atlanta's skyline.

"Our friend in the county commissioner's office thinks we need to get out in front of any bad publicity," Buddy said. "He's worried about the hearing on Friday."

"He's always worried," Ken said, running both hands through his hair, which was as thick and white as a mop, or a fancy dog. He adjusted one and then the other cuff link and he straightened his tie, which was a brilliant shade of turquoise with cranberry accents. "That's his job to worry."

A fat gray bird landed on the ledge outside Ken's expansive windows. Buddy got up from the table to give his throbbing back a break. "He says it's going to look bad for the planning committee if Arden Collier shows up with some long sob story."

"Hey, go away." Ken banged on the window until the bird disappeared. "Stupid flying rats. Those things are always crapping out there. I can't even open my windows when the weather's nice."

It's a hard knock life, Buddy thought. He remembered touring the building, as a kid, with Foster Gozer. The place was still under construction. Old Gozer had talked to the architect about installing balconies. They went with the oversized windows instead. Less expensive and a lower risk of jumpers. "He wants you to get on the radio today,"

Buddy said, "before the hearing, to talk about how much money we're going to make for the county and all that."

One side of Ken's mouth had curled into a sarcastic half-smile. "Not me. I'm not about to get on the radio. I believe that would be what we call your job." He didn't look at Buddy when he said it. He was too busy inspecting a row of purple orchids lined up like a bunch of horny old women on a gleaming credenza. "I'm the silent partner, remember? Silent means, no on-air time. Silent means invisible."

"Let's keep this between us." It was one of old Gozer's favorite sayings, whispered to Buddy whenever Foster, eyes shifting, shoved a wad of cash into his hands. Usually that had happened on Saturday afternoons, after a long week of back-destroying work, right before Foster returned Buddy to the red dirt yard of his mother's rotting duplex south of town. *"You don't need to tell anybody where you got this. Don't tell your mother."* The day they toured Ken's future office building, Buddy was a kid. He got to wear a yellow hard hat that was too big for his head. Foster had promised to take him to The Varsity for a chili dog and a frosted orange shake. He never made good on that deal. In front of spectators, Buddy was described by Foster as the son of a less-fortunate neighbor, and later, as the hired help—cheap labor on various building projects. Foster was fond of saying, if asked, how he felt sorry for the boy, growing up in those conditions, "with no advantages to speak of, and his father gone."

"Say, did you hear me?" Ken rapped his knuckles against the credenza until Buddy looked at him. "You still with me?"

"I tried calling that reporter who wrote about my company last week." Buddy was watching a man and a woman, far below Ken's window, as they slowly circled a small lake. His wife had never listened to him when they were married, and they had fought like roosters, but even so, he sometimes missed her—maybe not Rhonda, in particular, but the idea of having a family, people to care about him. From such a height, the couple looked tiny and inconsequential, the same way Buddy had felt whenever he had raked the Gozers' enormous yard and Parker's mother left him a plate of fried chicken on the back porch. "She wouldn't go for a follow-up story, but she'd recognize your name, if you called her."

Ken assumed a position of authority behind his massive desk, which reminded Buddy of the command module on the Starship Enterprise. "Yes, I'm quite sure she would recognize my name," Ken said, "which is exactly why I'm not calling her, or any other reporters. Look, there's going to be some bad press on this project. It might get ugly. Frankly, it raises all kinds of race relations issues. Why did you think I wanted you to be the front man on this? I can't get painted with that brush. I've got too much at stake. You've got less on the line. You're less vulnerable. You need to handle it."

"Dig that ditch a few inches deeper, would you?" How many years had Buddy worked as slave labor for Foster Gozer? Too long. He was glad the old man had finally given him a piece of land in Silver Park. Still, it was only a scrap, and the money Foster left to Buddy was long gone. One too many business deals had gone south. Buddy knew he deserved much more than he had received. He had earned it. As it was, he and Ken were going to need a string of special waivers from the county. They couldn't maximize their revenue potential on the narrow lot and have enough margin left over for all the mandated landscaping or the required space between their building and the road. "Look, we need to grease that guy's palms again."

Ken let out a noise like indigestion. "I thought we just did that."

"Yeah, but he's getting nervous again." It was clear Arden wasn't going to play ball, and Buddy had no idea what to expect from Parker when he saw her the next day. She didn't exactly have a track record for being agreeable. He remembered her mainly as an entitled princess, a pretty little girl who had made fun of him whenever he was wearing ripped-up work pants stained with paint and dirt. The county seemed like their best shot at making the deal work.

Reaching into his cavernous desk, Ken fumbled with a lock box, reached into it, and pushed an envelope across the desk. "That's the best I can do, and that's all I'm going to do. Make sure he understands that when you see him."

The flap of the envelope was still wet with Ken's spit. "I'll take it downtown."

Ken banged the drawer shut. "Remember, I'm in the background on this one. Leave me out of it. Nobody needs to know."

10.
ARDEN COLLIER

The woods were windless and quiet except for the steady rumbling of the waterfall, the faint call of a lone bird in the distance, and the muted crunch of Arden's boots moving through pine straw and twigs. Rarely, she might run into a lone hiker or a family having a picnic in Silver Park. More often, she was alone in her grandfather's forest. Her sketchpad felt strangely heavy. She clutched it to her bosom—pressing it over the exact spot where her button had flown onto Jared Astor's fancy rug. She locked her arms as if the paper, like her ideas, might disappear at any moment.

She had until Tuesday to come up with new work. Jared had at least given her that chance, a few precious days.

At the far side of the lake, she turned, gave Buddy's real-estate sign a kick, and kept going, across his property, up the hill. At the top, water tumbled over a rocky, moss-covered ledge. She sucked wind, climbing until her feet hit level ground again. When she squeezed through big trees set close together, spots of morning sun shrank to nothing, vanishing, leaving her in the cool, moist shadows.

Her uncle's secret shed looked as rickety as ever. Inside, the orange dirt floor smelled the same way food in a metal can tastes when it's been sitting too long on the shelf. A tarnished silver barrel had been abandoned in the shed; it lay empty in one corner. An agitated brown spider shook the center of its web, daring Arden to come any closer. Blackened coils of discarded copper pipes, cracked glass jars, and bits of cork littered the floor. A tin chimney poked through the roof, which was riddled with holes where the dust rose, swirling in the gloom.

Arden ripped a fresh piece of paper from her pad. She used it to cover a filthy wooden chair by the table where she planned to sketch new ideas. Wilma's husband had spent hours in the same spot, distilling the booze that killed him and left her blind. Arden wondered if Aunt Wilma or her grandfather had ever come to see George in his shed. She couldn't picture it. Her grandfather had repeatedly warned her not to go anywhere near the old still. He said the dirt was full of poison because metal had leached into it. She never dared to visit the shed until she was grown and everyone else was long gone.

Now, apparently, Buddy owned the land where George had spent hours alone, tending to his booze in the darkest part of the forest.

The paper stretched all the way across the table, which rocked, unsteady under the weight of her hand where she was gripping the pencil. As she stared, the vast network of blank white fibers seemed to pulsate like a lacerated vein. The whiteness of the paper strobed across her corneas, tapping out a Morse-code message of nothingness. She dropped the pencil, closed her eyes and rubbed them. Jared Astor was her only hope, probably for a long while, or forever. What would come next if she failed? She thought of her dark basement full of the clothes Joel had left behind when he moved to another city. She couldn't stand to think of his dress pants and long-sleeved shirts getting wet every time a hard rain seeped through the foundation of her house, but she couldn't bear to throw his things away.

Getting to Jared Astor's studio had been hard for Arden. She had grabbed her pocketbook as soon as Buddy's silver car, enveloped in a swirling bubble of red dust, disappeared around a crook in the unpaved road. Of course, Joel's rusty, disintegrating old truck wouldn't crank, no matter what she tried, even after she dragged a partially evaporated tub of gas from the shed to wet the engine—a trick he had taught her. She wound up walking all the way to Peachtree Street. After that, she stumbled along another road's gravel shoulder, trembling, trying to remind herself how much she needed an infusion of cash. Cars kept making her jump as they rocketed by. A man on a child's bicycle sailed downhill, knees cranking in opposite directions. "Hey, mama," was what he said, whistling at Arden for no good reason except to mess with her.

Later, a fire truck zoomed by while she huddled inside the bus stop. Her hands flew to her ears. A pregnant woman stared, expressionless. The bus finally chugged to a stop, spewing clouds of exhaust. Its door sank to the pavement long enough for Arden to climb the steps, head down, trying not to look at the pregnant woman's shifting backside. Sometimes, she wondered what it would have been like, if she had gotten pregnant before Joel left. Inside the bus, she blinked at the speed of trees, restaurants, and gas stations as they flashed across her field of vision like a spaceship carrying her into the future. By the time she reached Jared Astor's building with its gold accents, she felt shaky and hollow. Shielding her face with her hands, she stepped onto his ornate brick promenade, through a gauntlet of redbud, dogwood, and crepe myrtle trees planted symmetrically on either side of the stone walkway. His adolescent receptionist, impassive in her gold-hoop earrings, turned out to be another hurdle for Arden.

Before visiting Jared Astor, Arden hadn't left her property for six months. Her groceries were delivered every Saturday by a boy who left the sacks on her porch, along with a bill. While they were married, Joel drove her anywhere she needed to go. His big hands dwarfed the steering wheel. He had to crouch to keep his head from mashing against the truck's ceiling, which was constantly coming unglued in spots. In good weather, he left the back window open, for the breeze. The wind ruffled his starched shirt, lifting his necktie—a requirement for male teachers at Jameson Public Elementary School.

Crouched inside her uncle's shed, a wave of sadness gathered behind Arden's eyes like a summer squall while she thought about her husband riding a bus all the way to Greenville, where he had accepted a new job—a better one in a private school. Mostly, she missed spooning with him: the warmth of his belly against her back, the firm cradle of his hand below her heart. The paper, too white in the dark shed, throbbed under her fingers. She slapped the notepad shut, jumped to her feet, and stepped back over the doorsill.

The lop-sided stump was still there, squatting like a troll at the edge of a small clearing where her uncle must have cut down a few of the smaller scrub pines. In the middle, she could barely make out the remnants of an old fire ring, thickly shrouded with rotting leaves.

It made her think about another campfire when she was fifteen or sixteen, making out with a white boy. She couldn't remember his name. He had many oddly shaped freckles that merged into inky black spots. His gums were too big for his teeth. In the fire's orange glow, her friend Marcy had danced, stumbling, while Arden's date hurled an empty beer can into the flames, singing along with a Rolling Stones song about "Brown Sugar." Arden knew they were in the woods so nobody would see them together.

Back home, Aunt Wilma had been standing sentry under the naked porch bulb in her buttoned-up nightgown, waiting. She was on the top step, hands quiet against her thighs while Arden lurched from the car, calling her goodbyes to Marcy and the boys.

"I've been worried sick," her aunt said. In her eyes, the blue clouds floated left and right.

Aunt Wilma's fingers had felt sandpapery—itchy and irritating where they gripped Arden's arm. Arden had wanted so badly to break free, but she didn't want to wake her grandfather. He had been sick all week. It was just the three of them in the house by then. Her mother and grandmother had died. "I was on a date." Arden's mouth felt like it was full of gravel. She had to enunciate each word with extra care. "I get to go on dates, don't I?"

Aunt Wilma tightened her grip, pulling Arden closer. "That wasn't a proper date. That was a couple of white boys taking advantage. I'll bet they didn't even take you out for any supper. Did they?"

Arden's cheeks began to tingle. Her date had honked the horn on his father's car instead of walking up to her front door. She figured that was just as well. If Aunt Wilma had seen them, she would have scared them off. If Arden's grandfather wasn't sick in bed, he would have done the same. Arden jumped in the car while her aunt was out back in the garden, and off they went. They picked up Marcy next and stopped for a twelve-pack of beer. Somewhere on the far side of Chamblee, they parked in an unlit field full of blackberry bushes. Arden was so hungry, she thought about plucking a handful of the berries, but she couldn't risk getting her good dress dirty. She had saved up for it.

Her date spread a plaid blanket on the ground. He pressed his nose into her hair and frowned. "You smell funny," he said. "Like cooking grease."

His friend laughed. "That's the stuff they smear on their heads so they won't have Afros like Jimi Hendrix," he said.

"No," her date replied. "I mean, I like it. It's not a bad smell. It's like ham hocks or something. I like ham hocks."

On the porch with her aunt, Arden's eyes felt like they were swimming in her head. It took her a minute to realize Wilma was talking to her. "Tell me nothing happened," she said, squeezing both of Arden's wrists. "Tell me you won't be in any trouble now."

Trouble meant pregnancy. Trouble meant shame.

A flash of anger surged unexpectedly through Arden, which helped her sober up, at least a little. "He kissed me. I let him kiss me."

"What else?"

"You don't need to know about my private business."

Wilma shook a gnarled finger. "What you do is my business. The day you were born, you were so pretty, your Mama named you Arden, after the Garden of Eden. It's my job to make sure that garden doesn't get spoiled. What else did you do with that boy?"

"We kissed. That was all. I asked him to drive me home."

"I don't believe you."

Arden had shocked herself, yelling loud enough to make her aunt's hazy eyes bulge. "I don't care what you believe. I don't care if you disapprove. He kissed me."

"Hush," her aunt said, looking over her shoulder toward the church. "Sit down on the step right here."

Arden let loose after that, blubbering drunkenly and tugging to get her arms free. Aunt Wilma was bigger and stronger and she never let go. "I let him kiss me. I liked it. I can't stay shut up in this house where everybody's dying. I should be able to have some fun once in a while. I don't need you hovering over me all the time."

Aunt Wilma wrestled her onto the porch, whispering like she was saying a prayer, wrapping her arms around Arden, who wailed and struggled and kicked. "I'm holding you here so you'll have a better life than I did, so you'll be free and healthy when you're all grown up," she said.

Arden couldn't stop shouting. "Let go of me. Stop holding me down."

While she rocked back and forth, Aunt Wilma stroked Arden's hair and her cheeks where layers of makeup were dripping onto her chin. "I'm holding you so you'll know you're loved and you're not alone. You're going to meet a good man who cares about you."

"I won't," Arden said. "I'll never have the chance."

"You will so. Until then, my heart is in my hands and my hands have wings. These hands will lift you up from danger. These hands will keep you safe."

Arden had cried herself to sleep that night. Her aunt's words swirled through the worst of her bad dreams:

My heart is in my hands and my hands have wings.

In the clearing, Arden's fingers began to fly across the paper, tracing the memory of Wilma's twisted but muscular hands against a riot of wings in different shapes and sizes. She thought about the darkness that constantly lurked behind her mother's eyes. She remembered the shadows around her grandfather's fingertips where he clenched his ratty hat, cowering. She pictured his parents before him: her great-grandfather who bought his way out of slavery, only to die too soon. She thought about her father, the one she had never known because he disappeared before she was born. She imagined holding them, all of the people she had loved or wanted to know and keep safe, as Aunt Wilma had kept her safe, while the fear flew off them, finally, so they could be set free.

Sketching Wilma's face when she was fourteen, the year George had bartered for her, Arden remembered an essay from college about the Hebrew word for "little one"—*ketannah*—a child between three and twelve years old, plus one day. In earlier times, a little girl could be married off by her father. So many bad things had been allowed to happen to women and girls all over the world, in many different communities. Why that was so, Arden couldn't understand.

She flipped to a fresh page in her sketchpad and began scribbling as fast as she could:

Ketannah
Breath,
sweet and soured,
cigar-infused and strangling,
tight as the noose of premature
betrothal. Brown knees, knocking, her
only dowry, no need for permission, no
night watchman or impoverished
father planting the empty
pre-suburban seeds of
betrayal. The
jagged steel cup, cool
between her teeth, still-pointed.

No one saw the sip that blinds, no
funny uncle or friendly aunt, the antifreeze
liquor and corn so fused. She promised to
obey, his grip on her throat, the
tongue already twisted like
the road not taken, a
life she left
behind.

As she read it, Arden knew it was a classic shitty first draft of a poem. She could work with it. In another day or two, it would be better. Her inner self-critic, that nagging shrew, tormenter of artists everywhere, could shut the hell up. It was a start, a beginning to the thread she hadn't been able to find for so long. She would revise later. For now, she would keep moving forward with whatever was propelling her.

Aunt Wilma had succeeded in keeping Arden safe. Arden had met Joel in college. They were married before graduation. She hadn't been able to shake the fear she inherited from her aunt, though, and Joel couldn't live in the darkness, never leaving the little house her grandfather had built. After Joel left, she gathered the artifacts of her life around her, building a wall to keep out the rest of the world.

It's time to let my family's history fly free, she thought, *to let my life grow wings.*

After heaving a large rock, two-handed, at the already broken window of her uncle's moonshine shed, she ran all the way back to her house. Branches whizzed by her ears, slapping her cheeks and snagging her shirt. Her feet didn't seem to be touching the ground. Inside her brain, ideas kept swirling like the shifting rainbows on soap bubbles. She needed to blow them onto paper right away, to write them down and sketch them before they popped and disappeared.

A brown van was parked sideways with its nose at an angle and one wheel on her lawn. She couldn't see all of the lettering on the driver's side door, but she knew the man on her porch was a sheriff's deputy. Recognizing the tan uniform, she stopped in her tracks, watching while he knocked on her door. When no one answered, he cupped his hands against her front windows and peered inside. He was a big man with a belly that bulged over his black belt. The seams of his pants were pulling apart in the back. Clearly, they had been repaired more than once.

When she planted a boot on the bottom step, he turned with a start, asked her name, and handed her a piece of paper folded into the shape of a travel brochure.

"It's a summons," he said. "There's a hearing on Friday."

Arden noticed the ragged pink patches etched across the back of his hands and the side of his neck where his skin was otherwise a deep chestnut color. She thought about Buddy's bright red neck and his warning to her. "Is this about the county citations?"

The deputy nodded. "For whatever it's worth, I'm sorry. I remember your grandfather very well. He was a special person, one in a million."

She met his gaze, wondering if she knew him from high school, but his nametag—*William Bennett*—didn't ring any bells for her. Maybe he had been one of the many eager boys Aunt Wilma never let Arden date because he didn't go to the same church or his mother was known to go clubbing downtown on Saturday nights. Arden unfolded the summons to find the address. "I have so much work to do this week. Do I have to waste a whole day downtown?"

He repositioned his hips over his feet, peering at her through shaggy white eyebrows. "Yes, ma'am, you do need to show up. This is serious. Please don't make me haul a nice lady like you into jail. That would break my heart."

Arden tucked the summons between the pages of her notepad. "I understand, but it's going to take me so long to get there and back on the bus. I'm not sure what's wrong with my old truck over there. I haven't been able to crank it up."

William frowned, making his chin fold over itself. "You take it to a mechanic yet?"

"I can't afford one right now."

He stared at his shoes for a second, tapping his fingertips against his work pants. "Tell you what, my brother runs a garage. I'll send him over tomorrow."

Arden's face felt hot. "Oh, no, I couldn't ask anybody to—"

"Please," he said, smiling. "Everybody around here owes so much to your grandfather. You probably have a dead battery. It's no bother, really. My brother remembers you, by the way. I think you were his same age in high school."

Out of nowhere, a kind face from the past rushed toward her. "Jackson Bennett," she said, recalling how he had carried books for her some days, after school.

William's teeth seemed too big for his mouth when he smiled. "That's the one. I know he'd be glad to stop by tomorrow and say hello, see if he can help."

"He was sort of different, if I recall correctly."

William Bennett looked at the dusty tips of his shiny shoes. "That's right. He hears a different song than the rest of us. He's harmless, though. Gentle as can be and a very good mechanic. He'd be thrilled to see you again."

Something about the way he said it, with his head tipped to one side so he was looking at her with one eye, smiling with his big teeth, felt like a secret code he was trying to tap out. *My brother has a difference.* Whatever the message was supposed to mean, Arden couldn't decipher it. *You're different, too,* was her best guess.

The weathervane started to spin, letting out a rusty squeak while she watched him climb back into the van. William leaned through the open window, waving as the van creaked off down the road.

She hopped off the porch and headed for her gazebo where she scrambled to assemble plaster, the bucket full of water, brushes in every conceivable size, plaster, and rows and rows of paint tubes.

Her heart was in her hands. Her hands had wings.

11.

PARKER GOZER

Parker arrived twenty minutes early for the meeting with Buddy. She sat in her rental car, idling in a remote corner of the parking lot, sweating. The asphalt looked craggy as the Utah salt flats, festooned with iridescent greenish-black petroleum blooms the size of Buicks. His office, wedged in the middle of a dilapidated 1980s-era strip mall, looked pitifully small, squashed between a bodybuilders' gym and a pawnshop. A rust-colored roll of cheap tint covered most of his front window, except for one corner where the film had begun to peel. By his door, beige slices of paint littered the sidewalk, under an aluminum awning so big, it partially obscured his orange and white company sign.

The parking lot intersected with a concrete barrier between the strip plaza and an off-brand fast-food joint. On the plaza's other side, the pavement was jammed against yet another parking lot and an autobody shop. No trees, no hedges, not a single lousy blade of grass as far as Parker could see in any direction. Nothing but broken pavement and cigarette butts and shattered glass. Whoever had approved the landscape ordinance for that part of town deserved a life sentence handing out smiley-face stickers in a discount store.

Parker struggled to see the place as it had looked in the 1970s—the same spot where she had caught turtles by the dozens, as a kid, letting them scrabble around the bathtub with a lettuce leaf overnight before setting them free. She would detour into a swampy, shallow crater on her way home from school so she could scoop the turtles into a box or a bag or her shirttails. That was in the days before she knew better than to capture wild creatures. She had a hard time picturing the crater as she looked at the rippling asphalt, Rorschach patterns of abandoned gum wads, and a blue dumpster surrounded by leaking white garbage bags.

She set the parking brake and reached for her phone. A tan pickup truck rumbled into the parking lot. Parker waited to hear Jolene's voice. Smoke billowed from the passenger-side window as the truck stopped in front of the pawnshop.

"I'm here," Jolene said over the sound of a horn honking. "Oh, cool your jets."

In front of Parker, the tan truck disgorged a large man who chewed on a cigar while he grappled with a cardboard box. "Is this a bad time?" she said. "It sounds like you're in traffic."

"Chillax, you mordiot," Jolene said against a soundtrack of distant yelling. Jolene was a master at blending words like moron and idiot, or ridiculous and donkey. "No, no, it's groovacetic. I'm hands-free."

Across the parking lot, the man fumbled with his keys. When he finally managed to open the pawnshop door, he slipped inside with surprising grace. A line of crows were perched along a telephone wire, reminding her of an old Hitchcock film. "I know I'm always calling you for advice, but you usually know the right thing to say."

"You're going to have to start paying me at some point," Jolene said. Over the phone, her car's engine stopped. The car door opened and closed. "People do pay me to be their life coach, you know. It's not, like, a hobby."

"I know. Hey, why are you on the road so late?" Carpool duty ended at eight o' clock every morning.

"Someone's daughter called me." Jolene's feet *click-clacked* over the driveway Beamer's crew had poured for her after her second husband split. Jolene loved it, swept it with Clorox once a month. "She forgot to eat breakfast and she didn't have any money in her lunch account. I went back to school with a sandwich, a granola bar, and a ten-dollar bill."

Above the parking lot, three birds took flight, snapping the wire like a whip. The smallest of them stayed put, covering her head with one wing. The man stepped outside his shop again, torched the cigar, and sucked on it. His eyes had a faraway, pensive look. "I'm sorry," Parker said. "Thank you."

Jolene was working her drill-sergeant voice, the one Parker dreaded to hear. Usually it meant Jolene was about to assign Parker to meditate for thirty minutes or take a hike or do yoga. One time, Jolene had assigned Parker to read an entire self-help book, backwards. "You need groceries, too. There wasn't a teaspoon of milk at your place when I stopped by last night. You do have a little bit of Grey Poupon, in case anybody wants to know."

"You looked in my fridge?" Parker was mortified, remembering the half-empty jar of mustard lying on its side next to a shriveled carrot with a bite out of it and a can of tuna fish Joie opened but never ate. Irritation rose under her collar like a rash. Fat ropes of cigar smoke wound around the pawnshop man's balding head.

"Honey, no offense," Jolene said, which made Parker brace herself because she was pretty sure she was about to be offended, "but you need to finish your work down there and get back home to your family."

"I know. I'm doing the best I can." The words popped out too quickly, like defective firecrackers. "I'm the primary breadwinner. I can't walk away. Everybody's riding on me."

"Ha," Jolene said with a snort. "Exactly."

"Wait, that didn't come out right. I meant, there's the mortgage and our car payments and Joie's college fund and—"

"It's all about boundaries. You need more boundaries at work and in your personal life."

Outside the pawnshop, the man slid his hands into his pockets, blowing jets of smoke through his nose. "Okay," Parker said, "I'll start setting some boundaries right now. First off, stop rifling through my fridge."

Jolene let out a laugh that turned phlegmy. "Ha. Touché. Your point is well-taken, my friend."

"I understand your point, too, and I appreciate everything you do for me, but where was my husband during this inspection? He's also capable of driving to the grocery store. In theory. Right?"

"Oh, he was there," Jolene said in a feathery whisper. "I gave him a list, but you know how it goes. Some people can change, but your boy's a dreamer, girleen. You can't be mad at him for that."

Sure, I can, Parker thought.

The early-morning clouds hadn't burned off yet, but the air was thick and hot inside the rental car, parked on the blacktop without a speck of shade in sight. She cracked the windows, remembering the first time she went for a ride with Buddy, at thirteen, and he rolled his fingers up and down the inside of her arm. It was maybe a week after he told her about the girl who leaned over his car bumper, behind a bar. Her hair was curly and brown as wisteria vines in winter and she had a blue butterfly tattooed on her right shoulder, under her bra strap that kept slipping down. She was a laid-back chick, he said. The coolest. He didn't remember her name. He thought it might be Peggy.

"What should I do about this BILF business?" Parker said, circling back to their conversation from the previous night. She had called Jolene soon after hearing Joie talk about the mean boys on the lacrosse field.

"I've already talked to Howie," Jolene said. "He called Coach Billie, gave me a full report. Joie won't know a thing and the boys won't hassle her again. Fear not."

"You're amazing."

"Obviously, I know that. Hey, where are you?"

The man was inside his shop window, rearranging shelves loaded with watches, clocks, bracelets, tennis rackets, and cameras—artifacts from the lives other people had left behind. "I'm outside his office."

"What's it look like?" Through the phone, ice cubes clinked. Water ran.

"Urban wasteland. Cheap and rundown."

"See, he's not so big and bad anymore." Finally, it was quiet on Jolene's end of the line, no more jostling for house keys or flipping pages of her calendar or gulping a drink. Parker imagined her friend perched in her over-sized orange recliner, watching the bird feeder Beamer had pounded together in her side yard. "This is a stressful day for you. Try to focus on the positives. Do you at least get to drive a nice car while you're down there?"

"No, actually." Parker's irritation with Jolene was growing. "I'm in a smelly economy-class rental car. This place is giving me the creeps."

"There's no reason to be afraid." Jolene sounded maddeningly cheerful. "You've been lucky a long time. Seems to me, you hit the jackpot with good ole Dr. Tinley."

"I wouldn't exactly call my salary a jackpot." Parker knew her voice sounded bristly. "It's a nonprofit, remember? But yes, I get to do good work for the world. We're trying to help."

"Okay, but I think you'd have to agree, Buddy's one of life's unfortunates, still hustling for a buck. He made bad choices back in the day. That was ages ago. Good Lord, it was the seventies, remember? I never had a single driver's ed teacher or basketball coach who didn't try to put the feels on me and nobody gave a rat's ass back then. All the music we listened to was about men not being able to leave the young things alone. Opportunistic pedophiles were a normalized aspect of the pop-culture landscape."

"Where did you learn to talk like this?"

"Once again, I'm a professional life coach."

"So girls were prey. They still are. Pretty much everywhere. What's your point?"

"My point is, look around now. Who's more pitiful—you or him?"

Jolene did have a valid point. Not one Parker was ready to admit out loud yet, but a point.

"What do you think he wants?" Fabric rustled as if Jolene was shifting onto her knees, excited, ready to dive into the dark tunnels of emotional torment where female bonding or country music takes place.

Heat rolled up Parker's neck, burning the tops of her ears while she remembered the real-estate sign planted next to her Dad's park. "He wants my land. He can't have it, of course. The park's protected, but I'll bet he wants to try and steal it somehow."

"I can't believe you never looked up who owns that lot. I would've met the neighbors with muffins the day after my Dad died."

"No doubt," Parker mumbled, cradling the phone against her chin so she could massage her eyebrows with both thumbs.

Jolene breathed in, humming on the exhale. "Look, let's start with a positive assumption, okay? If we get disappointed after that, so be it, but we're going to think good thoughts and hope they come back to us."

"This is why I love you," Parker said with a sigh. "I do want things to work out for the best. I have a hard time imagining how that could possibly be the case."

"Well, let's try. What if he needs to sell that property because he's flat-broke and he wants to offer you first right-of-refusal?"

Parker hadn't thought of this. "I'd cash out my retirement. I'd sell my house or my soul to buy it."

"What if he's in a twelve-step program or something and he needs to make amends for past mistakes? Maybe he's trying to rehabilitate himself, but the memories are driving him nuts, so he wants to say he's sorry. How would that make you feel?"

Grief—rough as a rusty nail or a sudden death—rolled through her veins. What Parker remembered, when Jolene asked her, was the one time Buddy had said, "You know I love you, kid." They were locked together inside his freezing car full of cigarette smoke that swirled in frantic circles through bolts of winter sunshine. She knew he only said it to keep her quiet. Still, she held the words in her mouth like after-dinner mints, never quite swallowing them, gripping their sweetness between her teeth until there was nothing left. When Parker answered Jolene, her voice sounded skeletal. "That would feel good. I'd like to forgive him, but he's never asked."

"Try this for me. Find a pen and a piece of paper." Suddenly, Jolene was all business. "Write this down."

Inside the dashboard, red numbers clicked forward one digit: eight fifty-five. Parker slid a notepad from her satchel and opened her favorite fountain pen. "Ready."

"God, lift Buddy up and set him free," Jolene said. "Free me from my past. Forgive Buddy and release him to the universe. Amen."

Parker did as she was told, tore off the strip of paper, and thumb-pressed it into a pocket next to her kidney. "That's beautiful. I wish it could come true."

"Call me later."

"Thanks for the prayer. I'm sorry if I sound all wound up. I love you. I appreciate all you do for me."

"I love you, too, my sweet little worrywart. You've got this."

Parker signed off, glad she didn't let anything slip about working with Dylan. Jolene would have a field day with that one.

After rolling up the windows, Parker turned off the car and opened the door. Out of habit, she picked up her satchel, stared at it, and realized there was no need to drag luggage into Buddy's office. Cracking into the trunk of the rental car to stash her belongings ate up another minute. Parker couldn't find a button or a latch. Finally, she discovered the keyhole behind a decorative silver logo, tossed in the satchel, and slammed the trunk shut. After that, she checked all the doors to make sure they were locked. When she couldn't think of any other ways to kill time, she started walking as slowly as possible across the lot with her head down, choosing each footfall so her heels didn't get stuck in the gaping black tributaries that crisscrossed the pitted pavement.

She fingered the scrap of paper tucked into her blazer and stepped onto the curb by his office, wondering if he could see her, and if so, what he was thinking. The "Caldwell Developers, LLC" sign was hanging at a slightly crooked angle above the door, which was glass but not tinted like the front windows—covered instead with a dingy lace curtain on the inside.

Parker thought about a few terrible things she had done in her life, especially in high school, egging mailboxes and burning three-sixty holes into a rich family's lawn with her car one night for no good reason except that she wasn't sure where to point her adolescent spear full of endless rage. Those memories still made her cringe, at middle age. Shame singed her throat and the tips of her ears and her stomach did a flip-flop. If she could ever find the house where she did all that damage when she was sixteen, she would leave an anonymous note with cash in the mailbox, but she couldn't remember exactly where she had been that night. Beer had been involved. What Buddy had done was orders of magnitude worse, not even in the same solar system as egging mailboxes or trenching lawns. If he was indeed trying to get better, as Jolene said he might be, Parker couldn't imagine what he must be going through.

Her fingers on the sticky metal doorknob felt weirdly small and culpable, like a kid who had gotten into her mother's nail polish. Inside the dimly lit office, the carpet, worn as prairie grass, smelled of yeast and mildew, and Parker thought, *Silence of the Lambs.* If a moth appeared, she would freak out, without a doubt. A lone laminated-wood desk looked stripped bare, not even a sheet of paper in the ancient Selectric typewriter. A yellow light was shining through a door at the far end of the room, where she heard a soft *whooshing* sound and instantly channeled the suffocating perfume of funeral-parlor lilies. She remembered her father's constantly humming oxygen tank and his eyes above the plastic mask.

God, lift Buddy up, she thought. *Set him free.*

Parker moved toward the open door. All at once, he was standing in it, filling the whole frame, backlit so she only saw his silhouette at first. "Damn," he said, "you look good."

His hair was down, not pulled back into a ponytail. He was an inch or two wider at the waist, but his shoulders still formed a straight line— basically the same shadow as ever—and she could see, after a few blinks, the watery brown of his eyes, his papery freckled skin, and the wiry red lines along the sides of his nose. Although the beard was gone, his face couldn't be more familiar.

Parker stayed where she was, buttoning her jacket. Outside, a car horn honked, long and flat, a door slammed, and a bird that sounded like a hawk or some other type of predator shrieked above the parking lot. Looking around, she spotted a chair pushed against the empty desk. A second one was parked under a framed certificate too blurry to read. "Shall we sit here?" she said.

He shifted sideways in the light, smiling an old person's sad smile, and he waved her into his office. "Come on in. It's okay. Don't be scared."

Parker edged by him, keeping her eyes straight in front of her without looking up so they rolled right over his chest inside a denim shirt. He smelled of Right Guard and cigarettes. "Trust me, I'm not." She said it through her teeth and made a beeline for a black plastic chair on the far side of his cheap metal desk.

The seat felt slippery when she pulled it forward, like it had been wiped down with Armor All. She remembered the oiled leather in his giant sedan, that first time she rode with him—the shaky rush when he said, "Slide over." The car was only slightly smaller than his office. In one corner, silver and orange fish were gliding through bubbles in a blue tank where an air pump let out a loud *whoosh* every fifteen seconds or so.

Buddy lowered himself behind the desk, fired up a cigarette, and tipped his face to blow smoke at a lampshade with a burn mark on it. "Thanks for coming by," he said. "Long time."

On the shelf behind his head, a boy and girl with wavy auburn hair grinned inside a red picture frame. They were posing by a fake tree trunk. The girl's head was tilted to one side and her hair was swept up and pinned on one side, though it was loose on the other side. She looked a few years older than Joie. The boy, all thick neck and big teeth, might have been twenty.

Parker had seen Buddy's wife only once, outside a grocery store. He was loading food into a station wagon. Spotting Parker, he froze. Plastic bags dangled from his hands. In the next moment, his wife was there— long black braids and a pregnant belly. Parker was pretty sure the wife never spotted her. She dove back into her car and peeled off, forgetting whatever it was she needed from the store. "A son and a daughter," Parker said, nodding toward the photograph. "Good for you."

He blew more smoke, flashing his tar-coated smile. "That picture's really old. My son's thirty-five now. Can you believe it? I almost never get to see my kids anymore. My ex-wife remarried a long time ago."

His teeth were stained a deeper yellow than Parker remembered. The aquarium pump released another blast of air and she asked, after a pause, "How'd you become a developer?"

"Long story," he said. "What are you doing these days?"

"I'm married." She started to add, "I have a daughter," but she stopped herself. She didn't want him to know Joie's name. She didn't want him to know about Joie's existence.

A silver fish coughed out a pebble and darted for the surface. Buddy twisted his cigarette into an overflowing ashtray and he leaned back, shaking his head without taking his eyes off Parker. "I'm not kidding, you look great. How old are you now?"

"I'm fifty-two. You were ten years older than me when I was in middle school, so that would make you sixty-two."

"Well, you've hardly aged at all. How much do you weigh?"

Her mouth opened but nothing came out at first. Too many different zingers were crashing into each other, inside her head, including, *None of your damn business, you creeper,* and, *More than I did when I was fourteen.* Usually, whenever she replayed the sequence of important verbs involving Buddy, they were in numerical order in her mind, like so:

1.) *Listened to Buddy talk about what he did to Peggy and the other Cool Chicks.*
2.) *Rode in his car and let him roll his fingertips up and down my arm for a few months.*
3.) *Hoped Mom wouldn't die while she was in the hospital, sobering up, after my father moved out.*
4.) *Ran away, turned on and terrified, when he came up behind me in the record store.*
5.) *Slumped against him like an over-boiled green bean while he kissed me in his moldy basement bedroom.*
6.) *Watched him click the lock on his door, turn around, and reach down*

for me.
7.) Pulled up my knees, the way he told me to do.

"You have exactly two minutes to explain whatever it is you want," Parker said, checking the time. "Go."

The red rims of his eyes expanded. His fingers spread across the desk like a virus and, to her surprise, his mouth quivered when he opened it again. "I'm sorry," he said, sounding shaky while he stared at his chewed-up, tobacco-stained fingernails. "To tell you the truth, I'm pretty nervous. I didn't mean to get off on the wrong foot. I don't know where to start."

Lift him up, lift him up, lift him up.

"Look, I think I know what you're trying to do here," she said as quietly as she could. "I'm ready to hear it. I want to hear it. Go ahead. Just say it."

Say you're sorry.

He exhaled through his nose as if he was blowing it. "I appreciate you taking the time," he said. "That was the first thing I wanted to say before I said anything stupid."

Parker gave him a slow nod of affirmation, smiling slightly the way she did whenever she was sitting on the front row for one of Joie's choral performances. Again, the egged mailbox and trenched lawn of her youth sprang to mind. *People do things they regret. It was a long time ago.* "Okay. Keep going. I'm listening."

A plume of ink vapor floated off his desk, enveloping Parker's head as he unrolled a large map. She recognized the outline of Silver Park right away—winding unpaved roads and trails and sprawling tangled yards reduced to pale blue lines on a geometric diagram. The lake, with the road curling sharply below it, reminded her of a seedpod, tucked around itself, embryonic. Encircling it like a halo, her property hugged the shoreline from one side to the other, all the way across the waterfall, leaving only a small gray wedge exposed. "The Falls at Silver Park" was printed above the orphaned wedge. From there, a red arrow pointed to a brightly colored sketch of a high-rise building with a fountain by the front door and two tiny cartoon trees on either side of it.

"That's you," he said, tracing the lake with his finger. "This nice little piece over here is where I'm putting my building in. We've already got a buyer pretty much lined up."

"What the hell is this?" Parker asked, squinting.

Buddy lifted his eyes but not his chin so he was staring at her from under his spiky Old Man Winter eyebrows. "This is my property in Silver Park," he said, gut punching the pronoun.

She squeezed her eyes shut, shaking her head, confused. "Arden Collier inherited that whole place, except for the park. No way in hell she'd sell out to you."

He smirked, lips curled. "Nice mouth, kid. Nobody sold me anything. It was a gift from your old man, if you really want to know."

Through the wall, a loud *bump* followed the low wordless rumble of two people talking in the pawnshop next door. Her fingers felt diseased where she was gripping the edge of his slippery chair. The seat was cold and hard, nothing like the plush merlot-colored sofa at the reading of her father's will, where a lawyer had talked in his quiet baritone that sounded the same way a back rub feels. "That's ridiculous," she said. "I know what was in my father's will."

Raising his eyebrows as if he might be growing bored, Buddy cocked his head from side to side. When he yawned, his breath reminded Parker of the dead fawn by the lake. "Your old man gave it to me before he died," he said.

Her father's bamboo-colored eyes—brown and green, infused with light—had faded toward the end, taking on the same color as the sepia-tone photographs in his crumbling scrapbook of Piney Tangle. He never forgot her name, though. "You're lying. He loved that park. He wouldn't give you jack-shit."

"Settle down." Buddy dropped a stapler and a tape dispenser on either end of the map where it kept curling together. He cracked his knuckles. "I did his dirty work for a long time, okay? A boatload of crappy handyman jobs. He owed me. He knew he owed me."

"Bullshit. He felt sorry for you and you took advantage of that. He didn't know what a manipulative jerk you are."

"Whatever. Anyway, this is a great idea I'm about to tell you if you'll listen for two seconds without getting hysterical."

He didn't have to grab the back of her neck, the way he used to do. The memory was enough to shut her up while he stretched both hands across the blueprint again. Parker was thinking, as she eyeballed the distance between her chair and the open door, how he had jumped off her, slapping her leg like a high five. She had swiped at the stain with her favorite purple blouse while he peed with the bathroom door open. "A high-rise in Silver Park," she said. She took a breath to keep her voice steady. "What a brilliant, original idea. You could be a MacArthur Genius."

"Stop with the sarcasm," he said. "Look, there's money in this for you."

"I don't need it." She said it so loud, he flinched. Of course, she did need money, for Joie's college fund, but she wasn't about to take a dime from Buddy, not even if somebody held a gun to her head.

"Oh, come on, you might not need it, but you know you want it." His feathery smile was the color of jaundice and Parker knew he was having fun, messing with her. He smoothed a second map on top of the first one and said, in a lilting voice as if she might be three years old, "See the pedestrian boardwalk and the 'Stop-and-Look' signs by the lake? That's nice, right? Kids love that kind of stuff. You could make it happen."

"There's already a park by the lake." Parker was secretly working a little yoga magic on herself, pushing all the air from her lungs as slowly as possible. If she was going to derail his plan, which she intended to do if it killed her, she would have to learn as much as possible about it. "That looks to me like a big sidewalk next to a road."

Buddy licked a crack in his bottom lip. "That's exactly right. It's a new road with a vegetative buffer and these public installations and look at that—a little rain garden where it gets muddy in the spring. You'd be improving the neighborhood, and I'd cut you in on a percentage of the revenue."

"Why?"

"I need access." He was staring her down without blinking. "You've got me boxed in, kid. I've got other options, but cutting through your park's the easiest way to go, hands down."

"You can't put a road through there. It's designated historic."

"I've been promised a variance. It's in my pocket, if you know what I mean, but the executor of the park—unfortunately, that's you—would have to agree." He leaned back and wiggled his thumbs under his belt where his gut wasn't exactly big, but jiggling slightly every time he talked, softer than when he used to lie on his back, watching Parker with one arm tucked under his head.

"What if I don't want to go along with it?"

He flicked out his tongue and plucked at a speck of tobacco. "I'd have to cut a back door all the way around the neighborhood. That would cost me a hell of a lot more. I might even have to move a house with somebody in it. My backer's prepared for that, but it would be a real pain. Lawsuits, bad publicity, and all that."

A dotted red line on his map, faint but unmistakable, bisected the sloping yard where Parker had first met Arden's grandfather, Mr. John Collier. Mr. Collier had helped Parker's Dad with lot cleanup and construction work. She remembered him for his crinkly smile and his starched white shirts, buttoned tightly at his wrists and neck. He had never wanted to sell the little cabin he built in the 1940s. After he and his sister Wilma died, Arden stayed in the house, to hold the fort for her grandfather. "You've got some nerve," she said. "I ought to have you arrested."

Buddy smeared his lips with a thick balm. "What for?" He watched her while he rolled the tube of grease slowly between his thumb and forefinger. "There's nothing illegal about any of this, princess."

His lungs whistled when he exhaled. Parker thought about him pushing into her until it felt like she might split in two. "You know what I'm talking about."

He folded his hands together on his desk and looked down at them as if he was about to say grace. "I know it was hard for you when Rhonda and I got married. I'm sorry I hurt your feelings that way. I really am."

Her jaw dropped open. A fish bumped blindly against the glass tank. "I'm not talking about Rhonda. I don't even know Rhonda and I don't give a single flying flip about her. I'm talking about what you did to me when I was a kid."

His eyes were flat and dry and she realized he didn't give a damn about her, either, one way or the other. She was simply holding his proverbial meal ticket. "Please," he said. "I did exactly what you wanted. What about all that stuff you did to me, anyway? Believe me, I wished like hell I'd never touched you in the first place. You followed me around like a rabid fox after that. You knocked on my door in the middle of the night. You cried if I told you to go away. I was scared shitless."

Cigarette butts flew across the room when Parker shoved the maps off his desk. Buddy jumped to his feet, bumping the shelf where his kids were still grinning inside the red picture frame from so many years earlier. "What did you expect?"

"I never expected you to show up at my trailer that one time, after you left for college." He was talking so fast, spit pooled in the oily corners of his mouth.

"I thought you were my friend." It sounded lame, but it was the truth. She had been programmed to imagine he was the only person who would ever care about her.

"You walked right in, boo-hooing about some guy. What was his name—Beamer? I never expected all that. Tell me if that was my fault, too, because I don't see how. What were you, eighteen? Nineteen? I don't remember holding a knife to your ribs, kid."

A clump of white grease stuck to his upper lip where it was twisted into a half-smile. She didn't stop to explain why a girl in middle-school might chase after whatever grownup has sex with her for the first time. A shrink had given Parker the lowdown on that once. Something about being groomed first and oxytocin and conditioning, which may or may not have been pseudo-scientific bullshit intended to make her feel better at the time. Parker wasn't sure. Maybe she was mentally defective— damaged goods. She had a brief urge to slash him with her fingernails, but she didn't want to waste a perfectly good manicure. "You're not putting a road through my Dad's park," she said and she charged away at full speed.

Parker plowed across the moldy prairie-grass carpet in his front room, popped through the front door and stood there blinking in the sunshine for a split-second. The pawnshop man was tossing breadcrumbs to a pack of birds on the sidewalk. They squawked and scattered when she ran through the middle of their circle. "Hey," he said, "are you okay?" Parker kept moving until she was inside the smoky perfumed rental car again, cranking the engine so hard it squealed, rocketing out of the fractured parking lot.

The road looked blurry, rushing toward her. She swallowed hard and waited, wondering if she was going to be sick, which tended to happen when she was upset—but no, the air-conditioner was a big help. Her fingers groped blindly through her satchel until they hit a stick of gum. She shoved it into her mouth, replaying the verbs she always left off her list whenever she was checking it over a few zillion times:

8.) Cried when he told me to get out before somebody walked in on us.

9.) Sneaked back downstairs after midnight and knocked until he opened the door.

10.) Phoned him at work until he called me back.

11.) Ran down the driveway the minute I saw his car.

12.) Crawled onto the back seat.

There was plenty more. The list was in fact endless, stretching on for years, but Parker couldn't keep replaying it. She had to get back in the game—quickly. Dylan would be calling her soon about the press conference video. She also needed to get in touch with Arden, to warn her about Buddy's plan. After pulling into a used-car lot, Parker dialed Beamer's office number and sat listening to her breath, shaky and amplified by the phone.

"Sweetheart." He spoke before Parker had said a word. "Are you all right?"

Above the cars for sale, red and blue plastic triangles dangled from a rope. "You don't have to pretend," she said. "I know Jolene told you. I just left his office."

Two thuds, followed by chair hinges, squeaking. She pictured him leaning over his desk with both feet on the floor. "Come home, baby," he said. "I'm worried about you."

She closed her eyes and pressed her cheek against the car window. "I have to stage a press conference for this new donor." She sounded and felt like a robot. "I want to see you. I know it's a lot to ask, but could you bring Joie down here to Atlanta? School's almost over."

The phone went quiet. She couldn't hear him breathing, and for a minute she thought he had cut her off by accident, or hung up on her. She opened her eyes and sat up straight. By the used-car lot, a green light turned red. A rusty blue El Camino rumbled to a stop. "Are you still there?"

"Yep," he said, sounding angry, "never left, not leaving. You know that."

A gingery cat tiptoed along the road, sniffing dandelions. Parker used her softest voice, as if they were both tucked under freshly dried sheets. "She won't miss any tests. They don't do any real work the last few days of school. I'll buy the tickets. You won't have to do a thing."

"We can't afford that and she's got one more game," he said. "Listen, I want you to stay away from that Dirtbag. I don't care what Jolene says about letting him make amends or whatever the hell he's trying to do. Don't call him. Don't go over there. Don't trade emails. You understand?"

She was staring at the El Camino's flashing right blinker, wracking her brain for an answer. "Not really." The light turned green and the car shimmied straight through the intersection with its turn signal still blinking. "I went in there hoping to flip the page—finally, you know? I thought he might say he was sorry, but he wants to cut a road through my Dad's park. He hasn't changed a bit. I can't explain how awful it was. I wish you would fly down here and be with me."

More silence. When he sighed, he didn't sound angry anymore—only sad and exhausted. "I'm with you," he said. "I'm right here. I'd kill that lowlife if it wouldn't make things ten times worse, but it tears me up when you keep rehashing it. Are we going to have this same conversation when they're spoon-feeding us oatmeal in the nursing home? You need to move on. This isn't good for you, baby. Enough is enough. Yes, it was terrible what he did, but you can't change it, and it's time for you to get over it."

She shifted the car into gear, keeping her foot on the brake. Her scalp felt itchy and damp from sitting too long in the sun. "I told Joie she could come to Atlanta. She was so excited."

"Maybe later. She's got her game on Thursday and I promised to fix Jolene's garage door. It's been stuck all week."

Parker's phone buzzed.

"Video's ready for preview," Dylan's message said. "P.S., if life hands you melons, you may be dyslexic."

She took her foot off the brake. "Honey, I'm late," she said. "Joie's going to be sad when you tell her. Will you give her a big hug for me?"

"Let's talk again tonight," Beamer said. "There's a lot going on right now."

"You're right. Like you said, she's got her game. I can't believe I let him make me feel that way. It was a shock, is all, seeing him in person."

"Keep breathing. Call me later."

Parker pitched the phone onto the passenger seat. She turned back onto the road and lowered all four windows. Traffic was weirdly sparse, for Atlanta. She felt like the only actor on an abandoned movie set. She cruised by check-cashing services and shops selling mattresses and cold beer. With her hair whipping every which-way, she reached into her pocket for Jolene's stupid fortune-cookie riddle. She thought about spitting her gum into the middle of it or tearing it into confetti so she could toss it out the window. She tucked it into her satchel instead.

12.
ARDEN COLLIER

Arden excavated her grandfather's old phone by moving cereal boxes, dish towels, and pots off the table, one by one, remembering how her Great Aunt Wilma used to sit in the same spot to make a call, every hair gelled into place under a clean, white scarf, a blank notepad and two lethally sharpened pencils at the ready. The old lawyer might not even remember Arden's name anymore. She hadn't seen or talked to him in years, not since her grandfather's death and the reading of the will in a little house that doubled as an office next door to the Silver Park Funeral Home. At last, Arden managed to clean a patch of table large enough to plant her elbows around the phone. She knocked an ancient bag of flour off the chair, sat down, and dialed the number, hoping he was still in business.

She needed his help.

Philip Smith III answered the phone himself, after the first ring, and when she told him her name, he let out a laugh like church bells, ringing. "Of course, I remember you," he said in the thick, musical accent of an earlier generation. "Now, how could I ever forget my dear friend Mr. John Collier and his lovely, charming granddaughter?"

"I'm calling to inquire about your services." Arden was weaving her fingers through the loops of an impossibly long, tangled phone cord. "I've been summoned to a hearing later this week. I'm told the county could seize my home. I don't have anywhere else to go. Even if I did, I don't want to go."

She heard paper rattling, in the background. She pictured him shaking out a newspaper, adjusting the crease. "Yes, I've read about the citations," he said. "I guess you've been having a little trouble with the upkeep of your home, haven't you, dear?"

Her scalp began to tingle. She didn't like her personal business being all over the news. In the sink, a line of large, entitled-looking ants marched over a pile of unwashed dishes like they owned the place. "I was hoping you might be able to go with me on Friday."

"I'd be glad to help you if I could."

Her chest expanded while she cradled the telephone receiver, pressing his voice against her cheek like a lover's hand. "Oh," she said, breathless, "thank you."

"The only thing is, I'm retired now, dear, and I haven't kept my license current." His words hit her hard, squarely in the middle of her chest where she had been holding out hope. "I don't know any lawyers nowadays who take on *pro bono* cases. I know one fellow who's quite good, but he would bill you three-hundred and fifty dollars an hour, probably with a four-hour minimum."

Her breathing turned into a series of ragged, heaving blasts, laced with grief. "I don't have that kind of money. I don't have any spare money at all. I'm sorry for wasting your time. I don't know what I was thinking."

"Hold on just one moment." She heard a shuffling, followed by a crash and a sigh, through the phone. "I can give you some advice as a friend. That's the best I can do. Your grandfather taught me so much about true friendship. Did you know we served together as deacons in the church?"

"Yes, sir. I remember that."

"He always had a kind word for everybody. He told me once, 'If some white folks treat you badly, be as nice as you can to them. They'll feel ashamed and come back to you after a while, and then you'll know, and God will know you've taught them something."

"Keep your head down and your heart focused on God," was another one of her grandfather's favorite sayings. It made Arden's head feel like a crayfish being steamed to death.

The table felt gritty against her palms. She hated her grandfather's maddeningly meek philosophy, which was only slightly less annoying than her aunt's instructions about never calling a boy. Her heart began to thrum as she recalled the one and only time she had ever dared to dial a boy's house and got caught with the phone in her hand, asking for him. She wound up grounded—housebound with her aunt's clocks and porcelain figurines for a week's worth of long, dusty afternoons.

She shouldn't have called Philip Smith III. It was clear he couldn't help her and Arden didn't feel like listening to a bunch of Uncle Tom nonsense.

"He and my Aunt Wilma were old school," she said, as gently as she could. "They believed in being passive and subservient. Pretty sad, but that's how they were raised."

Mr. Smith made a tenuous humming sound. "Passive? Yes, maybe. As you say, your grandfather and I were brought up in a certain time and place, but I never thought of him as subservient. He was a very powerful man. He had an inner strength, the strength of his belief in God and what was right and wrong."

"Well," she said, staring with slumped shoulders through the kitchen window at her cluttered lawn where the sun was gaining its own strength, "I don't think his trick is going to help me this time. I can't rely on the county to feel ashamed later."

He asked if she had a pen and paper.

Arden tore a strip off a paper sack. She fished a red crayon out of a bucket. "Yes, sir." Her response sounded flat, resigned.

"I'm going to give you some phone numbers to call. I still know a few reporters in this town, and you'll need them there as witnesses at the hearing on Friday."

"Reporters?" Arden lifted her wrist off the paper.

"They'll shame the county for you. Make some calls today. Tell them the county is trying to bully you and unfairly seize your property for economic gain. Be sure you say it just like that—*for economic gain.* That's against the law, you see. Tell them a little bit about yourself and your family's history there."

The red numbers, blurry on the wrinkled brown scrap of paper, looked somehow menacing to Arden. She felt as if she had set a loaded gun on the table, or a boy's phone number. Could she really draw attention to herself in that way? Could she ask for help? "I understand," she said.

"My other advice is, go in there looking like a pillar of the community. Do you have a nice dress that's not cut too low at the top, or too high at the bottom? Something you might wear to church?"

She remembered Joel's hand in hers and their thighs touching while they sat on the church pew, their last Easter Sunday together. The linen suit had made her feel hopeful. "Yes. I have something nice I could wear," she said.

"Good. Go in there looking your best, speak up for yourself, and as I said, try to get those witnesses into the room. Those reporters. I'm sorry I can't do more for you. I'm not able to walk very far these days. I'll be thinking of you, though. I'll be praying for you, my dear."

Arden promised to report back to him later.

"There's one other thing I might be able to do, although ..." His voice trailed off. Arden waited. "I have one other idea. My granddaughter volunteers with the historical society. I haven't seen her for at least a year, but I could give her a call. The historical society has an excellent track record, influencing these sorts of situations."

From her kitchen door, Arden could see the steeple on the church where she was baptized alongside his head-strong granddaughter who insisted on wearing a necklace of red and yellow beads everywhere she went. "Oh, my goodness, yes. Vera Mae. She certainly made a name for herself with that jewelry on QVC. How is she doing?"

"As I said, I haven't seen her all that much lately." The words drifted, heavy and forlorn as wet leaves tumbling downriver.

The ants formed a vibrating mob on a dab of strawberry jam Arden had left on the previous night's dinner plate. "I'm sure she stays very busy with her company. She must travel all the time."

"She could find time to visit, but you see, dear, she's an atheist."

"Oh," Arden said, holding back an evil cackle. *An atheist!* She fought off a memory of her Great Aunt Wilma in white Mickey Mouse gloves, standing sentinel on the porch of Mount Zion Baptist Church, clutching her pocketbook, keeping tabs on any sinners who hadn't shown up for service. "I guess the two of you don't see eye to eye."

"She won't listen to reason."

"Well, I'm sorry to hear you're not spending much time with Vera Mae."

"I have two great-grandchildren as well. They've sided with their mother."

"That's very sad, sir."

"Maybe one day," he said, "the spirit will move her."

Arden thanked him and hung up. She made her way toward the hall closet, lifting her knees to step over boxes of mushroom soup, scaling a newspaper hill, squeezing between two towers of used canvases she was determined to repaint someday. Getting the closet door open involved another feat of strength, acrobatics, and will power. A pyramid of cleaning supplies had become wedged against the knob. She tugged until at last she could see the white and blue brocade of her Easter suit, still on its wooden hanger, encased in plastic. *Yes.* She knew where to find her good dress.

The long muscles along her haunches ached from all the climbing. As she replayed the phone conversation in her head, Arden began to feel unreasonably sleepy. Waves of exhaustion and sadness kept pushing against her eyelids. She wanted to lie down on a mound of sweaters in the hallway. She turned and headed back toward the kitchen instead, rehearsing aloud the speech Philip Smith III had recited to her about being bullied and threatened and illegal economic gain.

With the red phone numbers in front of her, Arden picked up the phone.

13.

PARKER GOZER

Dylan smiled at Parker, squinting in the sun while he smoothed paper napkins across the grimy checkerboard table outside Charles Van der Griff's building. His breath reeked of peppermint mouthwash and bourbon vapor. How long had it been since they performed acrobatic stunts all over his dorm room? Thirty-two years?

Time was running out. Parker couldn't afford distractions. They needed to finish the video script for Van der Griff's press conference, which would take place on Friday, ready or not. They had been working for three hours before her fingers stalled and hovered, paralyzed over the keyboard. Announcing a lunch break, Dylan had retrieved a large brown sack from the kitchen by his office.

Outside, he pulled two hard-boiled eggs, a tiny pack of salt, a pair of apples, and a partially flattened blueberry muffin from the sack. The concrete chair felt cool under her legs. A ladybug landed on her skirt, flapped, and crawled north, toward Parker's knees. Dylan's eyes, enlarged by reading glasses, looked especially green under the dogwoods. He handed her a plastic spoon-fork hybrid—a spork—and a cup of yogurt labeled "organic" in fancy cursive lettering. "So," he said, "you think my video extravaganza will work?"

She peeled the lid off the yogurt and swirled a strawberry cyclone through it. "I do, yes. You really pulled it out of the loop with that presentation. The human story is heartbreaking and the real-time flyover took my breath away. Thank you."

He produced a croissant, along with a miniature bottle of gourmet orange juice. "I knew you'd be starving. I know how you operate." The bottle crackled when he twisted the cap.

He was right. She had forgotten to eat breakfast. After the confrontation with Buddy, she was too upset to stop for food. "Wow," she said, grabbing the juice like a wolf starving on the frozen Yukon tundra. "I'm getting you pregnant tonight."

His beautiful, empty fingers froze in mid-air. "What?"

"Oh." Instantly, her face felt engorged, hot and swollen. The pavement seemed to ripple under her feet. "I don't know why I said that. I guess I—it's been a long morning. Something happened earlier, and then—hey, would you mind ignoring me for a minute? I'm pretty hungry. I'm sorry if I sound like a crazy person."

His eyes widened, child-like—so different from Buddy's squinty glare that made Parker feel like a chipped drinking glass, or some other form of damaged goods. She imagined Dylan as a kid, running through a dark field with a lit sparkler, and later, pacing back and forth in front of a chalkboard in college, gesturing wildly, full of wonder. He reached across the concrete checkerboard. "That's all right, friend," he said, patting her hand in a grandfatherly way. "Time to reprogram."

She planted the spork in her yogurt and sucked on a strawberry seed wedged between her molars. "Hey, I've got to figure out the rest of that script, man. I don't have another day to mull this thing over."

He bit into a croissant and tapped his lips with a napkin. "What have you got so far?"

"Science and technology promise a better way of life for young people all over the world—"

"Right, that's the flyover bit. We'll be zooming in on Nigeria." He opened a file folder containing his notes.

"Today, a child persecuted in Nigeria or Myanmar or Tibet can be saved by high-tech eyes in the sky. Those eyes are Charles Van der Griff's high-resolution satellite images analyzed by The Tinley Institute's patented algorithms for pinpointing minute changes to landscapes and structures. Someday, we might even be able to predict human rights attacks before they happen."

"Bingo." Dylan pointed at Parker. "There's your money quote. Then we cut to the photos of the little girl and her family."

Parker slugged more orange juice and kept going, reciting her video voiceover from memory. "This is Oba. She was six years old when her parents were killed in front of her, caught in crossfire between the Joint Task Force and armed gang members fighting for turf in an oil-rich region. She was seven when her uncle's arms were cut off by machete bandits."

Dylan peeled off his glasses, one ear at a time. "Poor kid." He mashed his thumbs against his eyelids. "She's beautiful."

He was wearing a freshly pressed linen jacket over an off-white dress shirt. No tie. A hint of skin, but not too much under the open collar, and he was nicely tanned. Very Miami Vice. A great choice for TV interviews. Parker approved. The ladybug kept tickling her knee. When she peeked down, the tiny creature was lifting her lovely spotted wings. Trembling, she took flight. Parker's storyline disappeared from her brain at the same time. "I don't know what comes next. We need a big finish."

He slipped one hand into his jacket and tipped an antique flask to his mouth—silver filigree in a leather case. Parker remembered the flask as a cherished gift from an uncle who used to take Dylan to football games, back in his college days. "What was that like when you were over there with your boss? You met this little girl, right?"

The bourbon smelled like cinnamon on steroids. Parker closed her eyes, picturing Arden's Aunt Wilma, who had kept a constant supply of hard candy called Red Hots in the pocket of her creased white apron. One Saturday, Wilma had popped unexpectedly into the hallway of Parker's house, exhaling the aroma of Red Hots like a fire-breathing dragon. She grabbed Parker's wrist with her fingers that felt as scratchy as the steel wool she used to scrub their pots and pans. Behind her, shadows flickered without a sound across a black and white TV set where she watched soap operas in the laundry room. Puffs of steam coiled from an iron. Her cloudy eyes floated in opposite directions. Her breath smelled like the spicy fire in the candy. "Don't ride with that man," she said, meaning Buddy. Parker had yanked her arm free before running out the door to catch up with him.

"Hey," Dylan said. "You okay?"

"I met Oba's whole family," she said, opening her eyes. "It was pretty much exactly what you saw in the video—kids kicking a rag around a dirt yard. Big orange and black oil plumes roaring in the distance."

He looked at her over his folded hands. "Tell me the rest of their story."

She pawed through her pocketbook until she unearthed a pen and an envelope with no writing on the back. "Oba and her remaining family members were evicted from their tiny plot of land, where their drinking water had been polluted since her birth," she said, scribbling. "Every year, oil companies spill more oil in the Niger Delta than the Deepwater Horizon disaster."

"What else? What was the deal with that creepy photo of the older guy?"

"Now at the age of eleven, Oba's been promised in marriage to a twenty-five-year-old as soon as she enters puberty," she said, cringing at the memory of the girl's future husband, towering over her. Parker couldn't look for long at the way he gripped the back of her neck. She had turned away when Dr. Tinley snapped the photo.

"Yuck," Dylan said. "You'd better circle back to the promise of science and technology before everybody gets depressed and heads for the exits."

"We're identifying children—identifying young people at risk like Oba," Parker said, stammering as she found the words. "Oh, wait a minute."

"What's wrong?"

"We can't name Oba in public. That could put her at greater risk. We'll have to use a pseudonym. Let's call her Abebi."

"Good thinking. Go on."

"Our joint research will leverage satellite-image analysis combined with first-person, on-the-ground narratives to pinpoint areas of village destruction and human displacement. Our longer-term goal is to identify patterns that could make it possible to predict human rights violations before they happen."

When she looked up again, Dylan was staring straight through her with a nearly hidden smile like he might be remembering something she would rather forget. *Oh no,* Parker thought, *not The Look.* "You're good at what you do," he said in a subdued, bedroom kind of voice.

Having his eyes locked on her felt like getting zapped in the temple by a stun gun. For a split-second, she was mesmerized. Mercifully, he blinked first, looking down at his notes. Parker jumped up, banged her knee on the table, and started flinging everything into the grocery bag, including his folder and her script. "It's getting late," she said. "I've got to call Beamer. You remember Beamer? My husband?"

He glanced at her again and fished his notes out of the bag.

"We'd better go." She clutched the lumpy sack against her chest. She was pretty sure the open bottle of orange juice was leaking straight through the bottom of the bag where she had propped it against her hip.

"Whoa," he said. "You're all wet."

Parker inhaled so hard, it sounded like she might be having an asthma attack. "What?"

He stood up, took the bag from her, and pulled a blue handkerchief from his jacket. She latched onto it and started blotting, happy as hell she was wearing the black skirt instead of the white one. "Oh, dear," he whispered. "I'm terribly sorry."

"Goodness," she said with a weak laugh, "it's not your fault. I've always been clumsy. You know that."

"No, listen." He set the bag on the table and shoved his hands into his pockets. "I think I went a little overboard yesterday when I was saying goodbye. I didn't mean to make you uncomfortable. The fact is, I'm grateful to be working with Tinley, and you—you're the best and Van der Griff knows that. He wouldn't have made a deal, otherwise. I can respect your boundaries. I want you to feel safe with me. Good grief, we're middle-aged now, right? I'd like to be friends. Okay?"

Parker folded the sticky handkerchief and handed it back to him. His shoulders didn't look so big when they were bunched around his neck. "I'd like that, too. Thanks."

A smile spread gradually across his face until his cheeks creased and his eyes crinkled. He clapped his hands together. "How's about giving me a ride home, old friend? My car's been on the fritz all week. I've spent a fortune on taxis."

"I didn't know Atlanta had taxis. Last time I called one here, it didn't show up for at least an hour."

"That's the other problem. Plus, no subway trains that go much of anywhere."

In the parking lot, she fumbled in her purse for keys to the rental car. When she turned around, Dylan was guzzling from the flask again. Parker opened her car door. He eased onto the passenger seat, hands trembling. "You okay?" she whispered, turning to face him. "Kind of early, Dyl."

"I'm going to quit soon," he said with a shrug. "You know, that nickname's funny. It makes me feel like one of those spongy little pickles on a cocktail tray. What are they called? Baby gherkins?"

"You're more of a nice big Vlasic, as I recall." *What in God's name was she saying?* Her mouth seemed to be surging forward, unchecked by her brain, like a jammed accelerator pedal in a car not yet recalled.

He laughed, reached across the seat without further adieu, and ran the back of his fingers down her cheek in a bold precision move only Dylan could pull off. Parker knew she should make him stop, but waves of heat lightning seemed to be crackling across her skin, for one thing, and secondly, she couldn't catch her breath. She tried to remember the last time Beamer had touched her that way.

She didn't move while Dylan's fingers slid through her hair, massaged her scalp until her eyes strobed shut a few times. She felt—and probably looked—like a junkie. His hand rolled down her shoulder. As lightly as possible, he pulled his nails across the inside of Parker's arm, all the way to her wrist, her wide-open palm, and the pointy vulnerable pads of her fingers where they hit the keyboard. She took hold of his hand, thinking she would push it away for sure, but it was unimaginably warm. When she tightened her grip, he smiled with blurry eyes like they were underwater, playing tea party in the neighborhood swimming pool.

Parker was having so much fun, pretending, she thought about staying underwater until her lungs exploded. Mustering all of her strength, she pushed him away instead. "Not a good idea," she said. The words sounded strangled. "I'm sorry, but no."

A shadow drifted across the windshield, muting his cheeks where they had turned pink from the booze. Too soon, his hand slid free, leaving Parker's poor cold fingers bereft as orphans. "I understand. It's probably just as well," he said. He was leaning forward, whispering in her ear. She could tell, as her heart pounded from the sound of his voice and the smell of the bourbon, how hard he was struggling for words. "There's no wood left in that forest anymore, dear, if you know what I mean."

She wasn't sure, at first, if she had heard him correctly. She bolted upright and stared at him, thinking, *Be cool, be cool, be cool.* He licked his lips and narrowed his eyes like he was straining to see a distant face that might never come back into focus. "You mean—none at all? Nothing?"

"Nope. Nada."

"Are you sure? Never?"

"I'm afraid not."

Grief's iron mask tugged at the loose skin along his jaw. He looked pinned to the seat, to his place in the world, to the Earth. Parker thought about the funeral home where someone had spackled orange putty onto her father's face before he was lowered into the ground. She watched Dylan's hands, full of anguish, his swimming eyes, and the lines around his mouth—shadows of gravity, imprinted on his skin, trails across the great divide of life and death, men and women, Dylan and her, then and now. He winked and smiled in a sad way. Inside Parker's brain, a dormant circuit flipped back to life. She knew what to do. *This is my job,* she thought. *This is my job. This is my job.*

"I was a Girl Scout for seven years," she said. "I can start a fire with an empty matchbox and a stack of wet kindling."

His eyes were closed. His tongue was out of his mouth before she finished the sentence and they were hermetically locked at the lips, after that. Bourbon flooded her mouth. She kept hearing an otherworldly keening like those hypnotic New Age recordings of whales. It was coming from her. Dylan seemed more focused on action than sound effects. He went straight for the boobs—no surprise there—but his speed and opposable-thumb dexterity, even nicely buzzed, were truly a marvel of human evolution. Inside the rental car, it was *Come In, Rangoon* hour at the ham radio club, all of a sudden.

"Not here, not here," Parker said, gulping for air while the mother of all hot flashes seared her prefrontal cortex. She shuddered to think of Van der Griff getting a gander at them flailing inside the Chevy Aveo. Once again, she silently cursed her failure to upgrade to the Mitsubishi Galant or Similar category.

"I'm home," he said in a husky voice and he came at her again with his mouth open. "Take me drunk."

In the nick of time, Parker turned her head. He slimed her cheek while she was twisting holy hell out of the ignition key. The engine whined, she hit the gas, and off they zoomed with Dylan's hand planted firmly between her legs. He kept whispering directions in her ear. What happened next was like watching inferior animation on an old VHS tape stuck in the fast-forward mode. Phone poles and buildings and trees and Starbucks coffee shops flickered by in a continuous, herky-jerky loop. They were in midtown when Dylan's tongue found her ear. As they careened into an underground garage in Inman Park, Parker miscalculated the angle of descent, causing the Aveo to briefly catch wind and lurch on the downfall. His head tapped the ceiling, dislodging his hand. "Damn," he said. "It's like a monster truck rally."

Inside, he darted unsteadily into his bathroom while Parker loitered around a wall-length mirror like an aging prostitute. She rotated her skirt until the zipper was in the back. She felt drunk: weightless and euphoric, not sick drunk. She thought about Beamer—she did, while Dylan kicked off his shoes—and she tried to picture the last time her husband had made love to her. It wouldn't come back to her. She wondered if Dylan might need to use the Jaws of Life. The idea made her start laughing like a crazy person until her eyes filled. The next thing she knew, Parker was crying, overcome with sadness.

What am I doing here? she thought. *I have to get out of here.*

She pushed the tears into her hair just as Dylan threw her over his shoulder, the same as in the old days, except one of his knees creaked like a haunted house. A funny thing happened after that. They made out sinking into an oversized chair, standing up, and rolling around on the bed. He was on top first, then Parker was straddling him, then he pushed her over again like they were a pair of tipsy sumo wrestlers. She strongly suspected the heavy petting chapter of the human sexuality textbook would need to be rewritten after their get-together. Still, none of their clothes hit the deck. Not even a sock or a lousy popped button. Parker figured he must be feeling self-conscious due to his lack-of-wood-in-the-forest problem. Otherwise, they would both be naked, craving cigarettes at that point.

Clearly, Parker needed to man the helm.

Pulling his shirt out of his pants was her first move. Immediately, she was rewarded by a glimpse of his tanned torso. She could have bounced a quarter off his belly but she didn't have one, so she bounced her hips off him instead, causing her aging back to spasm while she peeled his jacket and shirt off. Repositioning, she popped his belt, unzipped his pants and gave them a tug. She took a moment, as she was removing his navy blue boxers, to admire the subtle white piping along the waistband. This helped Parker act like she wasn't the least bit concerned about his poor pickled sapling, which was pasty-white, comatose and keeled over on its side.

"Oh, yes," she said, straddling his soft hips again while they kissed for the millionth time. Her mind wandered to TV commercials about sugar-free chewing gum and couples in side-by-side bathtubs overlooking scenic vistas while they waited for an erectile dysfunction medication to kick in.

He was mostly lying still with his eyes closed and a small smile plastered on his face. Parker felt like a failure, as if she had flubbed a big assignment at work. *Time for a new game plan.* They had never opened the heavy bedroom drapes—crimson and teal stripes, like a circus tent or a puppet show—and the lights were off, except in the bathroom. *Perfect,* she thought as she hopped to the floor. *I don't need a klieg light at my age.* As soon as she got her bra unhooked, she remembered the adhesive flesh-colored booster pads Joie called "the chicken cutlets." They allowed Parker to look symmetrical in clothes despite the lumpectomy from some years earlier. Turning her back on him, she ripped the pads free and winced. Both cutlets fell on the carpet with a soft *thwack.* One of them bounced a foot in the air before wobbling under the bed—not exactly the erotic ballet she was going for.

"Talk to me," she said.

"Sure," he said. "Whan that Aprille with his shoures soote, the droghte of Marche hath perced to the roote and bathed every veyne in—"

"No, please," she said, "not that." Dylan had always loved to recite the prologue to *The Canterbury Tales* in Middle English whenever he was buzzed.

Her skirt was unzipped by the time she remembered her C-section scar. She gave up on the striptease and went back to straddling Dylan, who appeared to be on the verge of sleep. Hope rose in her chest like a flock of wedding doves when she felt a tiny twitch, but when he wrapped his hand around both of her wrists, squeezing hard, she couldn't lift her arms or move, and it freaked her out. The whole room seemed to tilt. Parker told him to stop. Immediately, he let go. She pulled away and sat on the edge of the bed with her head in her hands.

Oh, my God. My poor husband. What have I done?

Remorse pulsed through her as Dylan groaned and flexed his spine. He was sprawled on his back, eyes open, watching her. His face was eager but leaden, like a kid who wanted to be told a story, although he knew the ending would make him sad.

"I wanted to see if I could make it work with you," he said. His hair was damp. He smelled like a distillery. He was speaking quietly. "You know what I'm most afraid of? I'm afraid of being alone forever."

Her eyes moved across the brass floor lamp on one side of the room and back to the red Victorian chair at the other end, but Parker couldn't think of a single thing to say to Dylan. She couldn't fix him—or herself, it seemed. He pulled the covers over his body. She petted his hair without talking. In another minute, he was curled in a fetal position, asleep or possibly pretending to be.

Standing up, Parker was surprised by the sight of herself in the vast spotless mirror above his bureau, a naked middle-aged woman, flushed with her hair askew. She had never noticed all of her scars in the aggregate: faded white lines from the year her breasts grew too fast for her skin, attracting Buddy's attention, the red zipper where she had found a menacing lump that turned out to be benign but had to be cut out, nonetheless, and Joie's bright pink escape hatch during the C-section. Parker's eyes filled.

Dylan's breath was slow and even and she realized she had just replayed, in microcosm, everything that happened with Buddy—a stylized version of her infamous verb sequence: *talk, touch, hope, kiss, hurt, cry.* Except she had been in charge this time, and for her reenactment, she had chosen a friend who told her *up front* he would only be able to pretend with her.

In sleep, Dylan transformed back into a boy. His soft blank expression reminded Parker of the younger man she had known, awkward yet fearless, and her father, terrified by the vanishing shadow of a cowardly old man. She thought, too, about herself as a girl, lonely and yearning, hopeful and guileless as they had all been at some point—maybe even Buddy.

Parker sat on the bed next to Dylan.

"I'm having a hard time," she whispered. He didn't stir. She kept going. "I felt like a ghost, growing up, you know? Invisible. My Dad had moved out and my Mom was sick. There was this guy. I was a kid. It twisted me up. It took a long time to come back to life, to find my voice. When my daughter was born, she brought me so much joy, I can't even explain how much. I thought the whole thing was behind me, after that, but it came back to bite me and I still think, deep down, it was my fault.

I *know* it was my fault, what happened with Buddy. Nobody could ever talk me out of that. People don't see it on the outside, but there's something wrong with me inside. You know? The things I do, I can't explain. I keep repeating the same old stupid patterns and I've got nobody to blame but myself this time. One of these days, I'll have to figure out how to forgive myself."

She dressed and retrieved her pocketbook from behind his front door, where she had dropped it. In a zippered slot, she found Jolene's prayer. "God, lift Buddy up and set him free," the prayer said. "Free me from my past. Forgive Buddy and release him to the universe. Amen."

Parker's pen hovered over it. She wrote "Parker" and then "Dylan" above Buddy's name. She was about to write "Dad," but an indigo tsunami of ink flooded the fibers when she pressed down again. Ink spurted across her fingers, jolting her back into a panic about the pale blue lines on Buddy's map and her father's foolish gift of land to the Dirtbag. Parker tossed the leaky pen into a trashcan without adding her father's name to the paper. She kissed Dylan's cheek, tucked the smudged prayer back into her bag and slipped out the door.

Her rental car seemed to glide on its own, without any direction from Parker. Before she knew it, she was headed for Silver Lake and Arden's house. *Somebody has to tell her,* she thought. Arden needed to know about Buddy's plan.

14.
BUDDY CALDWELL

Ordinarily, Buddy never bothered to pull his car off the road to make a phone call, but his eardrum was getting drilled hard by Ken's voice. Buddy veered into the parking lot of a bank with plywood-covered windows and a "For Sale" sign out front. It reminded him of the sign he had so far failed to remove from his Silver Park property. Along the curb, bouquets of weeds had sprouted amid long, bent blades of grass. The clinging arms of enormous dandelions had formed a ring around the base of the empty red brick building. Tangled knots of poison oak covered all but the uppermost leaves of a dogwood tree near the street.

"Why didn't you get that listing off the Internet? For God's sake, why didn't you at least take the sign off the damn lot?" Ken's voice pounded into Buddy's brain, as shrill and constant as a jackhammer. "We just got another inquiry about it. You had one job to do. It was the easiest thing in the world. I told you at least three weeks ago to get that property off the market."

Buddy fumbled for the full pack of Marlboro Lights he had purchased moments earlier at a convenience store. He had to wedge the phone under his chin and pluck at a gold strip with both hands to get the pack open. "I've been pretty busy, dealing with some of the issues we talked about, and we've already signed the papers. What's the big deal?"

Ken exhaled at full force, clearly trying to make some point Buddy couldn't quite figure out. "Cedar Point Associates. Remember them?"

"Yeah. I'm well aware of the competition." The cigarette crackled as Buddy held a lighter to it. At least for a second, the first hit of smoke and nicotine pulled the pain right out of his spine. Thinking about Parker and Arden, those two stubborn bitches, brought the agony rushing back on the exhale.

"Cedar Point's rep called our real estate agent." Ken's words were punctuated by a thumping sound, which might have been the side of his fist hitting the desk. "They saw the listing online. She said they actually sent somebody out to take a look at the site."

"So? It's not for sale anymore. If it's not for sale, it doesn't matter what they did."

"So now they can smell blood in the water. They're going to be watching to see if we can get ninety-percent occupancy in that building by the deadline." Ken had stopped pretending to discuss it in any kind of collegial way. He was yelling.

Buddy rolled down the window, feeling queasy in the heat. "Oh."

"Yeah, 'Oh.' You know the bank can pull my loan on this project if we miss that deadline, which I almost always do on these types of projects. They could reassign my loan if they wanted to play hard ball. Cedar Point's more heavily monetized than me. If I miss the deadline, the bank's going to see them as less of a gamble. They'll offer more collateral than I would ever be able to do. Is any of this making sense to you? Hello?"

"I hear you. I get it. I'll get it delisted," Buddy said, sitting up straight on the seat. "You don't have to worry."

"Oh, no? Even if I don't fall short on occupancy, the adjustable interest rate is going to skyrocket after the deadline passes. If I have any problems at all with liquidity, Cedar Point will take full advantage. They've done it before. They're ruthless sons of bitches."

Buddy tossed his lit cigarette onto the pitted blacktop and he reached for the car's ignition. He wouldn't be dealing with any of this shit if he could get Arden or Parker on board with his plan. "Listen, I'm doing it right now. I'm in my car. I'll drive over to Silver Park and take the sign down. I'll get on the Internet after that."

"I stuck my neck out for you." Ken was breathing hard. His voice had dropped to an ominous rumble, like a flash flood gaining speed and moving closer. "You had one job. Get that shit pulled down."

"I will."

"And another thing. Make sure you're ready for that hearing on Friday."

"I'm ready," Buddy said, wondering if he had told the truth. His fingers were soaking wet when he wrapped them around the steering wheel.

15.
ARDEN COLLIER

Sitting behind the wheel of her dead truck, Arden kept an eye on Jackson Bennett as he leaned under the hood. He was as tall and stocky as his brother, the sheriff's deputy—muscular around the shoulders, feet planted solidly on the ground, with a mouth full of over-sized white teeth that never completely disappeared behind his lips. His waist was big but tight, nothing loose lapping over his belt, where he had attached a string of noisy gold charms: a cross, a house, a heart, and a wrench. Wispy patches of white hair had formed over his ears and his cheeks were as creased as a road map somebody had folded and refolded too many times.

Arden tapped her thumb against the steering wheel, counting off the seconds as they slipped by. At sixteen, Jackson Bennett had been a tall, nerdy kid in big glasses who carried her books the spring before she got married. He had never been one of the popular boys. If he wasn't in the library, he was holed up in his father's garage, tinkering.

Jackson hadn't shown up at her house on time, unfortunately. She was expecting to see him the day after his brother handed Arden a summons. Finally, Jackson had appeared on Thursday, interrupting Arden while she was in a full-blown lather, trying to get to the thrift store. Philip Smith III would never approve of her going to the hearing in her ancient mud-covered boots and her one good dress. She needed to buy some used high heels, or at least a nice pair of flat shoes in a color that wouldn't clash with the Easter suit. When Jackson materialized in the side yard like another ghost from her past, she had been lacing up her boots, preparing to hike to the bus stop so she could go shopping at the Goodwill store with its rows of musty shirts, faded blue jeans, and tennis shoes that curled in on themselves from too much use.

He hollered for her to flip the ignition key again. "Nothing," she said, craning her neck through the truck's open window. The Goodwill store would close in an hour.

From behind the hood, metallic tapping noises ended with a click. "How about now? Anything?"

She climbed out of the truck, leaving the door ajar. "Sorry." Bending into the rusty engine next to him, Arden surveyed the white-crusted spark plugs, the motor caked with oily black gunk and a red rubber belt with deep cracks running nearly all the way through it. "Maybe there's no saving it."

"No, no. no. There's always hope. Ha ha haah. Always." He shoved a wrench into his back pocket and ran a green rag over his forehead, which had become more expansive since high school, now that his hairline had begun its retreat. He walked in a circle with his head down, laughing his strange laugh, which was not unlike a donkey's infectious bray, emphasizing the first and last syllables, *HA ha HAAH.* "We have to think this thing through. We've checked out the choke and the starter. You've got gas in the tank. I don't have my battery gauge with me. What we have to do next is, we have to try and jump-start it. Then you'll be able to drive it all over creation. You could even drive it over to my house if you wanted to."

Arden stepped away from him, thinking about her sketchpad, untouched since breakfast. She had left it on the worktable in her garden. She knew exactly what she wanted to create for Jared Astor. She wasn't sure she could get it all done in time, given the shoe shopping she needed to do, plus at least half a day lost in kangaroo court. "I feel so badly, you wasting all this time on me. What if you do all this work and it turns out to be hopeless? That would be just my luck, too."

Jackson stopped pacing. On his face, a small, tight-lipped smile formed, gradually expanding into a grin, and when he looked at her again, the forlorn cast to his eyes put Arden in mind of her grandfather's saying, *"Be good to everyone you meet. You'll see yourself coming back, after a while."* Had she been kind to Jackson in high school? She couldn't remember. He was different, as his brother had mentioned. She felt as though she could see herself, only younger, reflected in Jackson's expression.

He stepped away from the truck and made a church steeple with his fingers. "Now why would you think I'm wasting my time, being here with you? Ha ha haah. Can you believe the world has something good for you, and you deserve it?"

"What?"

"Ha ha haah." Jackson liked to laugh, which made Arden want to laugh, too. His upper teeth jutted slightly over his lower lip, giving him the appearance of a cheerful can opener. He kept tapping his fingertips together. "Can you believe?"

"I'm not sure what you mean."

Instead of tapping his fingertips, he switched it up, bumping his knuckles against each other. She liked his clean, funny-looking teeth. He seemed to have so many of them. "You remember what you told me when we were kids and your auntie wouldn't let you go out with me anymore?"

Arden shoved a clump of stray hair behind one ear, embarrassed by the movement of her lungs, which were cranking her chest up and down too fast. Her mouth had gone as dry as the red dust swirling behind every car that had ever passed by her little house without stopping to buy a single piece of artwork. "I remember Aunt Wilma giving me a lecture that first time I let you buy me a Coke."

His laughter rose up between them like a bubble, shimmering and precarious. "Well, I wasn't a Baptist. She didn't approve. Could you blame her? In Silver Park? Not being a Baptist made me an outcast and a freak."

He was close enough for her to smell the sweetness of his cotton shirt. She imagined touching the warmth of his face, the curling lines around his eyes where he was squinting against the sun. If she couldn't get to the Goodwill store before it closed, maybe she could stop there first thing in the morning, on her way to court. She could put the new shoes right on her feet and toss her old boots into the garbage can. Or maybe she could hide her messy boots in the bushes outside the courthouse and bring them back home later. She wasn't sure if she was ready to give them up. "She didn't approve of a lot of things. I think she wanted me to be a nun."

"Miss Wilma was a fine lady." He hunkered down over his work boots, the better to fish through his toolbox with both hands. "She was always looking out for you. Too many kids in this world haven't got anybody keeping them from themselves or the evil that's out there. She never looked away. She never gave up. That's love, in my book. Real love."

"Or child abuse. Anyway, there was no changing her mind once it got set. It never would've worked out for us to date."

He disappeared behind his ancient Ford sedan. When he reappeared, a pair of orange jumper cables dangled from his hands. "That's exactly what you told me back then. You remember? 'It's never going to work.' Ha ha haah. You were so dramatic!" He clamped the cables onto his car, cranked it up, and walked back toward her. "But I would have been happy to talk with her. You wouldn't let me."

She tried to picture it as he clamped the jumper cables onto Joel's truck: Jackson Bennett in high school, confronting the concrete blockade that was her Aunt Wilma after she adopted a particular position on something. The image made Arden smile. "She would've told you to go out in the yard and find her a switch for your backside."

"Girl," he said, "I would have testified to her. I'd be quoting some amazing scripture to her, straight out of the Bible. She would have been hanging on every word. You think I don't know my Bible verses?"

Arden let out a hoot like somebody shouting praise in church. "Mmm-hmm, I'll bet you do. I remember your mother had her own Bible streak, didn't she?"

"You know it. Methodist. You should have let me try to win Miss Wilma over."

For the first time, Arden noticed how pinpricks of sunlight had formed a constellation through the open hood of Joel's truck. Like everything around her, the metal was falling apart, crumbling to ashes. Jackson fiddled with the gold charms on his belt, smiling and watching her at the same time. His fingers were bare. No ring. She glanced at the position of the sun, trying to calculate the time. Goodwill would close at six o' clock. "Oh, that was so many years ago," she said. "A lot of things have happened since then."

"Whatever happened to good old Joel? He was a good man."

A tickling heat raced up Arden's neck. "He walked out on me."

"That bastard!"

"We got divorced."

"Same here. She liked the nightlife."

"Oh." Arden had to force herself to hold onto a serious look, to keep from grinning.

"I'm sorry about your marriage, and mine, too, but on the other hand, if things had worked out differently, I wouldn't be here with you now, trying to work up the nerve to ask you out. My brother said if I don't ask you, I can never darken his door again. Ha ha haah."

She let herself smile a little, although her lips felt like they might be wobbling enough for Jackson to notice. Was he angling for a quick hookup? He might be the kind of man who would take her to bed once or twice and disappear, never to be seen or heard from again. Her heart couldn't take another blow. It would shatter into a million pieces, a Humpty Dumpty mosaic of agony. She would never be able to put the pieces back together again.

"I've got a whole bunch of things going on right now," she said.

For a beat, he looked at her without talking. His mouth closed in a prayerful way, but before she had time to worry, a shadowy half-smile moved across his face. His teeth reappeared all at once, like the sun coming out from behind a cloud. "Good things can happen. There are all types of blessings in this world and good people everywhere. You have to believe."

She smiled back at him. "I'll try to do that."

"Jump in that truck and start her on up. Ha ha haah."

Across the yard, the front windows of her grandfather's house were lightless. Tattered blue drapes hid the worst of the mess from anyone who might walk onto her porch. Moths had chewed holes in the hem. Dust billowed from the fabric anytime she touched it.

Arden climbed into her ex-husband's truck, took a deep breath, turned the key and laughed as the old engine roared to life.

Through the truck's windshield, Jackson beamed at her, flashing a thumbs-up sign.

Again, he laughed.

Arden still had a half hour to find some new shoes. With a working truck, Arden believed, she could reach the store with time to spare.

16.

VERA VAN DER GRIFF

Vera Van der Griff, aka Vera Mae Smith of VMS Designs was airborne, dangling from a pink aerial yoga trapeze on the top floor of her home, from which she could see only the tallest trees, when the housekeeper, Raynell, delivered bad news.

"Mr. Smith called," she said, breathless from the hike up three flights of stairs. Raynell was kneeling awkwardly on one knee in order to speak face to face with Vera, who was upside-down. By the wall-length window, Raynell's eyes reminded Vera of materials for jewelry-making—aquamarine crystals, ringed with onyx. "He didn't sound well."

With her belly parallel to the floor and her arms and legs splayed in four directions, Vera's hands had gone numb from the loss of blood. If she didn't change positions, she would lose her ability to hang onto the stretchy fabric suspended in a complex pattern from the ceiling. She repositioned her grip, pulling and twisting until she was upright in the air. Blood rushed back into her hands, causing them to tingle. In the new position, unfortunately, her royal blue unitard was giving Vera an extreme wedgie. She wanted to pull the fabric out of her crotch, but she didn't want to interrupt her flow. "My grandfather called?"

Raynell stood up and smoothed her pleated skirt. "He said he wasn't feeling like himself." Her words came out in a mumbled rush, barely audible above the flute-centric spa music Vera had chosen for her workout. "He wonders if you could pay him a visit today. I asked what was wrong, but the connection got cut off."

Perspiration pooled along Vera's clavicle, which was one of the problems with being upright. It made her feel itchy all over. "What do you mean, he didn't feel like himself? Please speak a bit louder and bottom line me. I've got ten more minutes to go here. Then I'll have to get cleaned up. I also have to prepare for my conference call at four o' clock."

On the windowsill, an egg timer was grinding away as it ticked off the minutes.

The pale pink patches between Raynell's freckles took on a salmon color. "Maybe you should try to call him? He sounded so weak. I tried calling him back, but it went straight to voicemail."

Vera pictured her grandfather slumped on his bathroom floor in his trademark long white nightshirt, unable to retrieve the phone after he had dropped it. With a long exhalation, she pulled her legs from the yoga stirrups and hopped onto the floor. "He hasn't spoken to me since I published that op-ed about missionaries who try to convert uncontacted tribes."

"Mmmm." Raynell looked away and rubbed the back of her ear with one finger. "Arrogant, I think was how you described that type of missionary. We sure did get a lot of calls about that one."

"That was a year ago. If Paw Paw's having a problem, why would he call me, of all people? He's got an excellent nurse. I'm still paying her."

Raynell retrieved Vera's towel and handed it to her. "I'm not sure, Mrs. Van der Griff. Like I said, he didn't sound so good. It was a little scary. I didn't know whether I should call 911, or what."

Vera blotted her face, streaking the towel with blue eyeshadow, peach blusher, and bronze foundation. She tossed the towel over one shoulder. With the back of her fingers, she smoothed the slightly loose skin on her neck upward, hoping as always to defy gravity. "Tell Martin to bring the car around," she said. "I'd better go check on my grandfather."

It took Vera thirty minutes to shower, dry her hair, and step into a loose gold lamé pantsuit. In the back of the car, she applied foundation and lipstick only. Black iron fences, gates bearing gilded initials, rolling green lawns, houses as big as hotels, and statues of lions flashed by the car's tinted windows.

Nearly thirty years had passed since QVC, the home-shopping network, first put Vera and her jewelry on TV during the graveyard shift—she assumed because her skin was too dark for a daytime slot back then. On air, Vera had worn several necklaces simultaneously and a half-dozen bracelets on one wrist, thereby launching the lucrative concept of stackable jewelry. She couldn't possibly estimate how many instant noodles she had eaten before QVC, when she and a few women friends made jewelry in her basement apartment. Two years into it, she had arranged for Charles—then a handsome graduate student—to meet on her behalf with a buyer for the Sear's mail-order catalog. She easily got into the catalog. In 1986, QVC came along.

She had earned every penny of her good fortune, yet whenever she rolled through her neighborhood, Vera still felt amazed. Why her grandfather had refused to move out of his ancient house in a community that wasn't even hooked up to city sewer lines, Vera couldn't understand. He said he wanted to die on his front porch, with its view of the church. It was the place where Vera had been baptized, wearing a white lace dress and her favorite beaded necklace.

Except for the occasional repositioning of his hands on the steering wheel, Martin remained motionless in the driver's seat. The car continued gliding east on West Paces Ferry Road, through Buckhead, where he turned left, heading north on Peachtree Street until they got stuck behind a long line of cars near Piedmont Road. Again, Vera tried calling her grandfather as well as his nurse. Neither one of them picked up the phone. She could call 911, but it seemed an extreme measure, given that he might only be suffering from indigestion. In case of a true emergency, the nurse, Charity, would have called.

Vera leaned forward. "Is there no way around this mess?"

Without a word, Martin turned on the car's blinker, forcing the black Mercedes-Benz into the right-hand lane and through a parking lot, onto Piedmont, where he turned left and wound his way through a neighborhood of Cape Cod-style homes. Pulling back onto Peachtree Street, he hit the gas, headed for Brookhaven. At last, he turned left, toward Silver Park. Although Vera was tall enough to lean her cheek against the top of the car's window, she felt small and inconsequential, as soon as they had reached her birthplace. Already, she was bracing for the weight of her grandfather's judgment, which had been a constant all the years of her childhood, particularly after her mother died.

The car was rolling to a stop when Vera popped open her door and jumped out. With some effort, she refrained from running toward her grandfather's red brick cottage. The sagging porch looked more crooked than the last time Vera had seen it. Red dust swirled around her legs. The front door was locked. With her temples throbbing, she followed the wrap-around porch along the side of the house, peering into the dark windows until she had reached the back door. Out back, her grandfather was standing in the middle of his garden with a straw hat on his head and a long black snake writhing from the end of a stick.

"Got him," he said, laughing. "Hello, my dear."

"You're out back catching snakes?" Vera's high-heeled sandals were sinking into the newly turned soil of his garden, which took up most of the backyard. Rows of squash, beans, and peppers were juxtaposed with tomato plants inside metal cages and bushes dotted with purple flowers. He didn't look a bit sick. Vera would have to wing it on her conference call, having had no time to prepare. "I've been trying to call you for an hour."

Her grandfather lowered the snake into a burlap sack, which he tied and tossed onto the grass. "Don't worry. I'm not going to hurt him. He's non-venomous, so that would be illegal. I'll carry him over to the lake and let him loose there. That's usually what I do when one of these big fellows camps out in my garden."

Vera found her balance, tugged her heel out of the dirt, and stepped back. "Raynell said you weren't feeling well. I was about to send an ambulance. What's going on here?"

"I know this type of snake eats rats and insects. Most folks think they're good for gardens," he said, brushing dirt from his trousers, "but they do bite, and I don't especially want to step on one when I'm pulling up weeds. My reaction time is not as fast as it used to be."

As he made his way through a patch of eggplants, she watched the movement of his legs and the expression on his wrinkled face. He was as steady and clear-eyed as ever, at eighty-seven. He didn't seem to be having a stroke or a heart attack. At the end of the row, he stopped a few feet away and smiled. "Where is your nurse?" she said, looking around as if Charity might step out from behind a tree.

"It's Wednesday." He said it as if this explained everything and Vera had asked the dumbest of all dumb questions. "She never works on Wednesdays or Sundays. She attends church on those days. Of course, I realize that wouldn't be a limitation for you."

"No, it wouldn't be," Vera said. "In fact, I have work to do right now, so I have to go. You don't seem to be having any sort of medical emergency. If you could just confirm that for me, please, it would make me feel a whole lot better."

"Now, hold on, hold on." Her grandfather got a grip on her arm. He was surprisingly scrappy, given his halo of white hair and the eyeglasses as thick as Coca-Cola bottles. "I'm sorry if I worried you. I knew you wouldn't pay me a social call without a good reason, and I wanted to see you, dear."

Thanks to a brutal form of willpower, cultivated while Vera was working twenty-hour days for many years, she fought off the impulse to yank her arm free. His eyes brightened and his mouth widened into a beatific smile. Vera locked her knees. These were signs he was about to launch into a scolding sermon or spew forth a platitude, as he had when her mother died in childbirth, taking Vera's infant brother with her. Dolores had died from a completely preventable condition that nobody treated because she was poor and black. At the final viewing, Arden's grandfather had said that "God couldn't abide an unwed mother." The pronouncement had triggered a wave of head nodding among the members of Mount Zion Baptist Church.

Vera squared her jaw. "What do you want?" she said. "Why am I here?"

Lifting his chin, defiant, the old man released his grip. "I need a favor."

"I'm not coming back to your church." She turned to leave. "They won't even ordain women in that church. Forget it."

He followed her around the side of the house, toward her car, where Martin was leaning against the trunk. "Not that kind of favor," he said, sounding winded.

When Martin spotted her, Vera pointed at the car door. Swiftly, he opened it. "We've been over this. I'm an atheist. Religion never did anything good for my mother or me."

He winced as if she had scalded him. "Don't say that. You're angry because—"

"Goodbye," Vera said, smiling her brightest QVC smile. "Tell Charity I'll call her later to make sure she has everything she needs."

Vera ducked into the car. "I have a gift for you," he said. He blurted it out and stepped inside the car door, which prevented Martin from closing it. "It belonged to your mother. I want you to have it. Won't you come inside?"

In her mind, Vera was glaring at her grandfather from a distance, as if he might be any random old man with a straw gardening hat. His shoulders had curled closer together, during the long year of their estrangement. She pictured his silhouette in the rocking chair by her bed, where he used to read and read and read in her darkened room until she fell asleep, as a kid. That was after her mother's funeral. Vera had walked away from her clapboard home with its black plastic insulation and magazine photos thumbtacked to the walls. She carried her mother's fishing tackle box full of beads and jewelry wire, down the street to her grandfather's home.

"Is this another trick? Are you going to get me inside and splash me with holy water or something?"

"Mae Belle," he said, using a nickname from her childhood. "I have a beautiful necklace that Dolores made. I want you to have it. Please."

The inside of his house was as orderly as a library, with books lining three walls of the living room. Rugs, armchairs, and lace doilies were all positioned just so. The house felt damp, as it always had, being tucked under several towering oak trees that blocked the sky and constantly threatened to crash through the roof. Staring at her from the back wall, a white Jesus with a shaggy beard raised two fingers in blessing. Another one dangled in agony from a large bronze crucifix. Vera followed her grandfather to the back of the house, where his kitchen table overlooked the garden. A vinyl tablecloth with an unsettling yellow floral pattern covered his breakfast table. On it, a Bible lay open beside an empty teacup and a large hatbox covered with shiny purple fabric and rhinestones.

"After she passed away, I gave you all of your mother's jewelry, except for this one item," he said, pulling the box closer. "I suppose I wanted a keepsake. She was my only child, but I'm getting older now. Your mother's necklace belongs with you."

He closed his Bible, set it aside, and slid the hatbox across the plastic tablecloth. Vera's fingers felt heavy, reaching for it. "I remember this," she said, feeling six years old and as frightened as she had been the night her mother cried out and bled all over the bed. Between her legs, the midwife kept pressing towels while she prayed, until Dolores turned gray and still. The midwife called on God, but she called no paramedics. "This used to be under her sewing machine. She had a green felt hat with a flower on it."

Tap, tap, went her grandfather's fingers on the table. Outside, a rooster crowed. "She turned it into a jewelry box at some point. This was her senior project at Spelman College."

Smoothing the bumpy lid of the box, Vera took a deep breath. "She never got to finish her art degree."

"But you did."

"Yes, I did, and I'm truly grateful that you paid my way through college." Vera had never told him before.

"Go on and open it."

Briefly, she lost the ability to breathe. The piece was as large as the box—at least a foot in diameter with concentric circles of tiny red, yellow, and green beads in an intricate pattern. The circles were accentuated by vertical strings of tan shells that extended outward like rays of sunlight. "It's a Massai wedding necklace."

"She was studying those designs in school."

"I tried to make one when I was a kid, but it was only a couple of strings. Remember?"

His laughter filled the small kitchen. "Yes, indeed, I remember. Your neck turned red and green, like it was always Christmas time. Nobody could make you take that thing off, not for church or school or bathing."

"It was my connection to her." Vera had spent whole afternoons sitting by Silver Park lake, alone, trying to string necklaces and earrings the way her mother had done. Lifting the enormous wedding necklace as gently as possible, Vera held it to the light to inspect the needlework. It was as beautiful as those she had seen in Kenya, when she and Charles went on vacation there. "This piece would have been worn by a woman of substance. In Massai culture, the red beads symbolize power. See these vertical lines with shells? I guess Mama didn't have cowrie beads, so she used dime-store shells, but that's a very interesting choice. The vertical lines represent the number of cows in a woman's dowry. Green is for the land she owns. A woman wearing this necklace would have been recognized as very powerful."

"That's exactly why you should have it."

Vera's eyes filled and cleared. She set the necklace back into the box like she was lowering a sleeping infant into its crib. "It wasn't fair, what happened to her. She had dreams for her life." Through the window, the snake bag lay motionless on the grass. "You told me God had punished her for getting pregnant without being married."

Her grandfather folded his gnarled hands and dropped his head over them. "I should never have said such a thing, especially not to a little girl in terrible grief. I wasn't in my right mind at the time, but there's no excuse. I hurt you, and I'm truly sorry. I loved your mother."

Vera didn't move or breathe or speak.

"I ask your forgiveness," he said. "I ask it sincerely."

In a wink, many years of pain disappeared, extinguished by his simple apology. She stood up and hugged his neck. "It's all right now." Around his collar, she smelled the familiar sweet tang of his favorite cologne. "I'm doing just fine. I love you."

When she sat back down, he dabbed his eyes with a paper napkin. "God is great," he said. "Shall we pray together?"

"Paw Paw!" Vera reared back against her chair, ready to bolt. "You promised."

Again, he laughed. "See what I did there? I got you good."

"Ha ha," she said, uneasy as an amateur skater on spring ice. "Okay, then."

He set both hands face-down on the table. "Now, I must ask a favor of you, my dear."

"Go on." Behind him, a green plastic wall clocked showed the time as three-thirty. Her work call was at four o' clock. If he needed money, all he needed to do was ask. "You can be direct. What's the bottom line?"

"Do you remember Arden Collier?"

"Of course. Your friend's granddaughter. I own two of her best *dikenga* figures. I bought them from that insufferable art dealer, Jared Astor." As children, Vera and Arden had never been especially close, although they were baptized together. Arden was painfully shy—never made eye contact—and she wasn't allowed to play outside without supervision. Like all the other kids in their neighborhood, Vera had been petrified of Arden's strict aunt.

"She's hit on hard times."

"I read about that. The word in the art community doesn't sound good. Folks say she's not creating any new work. It's very sad. She's got real talent."

"There's a hearing on Friday. I believe the county intends to seize her property under eminent domain law, but it has historical significance to our community."

"You know I'm president of the historical society."

"I do indeed know that."

Vera stood up and straightened her sparkly pantsuit. "Consider it done."

When he grinned, wrinkles radiated across his cheeks, all the way to his earlobes. "My powerful granddaughter," he said. "My Mae Belle. I'll write down the time and place."

She kissed his impossibly soft cheek. "Let's have brunch on Sunday."

"Saturday would be better for me, dear. I stay pretty busy on Sundays."

"Oh, right. Sorry. Saturday it is, then."

Back in the car with the purple hatbox, Vera completed her monthly conference call with the chief operating officer of VMS Designs. After that, she placed several other calls, all of them on Arden Collier's behalf.

17.
PARKER GOZER

Parker tapped and tapped and banged on Arden's red double doors until the side of her hand was throbbing. An old brown truck sat idle in the scruffy-looking yard, but Arden wasn't in her garden with its whistling, multi-colored bottles. All Parker could see when she peeked through the front window was a leaning tower of clothes, toys, and unidentifiable junk. Maybe Arden wasn't even living in her grandfather's house anymore.

Would Arden still have long braids and the slow-spreading, sneaky smile? Had she ever stopped being furious about the loss of her grandfather's land? Parker wondered. Across the yard, pink and orange scraps of morning light flickered through the trees. She didn't care if Arden slammed the door in her face. She couldn't imagine a road slicing straight through the magical figures in the sculpture garden out back. She needed to warn Arden about what Buddy wanted to do.

An old wooden swing was chained to the porch ceiling. Arden's grandfather had installed it for her and Parker, when they were girls. She sat down to write a note, remembering the times she had visited Arden's house when they were in grade school. Arden's hand was usually sticky and mustard-stained, but Parker loved to hold it anyway. They had been ruthless in their abuse of the porch swing. They pushed off hard, pumping their legs until the back of the swing crashed into the house. Zooming forward again, they kicked the rafters with their heels, laughing.

The incessantly spinning weathervane, the clucking chickens, and Arden's secret smile, so close, had become imprinted on Parker's heart, the cloudy retina of memory, and her dreams for Joie, who swore she could never survive living more than a mile from her best friend—a five-minute trip, running all the way. Parker had been sad when Arden didn't come to the dedication of Silver Park, and later, when she peered over the gold chain on her door before clicking it shut. At the dedication ceremony, Wilma had read a beautiful letter about her brother, Arden's grandfather. Parker had mailed it to Arden, afterward. Arden never wrote back.

After tucking the note between Arden's doors, Parker decided to kill time at the park. Maybe she could knock off a dozen more calls to reporters, to pitch Van der Griff's press conference.

The rental car hit a deep rut at the end of the road. Her head bounced hard against the ceiling. Wincing, she parked under the trees and sat rubbing the top of her head while her eyes watered. She pulled down the visor to check her eyeliner, which was oozing down her cheeks. Staring back at her, the sight of her own eyes took her by surprise—shocked her, even. She was deeply ashamed to look at herself after what she had done with Dylan, and she knew there was no going back. She would have to tell Beamer, and Beamer would never forgive her.

She had inherited her father's eyes, which were green and brown and full of light. As she swiped at the black puddles on her cheeks, she pictured him smiling sadly up at her those last few days when he was in the hospital. The oxygen tank had sounded so lonely, like wind through a wintry field. His room felt smaller and smaller because of all the flowers, especially the horrible lilies with their sickening perfume that stuck to her skin and her clothes for weeks after he died. A plastic tube snaked under his nose and over his funny protruding ears, big as the handles on a jug. Wispy bits of hair, untrimmed for months while he was sick, looped across the pillowcase under his head. The hospital window illuminated the left side of his softly creased face. One bright pink ear looked translucent and his left eye was shining, while the other one drifted in a shadow, brown and droopy, not unlike Dr. Tinley's eyes. Red lines had glowed along the sides of her father's nose and through the whites of his eyes.

Staring at herself by the lake, all of her muscles went wooden. Behind her eyes, her father's face tumbled into focus on top of her own. She had heard him talk about the loss of his father. She never completely understood it before. He shouldn't have left part of Silver Park to Buddy. Maybe he felt as though he had to do it, to give something back to his younger self, to make himself whole, finally.

The rental car seemed to be eating her alive. The backs of her legs were stuck to the car's cheap upholstery. Thinking about Buddy made her physically ill. She pulled and pulled for air, but she couldn't get enough oxygen. She bolted from the car, leaving the door ajar while she ran toward the familiar path that would take her to the waterfall. She wanted to sit on the same rock where she and Sid had seen the starlings. For the hundredth time, she wished he could be there with her, alive, ready to tell her one more time that she would be okay.

The waterfall rumbled, low and steady as Parker moved closer to it. Surprisingly, she passed a young couple, holding hands as they walked slowly along the path. Maybe word of the park was getting out, after all. Parker nodded and kept walking. On the far side of the park, the sight of the dead fawn made her stop in her tracks. She stood staring at it, one hand over her nose, mad at herself for failing to call the groundskeeper earlier in the week. The fawn had fully rotted and it was soupy in the middle, from the rain. In the lake, a fish jumped. She heard footsteps through the pine straw. When she lifted her head, Buddy was there. He hesitated when he saw her, frozen with a cigarette between his thumb and forefinger.

For a second, Parker felt confused—completely disoriented. Never before had she seen Buddy in a suit and tie, wearing glasses, for one thing. Also, Silver Park was a sacred place, for her. It was where she and Sid had watched a murmuration of starlings, where he had told her she was going to be okay. It was an enchanted place—the scene of her first kiss with Beamer. To Parker, Buddy's presence in that unspoiled place felt like the worst kind of violation. He didn't budge. His shadow seemed to zoom closer, then farther away, over and over again, throbbing, like a heartbeat.

Parker locked her knees, for balance. "You shouldn't be here," she said. "Who do you think you are?"

He let out a snorting laugh. "What do you mean, who am I?" He was squinting with his mouth open. "I'm the guy who's putting a building right over there. Right? My lawyer's going to be in touch soon, by the way. I hope you didn't think I'd let it go just because you yelled and ran out of my office like a snot-nosed kid before we even finished our conversation."

Near her feet, a fly hovered, buzzing furiously over the fawn's cloudy, wide-open eyes. "You don't belong here."

"I don't, huh?" He turned his head, glaring at Parker sideways. His cheek flashed red while he puffed up his chest. "I didn't expect to see you here. Is this the part where you go all psycho on me? It'll be like the good-old days. Do me a favor. Flirt with me at the same time. That's the best. So confusing."

The smell engulfed her. A gamy, rotten taste filled her throat when she swallowed. "Don't you dare try to say I'm crazy. I'm having a normal reaction to a messed up situation. You never should have been anywhere near my family in the first place. My Dad took pity on you. He shouldn't have done it, but he did."

She didn't blink while he stared at her. Finally, he looked down, wrinkling his nose. "I see you've found the coyote's latest present," he said, blowing smoke. "What are you doing here, anyway, dressed up all fancy like you're going to a tea party?"

"You're standing on my property," Parker said. "What are *you* doing here?"

"I need to pick up my real-estate sign. I don't want anybody else making a competing bid at this point."

"Did you think I was going to let you get away with it? Were you expecting to do what you wanted and go on with your life like it never happened?"

He rolled his eyes, laughed, and lipped the cigarette again. Smoke curled around his head until he looked like a ghost, wavering on the edge of memory. His elbow bumped her shoulder when he stumbled by her. "I don't know what you mean, and I don't have time for this. I need to take that sign down and get back to work."

Parker grabbed his wrist without thinking. "I'm talking to you. Why won't you tell me you're sorry so I'm not stuck in this same place forever?"

His tobacco-stained teeth, crooked and brown around the gum line when he smiled down at her through a cloud of smoke, made her fingers feel frozen where she was touching him. She pulled her hand back, clutched it against her belly, and held her ground. He flicked his cigarette over her shoulder, into the lake. Parker flinched at the *hiss* as it landed. "You always were such a spoiled brat," he said in a voice like a lullaby. "You're a pretty girl, but you sure as hell know it, don't you?

Remember calling me a hobo every time I wore my work pants with the paint splotches on them?"

Her cheeks and forehead felt scorched, probably from the midday sun and the glare off the lake or the shame that had taken root in her lungs. She shielded her eyes with one hand, staring at the shadowy line of trees behind him. "I was twelve years old when I said that."

He looked at his feet. His eyebrows were fused together. "Your old man wasn't twelve," he said, nudging the fawn's hoof with his boot. "He should've known better than to treat me liked the hired help."

Parker thought about saying goodbye to her father, the smell of Old Spice and the blood on a wet bandage where the tube had rubbed his arm raw. In his eyes, crescents of color disappeared, brown slipping into white. For a second, she imagined killing Buddy and rolling his shattered body into the lake. "You were the hired help," she said, surveying a rock near the shore. "He treated you damn well. He gave you a job."

"Yeah, hauling bricks and all the other shit work nobody else wanted to do." Buddy locked her down with his eyes. "Nobody paid my way through college, kid. I couldn't get braces and nice white veneers for my teeth like what you've got there. I wasn't privileged like you were. I never even met my old man, and my mother came from the wrong side of the tracks. Your mom treated mine like crap, by the way."

The image of Buddy's mother Myrtus, the spindly woman with brown teeth, curdled Parker's stomach as the wind shifted and she got another whiff of the fawn's decomposing flesh. The woman's eyes had looked hollow the only time Parker ever met her. Myrtus had knocked on their back door and handed Parker a red velvet cake covered with tin foil, for Christmas. Parker cringed, remembering how her mother had dropped it upside-down into the trashcan, later. "My mother said she stole our silverware," Parker said, "that one time when she cleaned our house."

"Bullshit. That's a total lie. Your old lady wasn't such a prize herself."

The tip of the cigarette glowed as red as the lights on her father's car, vanishing. A choking blanket of smoke was hanging between them, obscuring his face. Her eyes burned. She squinted through the haze at the outline of his jaw, his high cheekbones, and his shoulders looming over her. For a moment, she felt like she was talking to her father. "Why did you let me get hurt that way?"

His breath came in loud, ragged spurts, as if he was running uphill, against a headwind. "All you ever thought about was yourself—you and your drunk mom with your maid and your daddy's money." His mouth twisted around his horrible rotten teeth. "Did you ever for one minute think about how hard it was for me, being around you people?"

"You were the grown up. You should have been thinking about what was best for me." Her voice sounded oddly distant. It reminded Parker of her father's breath, whistling in and out as he lay curled on his side, fast asleep with his mouth open. His lips had cracked and turned purple, on the last day.

"You had parents. Too bad your mother stayed wasted all the time."

The smoke in the stagnant air and the smell of dead game were spinning inside Parker's stomach. She opened her eyes as wide as she could stretch them. They began to sting and tremble from the effort, but she still couldn't see him clearly. "My mother was sick."

He shrugged. "Whatever. She was a drunk."

"She was an alcoholic. It's a disease. I had two parents. You should have been there for me. You left us. I was thirteen and I wound up being preyed on because there weren't any grown-ups paying attention."

He tipped his head to one side, with his mouth hanging open. "What in the hell are you even talking about now? I had my own stuff going on. You weren't my job."

He was right there in front of her. Parker knew who he is, but at that moment, she didn't know. She had so much to say to her father. "I *was* your job. That's exactly what I was. I needed you there. You left me in harm's way."

"You're nuts," he said, shaking his head and letting out part of a laugh. He turned his back and took two steps. "It wasn't that big a deal, anyway. You need to grow up and get over yourself, princess."

At last, Parker's eyes came back into focus. She laser-scanned Buddy's smug face.

"I got over all that stuff a long time ago." It came out as a full-on scream. Her nose was running. "I found a job. I got married. I had a baby. I went on with my life. Now you're setting me up all over again. I'm right back here. I'm trapped where I don't want to be, still tied to you."

He waved her off with one hand and kept walking.

"I loved and trusted you," Parker said, grabbing the back of his jacket with both fists. "You hurt me and you never apologized."

As Buddy turned to face her, she yanked his sleeve, hard. He tripped, pitched forward, and went down, grunting when his shoulder slammed against the ground. His body turned rock-still. For a split-second, she wondered if he might be dead.

Good, she thought at first, but her heart quickly started to bang in double-time. She pictured the police car she would have to call, the inside of a cold cement prison, and Joie growing up without her mother. "Oh, my God," she said. "Are you all right?"

Finally, he rolled onto his side and sat up. When he looked at her again, Parker recognized him. He was the memory she had been trying to push down and pave over, for too many years, the same way Atlanta had been getting paved over since her childhood. He had turned into an old man, ruined, with a wrinkled face that was twisted in pain. "I've got a ruptured disc, if you really care, which I doubt," he said. "I had surgery last year but it didn't work. I need to let them cut on me again. I've got to make some serious money first. I've never had any fucking healthcare insurance in my life."

His eyebrows were bunched together. Parker felt a sudden pinch of sadness for him until she remembered being a teenager, riding the bus to the women's clinic, alone—all her summer-job money zipped into her backpack in twenty-dollar bills. *That's how the cool chicks deal with these things.* "It's a miracle I only got pregnant," she said. "You could have given me herpes or something worse. Thank God nobody was getting HIV back then."

Buddy squeezed his eyes shut. "You can't imagine the pain."

"I'm not buying this. You want me to feel sorry for you, the way my Dad did, so I'll do whatever you want me to do. I'm not helping you with your development plan. I'm not coming to your pity party, either. Stand up and face me like a man."

He leaned forward, clutching his head in his hands. "Jesus, give me a minute, will you? My last pain pill's finally kicking in. I've been living on these damn things. I've got to make this deal work so I can fix my back and feel like a human being again."

A silky ribbon of wind slid across her skin. At the water's edge, a tiny wave tapped the base of a tree, receding and swelling again. "This place is everything to me," she said, mostly to herself. "I can't believe Dad left you a piece of it. Why would he do that to me?"

"Oh, boo hoo," Buddy said, pretending to laugh. "Poor kid. You've had a silver spoon in your mouth from Day One."

"That's not true. I work hard."

"Everybody jumps through hoops to do your bidding, all the time. You've got the best piece of property in Atlanta. All I got was your old man's leftovers—a little scrap some dumb-ass used as a dumping ground for old radiators and shit. I'm going to have to pave all that crap over and pray to God my backer doesn't ask for soil tests."

"What?" Parker wasn't sure what he meant, or exactly what she had heard. *Radiators?*

He shook his head. "Nothing, I'm just mad, okay? I'd like a fair shake, for once."

His shoulders kept listing, back and forth. He looked drunk. She wondered what kind of pills he was taking. She would be damned if she was going to carry him out of there. "Stand up," she said again, staring him down. "Apologize to me. Tell me you're sorry."

When he blinked, his eyelids stayed closed a half-second too long. "Come on." He was slurring his words. "Take it easy. I'm hurting."

Parker dug her heels into the ground. "You keep talking about yourself. I'm sorry you've got a bad back, but I've had to deal with pain, too. You never heard that, never saw it. I've got a voice and I'm using it. Get up. Apologize. Let's get this over with, once and for all."

His eyes drifted briefly out of focus. What Parker wanted him to say was that he did hear her, and he could see her pain clearly. She wanted him to say if he could go back in time, he would do things differently. He would be the family friend she had needed for him to be, not some wasted fuckup who always felt he was cheated out of his entitlement. She wanted him to apologize, sincerely, from his heart, so she could let the old pain go, finally. She was longing to say, "Yes. I forgive you. Go in peace."

He didn't say any of those things. He only stared at her with his glazed, dead-looking eyes, indifferent as a coyote. Parker remembered what Jolene had told her once, about forgiveness. She said it was like Buddy was halfway down a dark well, dangling from a rope, and Parker was holding the other end of it, refusing to lift him up even though she had the strength. She had been struggling to hold onto her end of it.

Jolene was wrong. Parker didn't have to lift him up. All she had to do was open her hands and let him fall.

A vibrating heat drained through her neck, down her arms, and off her fingertips. Her breath slowed. The air shifted. A light wind smelled faintly of wisteria. Parker thought about a slightly different version of Jolene's prayer. *God, free me from my past. Release Buddy to the universe. Amen.*

She opened her mouth and let him go.

"Get your sign and get out of here," she said over her shoulder. "I'm gutting your big development plan if it's the last thing I ever do."

18.

ARDEN COLLIER

Blank, unfamiliar faces peered at Arden from benches that would have looked like church pews if they weren't in the county government building—the center of all evil in her life. She hurried up the aisle toward a head table, which was elevated on a riser and supported a row of dormant microphones. A man in a bow tie and amber-colored glasses nodded, smiling in a tight-lipped way. Across the table, he pushed a clipboard holding a sign-in sheet. Nearby, a gray-faced deputy frowned, arms crossed, swaying slightly over black boots.

"Did you want to be heard?" The clerk's voice was surprisingly melodic and friendly. It echoed around the room where the fate of her grandfather's cabin—her home—was about to be decided by strangers.

Her mouth quivered halfway between a smile and a reply. Such a simple question, yet it was hanging in the air, along with his ballpoint pen, cocked and fully loaded. The clerk peered at Arden through his tinted glasses. Behind her, a few muffled whispers rose from the benches. She had to derail Buddy's plan, but in the chilly vacuum of the hearing room, she felt voiceless—stunned into silence. Lined with cheap wood paneling, the place was both sterile and dusty, like the homemade pine coffin her grandfather had built before he died.

Raising his eyebrows, the clerk rearranged his pen and clipboard. At the edge of his sign-in table, a small nameplate said, "Chandler Langston."

Across the room, a door squeaked and Buddy rolled down the aisle with a bouquet of rolled maps and several posters under one arm. He was limping the way he had done at Arden's house, but he was strutting at the same time—kicking his heels out, shaking hands, and clapping people on the back. He sneered, wagging his head, when he saw Arden.

She turned back toward Chandler the Clerk and straightened the jacket attached to her one good dress. It was white with blue trim and thickly embroidered across the shoulders. When she had put it on for the first time, for Easter Sunday, Joel took one look, laughed, and said it made her look like a naval officer or a drum majorette.

"Long time no see," Buddy said. He wrapped an arm around Arden like a lasso, yanking her toward him. He was pretending to give her a quick, friendly hug—clenching his cigarette-stained teeth at everybody. In truth, he was body slamming her. "Good to see you."

Her cheek got mashed against the smoky wool of his scratchy jacket, which momentarily knocked the wind out of her. The tips of his fingers pressed painfully into the side of her breast. "Get your hands off me," she hissed, struggling. "Don't touch me."

He fist-bumped her padded shoulder with his knuckles. "Hey, don't bother standing in line," he said, pointing. The freckled, knobby bone of his wrist protruded from its cuff, reminding Arden of Frankenstein's monster. The sleeves of his jacket were much too short. Across his stomach, a single buttonhole strained to hang onto its button. He kept fiddling with it while he waited for her answer. "You're already on the agenda."

Arden turned her back on him and scrawled her name on Chandler's yellow notepad, ignoring Buddy's instructions. She found a seat on the front row of benches, across the aisle from him.

"Quiet, please," the gray-faced deputy said as four committee members filed into the room, assuming their positions behind the elevated table.

A small, cinnamon-colored woman with round, buoyant cheeks moved into a spot marked, "Esther Fielding, Chairperson." She sniffed, parked an orange pocketbook at her elbow, and slammed a gavel. "Come to order," she said. "What's the job today, Chandler?"

The clerk turned the pages of a white binder. "Third and final review of the commercial grading plan for Silver Park Lot 14B," he said, making the task sound like a breezy beach walk, "contingent upon access for services."

Esther folded her slender fingers together. "Oh, yes. Our friend Buddy Caldwell." She flashed a pair of dimples.

Buddy lifted his big jaw, smiling around locked lips, like a cat savoring an injured bird.

"The Falls at Silver Park," Esther continued. "No historic-lot variance on the one side of him there. Protected status on the other side. We're back to looking at access for services. What's the order of business?"

"We have a rather full agenda," Chandler said. "Public comments."

Esther groaned and pulled a stick of gum from her pocketbook. "Okay, make it quick," she said and she waved at Buddy. "We've all heard it before."

Buddy unrolled and clipped a map onto an easel. Arden narrowed her eyes at the blue geometric shapes of a site drawing and the bright red line that sliced straight through a lot she recognized as her grandfather's estate. "The Falls at Silver Park will generate an estimated $959,000 a year in new revenue for the county in its first year." Buddy was all teeth and wind, grinning with his chest puffed up, swaggering in front of his poorly drawn cartoon.

At the head table with Esther, a man in a salmon-colored polo shirt let out a faint whistle.

Esther smiled again, revealing a green gum wad between her molars.

A young woman with a wispy ponytail hurried by Arden, followed by a large man carrying a camera. He attached the camera to a tripod and snapped on a light. Instantly, the room's funeral parlor chill turned as warm and bright as a carnival. The woman dropped a small recording device onto the head table. Finding her seat, she began scribbling on a notepad.

Thank you, Lord, Arden thought. *Reporters. Two of my witnesses showed up.* Philip Smith III had been right: A little publicity would help her case with the county. She only hoped Jared Astor wouldn't be watching the TV coverage.

"On second thought," Esther said, glancing at the camera, "let's go over the plan one more time, Chandler. The public should know what a good thing Mr. Caldwell is planning to do for the community there."

Chandler lifted a sheet of paper and began reading it so closely, it was nearly touching his nose. "Mr. Caldwell's development application was approved pending his ability to show proof that he can establish access," the clerk said.

Tilting her face toward the camera, Esther swallowed before smiling broadly, exposing a small gap between her front teeth. "That means, if I understand correctly, can he get a road in there as well as a line out to the county sewer system?"

"Yes, ma'am," Buddy said, unbuttoning his jacket. "That's exactly right, and I'm prepared to answer that."

Outside, a siren blared. Esther stuck her fingers in her ears, waiting. "Okay, then," she said after the blaring stopped. "Let's hear it."

Buddy whispered into Chandler's ear.

"Madam Chairperson," the clerk said, scanning his sign-in sheet, "I've been reminded that a Ms. Arden Collier is here to discuss her role in the access contingency on the commercial grading plan for Silver Park Lot 14B."

"Step forward, Arden Collier, wherever you are," Esther said, waving her hands. "Use the microphone at the front of the aisle."

Under the padded yoke of her brocade jacket, Arden's shoulders kept shaking. She felt strangely small, walking to the front of the ugly room. The light from the TV camera warmed the side of her face. A gust of her shaky breath blasted through the microphone and she coughed, jerking her mouth off the dimpled foam knob. "I'm not completely sure why I was called to be here," she said, choking on an old sorrow. The stringy muscles in her legs rose and converged, vibrating. She clutched her skirt with both hands, fighting a childish impulse to run. Her voice sounded wobbly and tentative—a vocal clone of her grandfather whenever he was around white people. If only she had a bucket of red paint at that moment, she could fling it against the walls of the dusty hearing room, or at Buddy's face.

"Madam Chairwoman," Buddy said, "Ms. Collier owns Lot 13, adjacent to my property." His hand groped a sprawling, misshapen rectangle on his map. One finger found the number and rolled down, tracing the red line where Arden knew he wanted to amputate half of her beautiful, fragrant yard. "Unlike the property on the other side of me, Lot 13 is unencumbered by historic designations. I've offered to purchase her property at a rate above market value. That would allow me to get a road and a sewer line into Lot 14B."

Esther tapped the table with two fingers. "You have the paperwork with you?"

Buddy adjusted his wine-colored tie with both hands. It was the same one he had worn the day he stopped by Arden's house unannounced. Even from across the room, she could see the fabric was flimsy, rubbed raw by his grubby fingers. Probably it was the only tie he owned. "We haven't quite gotten to that stage," he said, "but I believe Ms. Collier might decide to give her verbal consent today."

Esther propped her chin on her hands, eyes moving back and forth across Arden's face, left to right, as if she might be reading a book. "That right, Ms. Collier? Speak up now, so we can all hear you."

"He gave me a number—one number so far—but I," Arden said, stuttering, "I haven't said yes to anything. I don't even have a real-estate agent or a lawyer."

At one end of the head table, the man in the salmon-colored polo shirt opened a folder, planting his elbows around it like he might be protecting a plate of food.

Esther glanced at him, nodding, and she lowered her eyes. "I see," she said. "That's too bad. I'm sorry to hear that. I hope you'll reconsider."

Buddy grabbed a poster that was propped face-first against the wall. When he flipped it onto the easel, Arden gasped. Enlarged images of old tires, sawed-off soup cans, bits of broken pipe and cracked bottles—teetering stacks of her unfinished art projects—made the periphery of her garden look like a junkyard in a series of huge color photographs.

Arden flung her arms in Buddy's direction. "Who said you could take those?"

The man in the polo shirt raised his hand. "Esther, if I may?"

"You may," Esther said. "Go ahead, Vincent."

"As a routine part of our assessment, all of the surrounding properties were visually inspected and—"

"You didn't have my permission." Arden's voice was muscular with indignation, plunging and leaping off the room's dingy paneling. "You had no right."

Vincent inhaled, turning a sheet of paper face-down on the table. Arden wanted to punch the half-smile off his face. "Inspections were limited to observations from the county right-of-way," he said, although the images had clearly been taken at close range, from her yard the day Buddy trespassed on it. "We also reviewed property records."

"Cut to the chase," Esther said. Her fingers were splayed in front of her as if she was determined to keep the lid on a pot of boiling grits before they splattered all over the kitchen. "What are we seeing in these photographs?"

"The photographs provide extensive evidence of urban blight," Vincent said.

Arden bared her neck to the ceiling and her moan was soft—delicate, even—but prolonged. "What are you even talking about now?" The deputy bounced on the tips of his black boots, alert, as her voice kept rising. "Who do you think you are?"

Esther leaned over her elbows, thin but boxy around the shoulders, severe as a tank, glaring at Arden. "Eminent domain law generally prevents our municipalities from taking private property for development purposes, but we are well within our rights to prevent urban blight that is a detriment to other citizens' rights. Your property is most definitely blighted, Ms. Collier. Tell us more, Vincent." She stared into the camera lens. "For the record."

In the corner, Buddy shifted his weight from one leg to the other, arching his back. While Arden watched him, he turned his head and stared at her. His gaze, piercing at first, flattened into contempt, followed by indifference. She thought about a shark's eyes, with the membranes that roll back as it devours its prey alive.

Vincent turned the pages of his file so fast, it crackled like it might catch fire. "Not sure where to begin," he said, extracting more photos from a manila envelope. "Septic tank citations—three years in a row. Complaint from a neighbor concerned about the odor, the pile of used tires and the constant unwanted noise generated by a collection of old bottles. Large volumes of debris visible from the road shared by a number of property owners in this community—"

Esther nodded. "She's been given multiple opportunities to respond?"

"She has." Vincent closed the file as if that was it. *All there was to say.*

Arden covered her mouth with her hands—quiet, spent. "I'm an artist," she said, mumbling through her fingers. "How am I supposed to create anything without my materials?"

Esther turned toward Vincent. "What's the status of tax payments?"

"Her tax payments are up to date." He said it in a voice of surprise.

Arden stomped the floor with one of her flat dress shoes from the Goodwill store. "You can't evict me," she said. "I'm a tax-paying citizen."

Ignoring Arden, Esther never took her eyes off Vincent. "I suggest we give her thirty days to respond to the citations."

"Madam Chairperson," Chandler said. "The other public comments?"

"Right," Esther said, frowning. "Have a seat, Ms. Collier."

Arden's face felt heavy and frozen with grief when she turned, stumbling back toward the front row. The new shoes pinched her toes.

"Maura Levine," Chandler said, reading through his colored glasses. "Historical society representative."

A woman with ringlets of shiny blonde hair walked to the microphone. Instantly, the reporter perked up, snapping her fingers at the man with the camera, who zoomed in on Maura. "The Falls at Silver Park will disturb a delicate ecosystem that's protected under historic designation," she said, reading from a statement that had been hand-written on pink paper.

Had Arden ever seen the blonde woman before? She didn't think so. She didn't recognize her from TV. She rarely saw any white people in her neighborhood unless they were cutting through to get to the main road. Philip Smith III must have set aside his disdain for Vera Mae's atheism long enough to ask for her help with the historical society. God bless him—and her.

"This development will also negatively impact the culture of a traditionally African-American settlement," the woman continued. "Community notifications and the county's environmental assessment have been insufficient. As a citizen, and on behalf of the historical society, I urgently request additional cultural and environmental review. I'm confident this will convince you to deny Buddy Caldwell's request for a building permit, and especially his application for an unprecedented number of landscape and building ordinance waivers."

Esther yawned, eyes closed, stretching her jaw until it popped.

Vincent bent over the table with his shoulders bunched around his ears. "One important correction, Miss," he said, pointing a short, thick finger at Maura. "The environmental assessment was exhaustive. I take strong exception to your allegation that it was insufficient."

"The historical society disagrees," Maura said. "Your inadequate assessment was an unfortunate joke."

"Next," Esther called.

Chandler peered at his sign-in sheet. "Hershel P. Johnson. Historical society representative."

Esther looked at Vincent sideways.

A young man in a blue blazer and a red tie stepped to the

microphone next. He had a feathery soul patch on his chin and brown sandals that made Arden think of her Great Aunt Wilma's painting of Jesus.

Maura handed the pink paper to Hershel. Immediately, he began reading it. "The Falls at Silver Park will disturb a delicate ecosystem that is protected under historic designation," he said, voice cracking with emotion every third word.

"All right, all right," Esther said. "I get it. Does anyone here have a *different* public comment to share?"

Arden looked around the room. Two other men and a woman in a turban sat stone-faced at the back of the room. Buddy strutted in front of Arden, watching her, and he lowered himself onto the bench next to her. He massaged the back of his leathery neck, under the oily ponytail. Her whole body stiffened. He was sitting close enough for Arden to smell the medicinal tang of his aftershave lotion.

Vincent cleared his throat in a dramatic way.

"We need to move this along," Esther said. "I'd like to make a motion to—"

"No," Arden said, on her feet now. Her voice bounced off the domed ceiling and the glass-entombed portraits of dead white men. "I want to be heard." The words rippled in faint echoes. She gasped for breath.

Behind her, someone clapped. "Yes," the blonde woman said. "Speak up, Ms. Collier."

"I want to be heard," Arden said again, louder. "You're going to hear my story."

19.

PARKER GOZER

Behind Van der Griff's auditorium, Parker stepped over a series of power cables that had been duct-taped to the floor, wound her way through stacked chairs, and opened a door marked, "Green Room"—the speakers' waiting room. She wasn't expecting much more than a closet, given the facility's overall shabbiness, yet inside the Green Room, she found four chairs covered in brown velvet beside a gleaming granite counter attached to a wall-length mirror. Theater seemed to be the whole point of Van der Griff's facility.

A heavy sweetness infused the room. Red roses were wedged tightly into a crystal vase next to a bowl of fresh fruit and a cooler full of soft drinks. Taped to the vase, a tiny white card said, "Good luck, Parky."

Dr. Tinley. His kind gesture would have meant more if he had spelled her name correctly.

In front of the mirror, Parker was unnerved by her image, skinny and pale—an unfamiliar face without makeup. Taking a seat in front of the glass, she checked her phone for messages in case Dylan had called to explain why he was late. His late-night voicemail had been slurry as hell. Parker could barely understand what he was trying to say. Something about a change he wanted to make to the script. She figured he was probably fighting off a terrible hangover, running late while he sucked down extra cups of coffee. She pictured him swallowing aspirin, gobbling breath mints, and fumbling with eye drops designed to erase bright red cobwebs.

On the wall behind her, a large clock ticked forward. She needed to slap on makeup and get back out front with Van der Griff and Dr. Tinley. She had left them alone by the stage, telling them not to worry about a thing because Dylan would be there any minute. Frowning at her likeness, Parker slathered a greasy putty like primer paint under her eyes. She tied back her hair and piled on the foundation, taking care to cover her neck so she wouldn't look like somebody wearing a Halloween mask. The effect, after she inspected her work and applied lipstick, reminded her of a smiling, animated corpse, which was exactly how she felt.

Her phone, parked on the counter, lit up. Right away, Parker recognized Beamer's jazzy ring tone. She opened a bottle of eyeliner with one hand, simultaneously answering the phone with the other one.

"There you are," he said. "Why haven't you answered any of my calls? Jolene's been worried sick."

Welcome to my world. We only communicate when you feel like it. "It's crazy here." She was tracing her eyes with the miniature brown paintbrush. "I've only got a second. I need to get this press conference going."

Beamer sighed. "When are you coming home? Joie won her lacrosse game last night. She was the highest-scoring player."

Parker's hand froze in mid-air. Her eyes felt beyond tired. She had to blink to keep from tearing up. "I wish I could have seen it. She must be on top of the world."

"Will you be home for church this Sunday?" His voice had a sharp, guilt-inducing edge to it. Parker pictured his Stubborn-Mad Look, with his big chin pushed forward and his lips pressed together. "There's a picnic after the service."

At the far end of the counter, a melting clump of ice cracked. A Diet Coke sank lower into a silver bowl. She glanced at a banana, cringed, and stared at her painted eyes in the mirror. "Let me call you back after this press conference, honey." She swiped furiously at herself with a mascara wand. "There's a lot going on right now. Dr. Tinley's all keyed up and this guy Van der Griff's really a handful. Even worse, my headliner's a no-show at the moment. Can I catch up with you after this nightmare is over?"

"Who's your headliner?" Beamer sounded bored. "Some movie star again?"

Parker spit it out without thinking it through first. She should have taken a breath instead. "It's a funny thing. You remember Dylan Jones from college? He's kind of a big deal in satellite tech these days, and it turns out he's—"

145

A loud *bang* rocked her eardrum, through the phone line. She imagined Beamer's empty coffee mug slamming down onto his desk. She had forgotten how much Beamer hated Dylan. "What are you talking about? You mean you're down there with that loser? You never told me anything about that. Don't you think that's the type of thing you should have mentioned to me?"

Holding her breath, Parker checked the time again. If she cried, she would have to start all over again with the makeup. "It's not like I can ever reach you. You don't turn on your cellphone. I asked you to come down here and be with me, remember? I practically begged you, but you wouldn't do it."

"You could have told me you're in Atlanta with Romeo. I have a phone at work, too, you know. It rings and everything."

"It rings, but you never answer it."

"I do answer it."

"Look, sorry, but I'm completely exhausted right now." Parker didn't approve of how whiny she sounded, like a rapidly deflating balloon, but she couldn't seem to stop herself. "I feel like I might throw up. Honestly, I don't know if I can keep doing this job. It makes me feel like a machine, you know? Like I'm on autopilot all the time."

Beamer's laugh sounded snarky, like a dart hitting a board. "Great," he said, stretching the word. "First you're hanging with The Loser, now you're ready to quit your job? How's that going to work? We can't pay the mortgage on my income."

Parker's smooth, expressionless face looked foreign to her. "You're tense." Her voice sounded mechanical. "You need to have sex."

"Don't make a joke. That's not funny."

"I wasn't joking. Those are my primary functions in our marriage— to make the money and service you. Right?"

"Stop it. No, that's not right at all. You're being crude."

"I'm being honest. I can't win. I just told you, I'm so stressed-out, this job literally makes me sick. You don't care. It's all about the paycheck, like I have a dollar sign painted on my forehead. I'm in Atlanta to help support our family. You're pissed off because I'm not there."

"I'm pissed off because you didn't tell me about being down there with your old boyfriend."

"I want out." She said it quickly, the way she might rip off a hangnail or pull a loose tooth. She had never said it out loud before. She had thought about it, off and on, at the blurry edge of awareness, for at least a year. "This isn't working for me anymore."

Behind her, the door creaked open.

"Fine," Beamer said. "Move to Atlanta."

Dr. Tinley looked like a million bucks in his understated navy blue suit and tie with a nicely contrasting red scarf tucked into his breast pocket like a prom corsage. His eyebrows kept pressing together in the middle. "Van der Griff's beginning to lose it," he said. "Where the hell's Dylan?"

Beamer hung up.

Clicking off the phone, Parker stood up to face her boss. "He drunk-dialed me last night. I couldn't even understand his message. I suspect he's trying to pull himself together."

"This needs to work," Dr. Tinley said, pointing a finger at her. He tilted his chin back and looked down his nose at Parker as if she might be a patient from his past life as a pediatrician. "What's happened to your lovely face, dear?"

Her fingers flew to her forehead. She had rolled around in her hotel bed all night, reenacting ancient conversations with her Dad until five o' clock in the morning, when she had finally slipped into a tortured coma-like state. At eight o' clock, she had scrambled like a madwoman to get to Van der Griff's place on time. "I haven't quite finished my makeup."

Dr. Tinley lowered his gaze until he was staring grimly at her over a small second chin. "We won't get the rest of the money until we pull this off." He said it in a quiet monotone, without blinking, like a hypnotist. "Van der Griff's a little nervous. You want my advice? Everything needs to be calm and perfect and beautiful, which means you need to get Dylan here now. I don't care how you do it. Just get it done."

Parker swallowed hard, trying to remember how long it had taken to drive to Dylan's house. Half an hour or more? She might be able to make it there and back in time if she didn't hit too much traffic. "I'm on it," she said.

"Good. I'll keep our sponsor busy. You think we'll get good press turnout?"

Assuming real news didn't break out, Parker expected about a dozen reporters to cover the event. On-site so far, the sparse media scrum included Keith Richards—a short, round BBC reporter who looked nothing like the Rolling Stones guitarist by the same name—interns for *USA Today* and the *Wall Street Journal,* and—miracle of miracles— Georgia Portman, the kind-hearted *New York Times* reporter who just happened to be in Atlanta on another assignment and seemed to feel sorry for Parker. Another eight reporters had promised they would try to make it, either in person or online. "Absolutely," Parker said, gritting her teeth. "Be sure to remind Mr. Van der Griff about the webcast. Even if we only have a handful of reporters on-site, we'll have many more watching online."

Dr. Tinley's eyes went thin. "We'd better have more than a handful on-site."

As soon as he was gone, Parker tried phoning Dylan one more time, without success. She tossed a soda into her bag, grabbed a pastry, and bolted for the exit. Traffic wasn't too bad, mid-morning, thank God. Only once, she got stuck behind a city bus and a garbage truck before hitting a clear stretch of North Highland Avenue, beyond Manuel's Tavern. Outside Dylan's place, she swerved into the parking spot and darted into the lobby behind an old woman fumbling with a collection of plastic grocery bags.

Repeatedly, she pounded on his door.

"Ugh," Dylan said when he finally appeared. He glanced at her with one eye and walked away. Shoving her foot through the door before it slammed shut, Parker slipped into his foyer, balancing the Diet Coke, an almond croissant, and her satchel.

Dylan stumbled, naked and farting, into the bathroom. "Early," he said, leaning over to suck water from the faucet. The sloppy lapping reminded her of a dog, or oral sex. Her fingers, wrapped around a chunk of ice stuck to the soda, felt freezer burned—numb and strangely hot at the same time as she headed for his kitchen. She remembered Beamer, handing her a mug of coffee through the shower curtain back home. Acid bubbled in her stomach.

"Why didn't you answer the phone?" she yelled, parking her stuff on a marble counter. She pulled open the heavy curtains in his living room and fumbled through her bag for a bottle of maximum-strength pain relief pills.

"Exhausted from our marathon of love," he called back before burping.

148

Panic surged up from Parker's gut, sour. She had fifteen minutes, tops, to bring him back to life and make him look presentable enough for the cameras. "The press conference is at ten o' clock," she said, smashing four pills with the back of a knife. "Did you forget?"

Dylan's red face looked poached when he peered wide-eyed around the bathroom door. A deep crease in his right cheek resembled the folds of a tangled sheet. "What time is it now?"

"Five minutes after nine." She whipped the pulverized medicine into a glass of water.

"Shit," he said, stumbling across the room. He shoved one foot through his navy-blue boxers—the same ones she had pulled off him the night before. He lost his balance, fell onto the couch, jumped up, and hopped into his pants. Thin, sagging handles of flesh quivered on his hips, loose and pimply in the hard morning light. "Way to give a guy notice."

"Have a seat," Parker said, swiveling a stool in his direction. She slid the Diet Coke, the chalky water, and the pastry in front of him. Talent Management was a thing she knew how to do. *It's not my first rodeo,* she thought. *It's not my first rodeo.* It occurred to her how she was a real drunkard's dream. "Drink up."

Dylan's fingers jerked. The lip of the glass clattered against his teeth. Parker nudged the croissant closer to him. His Adam's apple bobbed four times before he lowered the glass with both hands. He tried without success to focus his bloodshot, wavering eyes on her face. "Hey, I'm sorry about yesterday," he said. "Give me another try, sweetie. Best two out of three."

Parker winced. Shame and fear kept washing over her like recurring nightmares. "We'll talk later. We've got to get through this press conference first. Your boss is a nervous wreck. Mine's not much better. He's scared shitless he won't get the rest of the money unless I knock this one out of the park and I—"

"Let me guess." Dylan threw his head back and laughed with a sliver of almond stuck to his lip. "It's all up to me. No pressure, though."

She groped inside her satchel and shoved a binder at him. "Look, that's the playbook—the script, the choreography, everything. All you need to do is keep it in front of you and follow along. Easy."

He parked his elbows on the counter and moaned into his lovely hands, revealing a tiny bald spot, tucked under a flap of hair. Parker was beginning to understand why *National Geographic* had dumped him. "Jesus," he said. "I'm so sick of this job."

"Listen, listen," she said, clacking her wedding ring against his sleek counter until he lifted his head. "I need for you to focus here. Focus! Focus! Remember why we're doing this. You're going to explain how you analyze satellite images. Tell them how many villages were destroyed in the Niger Delta last year. Give them the percentage increase in gas flares since 2000. Talk about the black water and what it does to the kids there. This research can make a real difference in the world."

He leaned back, yawning, pulled out a bottle of eye drops, and tipped his head. He let the liquid roll all the way down his cheeks. Smiling, woozy, he reached for her waist. "Come on, let's try again. Sometimes I'm better in the morning."

Parker stepped away from him. "Stop it. I don't want that."

"Hey, I've got meds. I didn't use them yesterday because they give me a five-hour hard-on and then I feel like I'm having a heart attack and my tongue turns blue. But who cares? We'll sleep when we're dead, right? Better living through chemistry, as they say."

His voice sounded like the buzz of a moped that was running out of gas. His breath smelled like an open bottle of bourbon. *I can't fix him, I can't fix him, I can't fix him.* "You know what the real problem is," she whispered. "Your job is not the problem. You're going to have to face this thing with the booze. You know that."

He licked his lips. "Are those your terms? You'd be with me if I took the pledge?"

"No, that's not what I meant. I'm just saying, think about your health and what you're doing to yourself. It's about you, not me. Anyway, look, I'm married. You know that."

He gulped the rest of the water, belched, and dropped the empty glass into the sink. "I can't believe I let you do this to me again," he said. "Fuck."

"I made a mistake." She was surprised by her sudden tears and roaring voice. "I take full responsibility and I'm sorry, but I thought you were flirting with me and it triggered something from a long time ago, and I—I don't know."

"Me? Flirting? What are you even talking about? When?"

"Yesterday," she said. "Outside."

Dylan blinked, swaying on the stool. "You were the one who was flirting. Pretty blatantly, I'd say. I mean, pickle jokes? Good God. You could've done better than that."

He was sitting in front of a massive, surprisingly ugly painting of a tropical garden. All of the details were exaggerated. Parker thought about the flowery watercolor jungle she had painted for Buddy when she was fourteen. She had signed it, "Love, always," and she shivered at the end of her mother's driveway after midnight, waiting to see headlights. After picking her up, Buddy had parked at a construction site, where he pulled out a joint as well as his penis. Parker left her painting on the front seat, an hour later, when he dropped her off.

Across the counter, Dylan's eyes were clear and less wobbly all of a sudden. The pastry and aspirin were working. She touched the back of his hand. "I'm sorry," she said and she checked the time. They urgently needed to be in motion. "I'm a horrible, disgusting person. Will you help me anyway? We've been friends a long time and my family's counting on me. I can't blow it."

He bit into the pastry. "You're the boss," he said, snarling with his mouth full. "All I've got to do is baffle them with some technological bullshit. My specialty."

On the bright side, Parker could tell his brain was shuffling slowly back from the swampy land of the Bourbon Zombies. He was also turning at warp-speed back into the mildly snarky, arrogant version of himself—the Dylan Jones of TED Talk fame. She shook her head, holding up one hand like a traffic cop. "No," she said. "Don't start getting cocky on me. Unless we're announcing a waterfall on Mars or the capture of a woodpecker believed to be extinct, we've got to approach this thing humbly. The Tinley Institute is a do-gooder nonprofit. Be sincere. Please, Dyl. You've got to sell it."

Dylan shrugged and flashed his swaggering half-smile. "Okay, okay." He wiggled a pair of reading glasses over his nose, scanned the playbook, and slammed it shut. "Let's do her."

They made it back to Van der Griff's building in fifteen minutes, flat. Parker only had to stop once to let Dylan puke onto a grassy strip by the side of the road. He seemed better, after that, and he even smiled a little when she handed him three sticks of spearmint chewing gum.

Inside, Dr. Tinley was waiting at the back of the auditorium. His shoulders were pulled back, straight and rigid as a Marine—his take-charge posture. Parker surveyed the room: Two camera crews, one photographer, and four other reporters, all looking bored. Not too shabby on two days' notice, thirty miles beyond Atlanta. *So far, so good.* Her boss smelled lemony. She wanted to bear-hug him around the neck, she felt so relieved to be back in time with Dylan. Instead, she squeezed her clipboard and smiled without showing any teeth. "Everything's going to be okay now," she said.

"You took long enough." Dr. Tinley touched his upper lip and stared at the slight sheen of sweat on his fingertips like he couldn't quite believe it. "I had to greet your guests for you."

"Thank you. I appreciate it."

He jerked his thumb and looked away. "You've buttoned your coat wrong."

He was right. One side of her jacket was hanging two inches lower than the other. "Would you mind doing the introductions?" She started realigning her buttons. "I have to monitor the webcast in case anybody asks a question over the web."

"I thought you just wanted me to look pretty. I didn't prepare any remarks."

Parker pulled out three index cards. "The script is on the teleprompter, or you can *ad lib* from these cards." Dr. Tinley wasn't a fan of teleprompters. He said they made his eyes look like they were bulging out of his head. "You always do such a wonderful job. Do you mind?"

"All right, all right, already. Shit." Her boss grunted, bear-like, not at all his usual friendly self. The pressure was clearly getting to him. "There aren't any reporters here. We're starting in ten minutes. This is embarrassing. What are you going to do?"

"It's going to be great," Dylan said, giving Dr. Tinley's shoulder a squeeze. "This isn't our first ride around the ring, sir. No worries."

Dr. Tinley flinched and pulled his shoulder free.

"I have to set up my laptop," Parker said in a robotic voice. "Don't forget to tell your new sponsor about the webcast. That should make him feel better. This is a pretty good turnout, considering."

Dylan peered at her from under his eyebrows, rubbed an imaginary brown spot off his nose, and slipped down the aisle. Parker followed him.

Up front, Van der Griff twisted in his seat, the better to glare at them. Dylan shook hands with the reporters, warming up the audience. Dr. Tinley hustled back toward the stage. When Parker nodded, he climbed the steps with Dylan and Van der Griff, who looked uncomfortable in a tight jacket and tie instead of his usual baggy lab coat with his name stitched on the pocket.

Bring it, boss, Parker thought.

Dr. Tinley did not bring it, alas. His nostrils flared when he stepped behind the podium. His chin wiggled and he stifled a yawn through his nose that got amplified by the microphone. "Hello," he said, tapping it. "Is this thing on?"

Parker sucked in a breath and held it.

"Good morning," he said. "Thank you for being here to learn about The Tinley Institute's latest initiative. You've heard about our efforts to leverage technology in the service of human rights in places like Myanmar and Tibet. Today, we're going to tell you about another innovative effort to identify children at risk in Nigeria."

On the big screen behind him, the children in Dylan's video kicked a rag ball around a dirt yard while orange and black oil plumes flared in the distance. Below the stage, the press kit table was empty, which meant the TV crews had grabbed her press release and copies of the canned video footage.

Leaning forward, she clicked a toolbar on the webcast to check attendance: Twelve online viewers so far. No reporter questions. A line of text popped into the white box below the video window. It was Parker's old buddy Bart, the reporter with the Associated Press, the one whose presence at dinner had helped Dr. Tinley score the funding from Van der Griff in the first place. Her heart skipped a beat. One story on the AP wire could be republished by two-hundred other media outlets overnight. "Hey, kid," Bart wrote. "Your boss could be a cure for insomnia. How's it going there?"

Parker's eyes nearly crossed from frowning. Questions and answers typed into the free-text box could be seen by anyone watching the webcast. "Thanks for joining us, Associated Press!" she typed back. "VERY glad to have you with us. Please be sure to ask a question after our speakers finish their presentations."

"Okay, and if your boss starts talking again, please release a live squirrel into the proceedings so I won't pass out from boredom," Bart typed back.

Her photograph of Oba, the Nigerian pre-teen with huge brown eyes, appeared on the display screen behind Dr. Tinley. "All over the world, children at risk need our help and protection," he said. "So that we don't put her at greater risk, I'll call this child Abebi. She is only one young person in a single village in Nigeria where war and the quest for oil to fuel the energy appetites of industrialized nations have torn families apart. Abebi lost her parents to unspeakable violence. She lost her home, too, and her drinking water has been contaminated as a result of unethical practices by oil producers."

Dylan unfortunately chose that exact moment to pour himself a large glass of water from the pitcher Parker had left on the table—no ice, since ice cubes would make unwanted clinking noises. When it was his turn to speak, though, Dylan didn't let her down. He was flashing his charisma on its highest beam. "Today, high-resolution satellite images offer a way to keep high-tech eyes in the sky on vulnerable children like Abebi," he said, moving back and forth in front of the screen. "I'd like to show you how this technology works."

"Ho hum, old news so far," Bart wrote into the box below the webcast. "I hope your friend's video is pretty freaking cool. It's double-coupon day at Macy's. I need new socks. I have a life, you know."

Parker opened her Twitter account and fired off a private message to Bart. "I love you," she typed, "but please stop joking around on the live webcast. Everybody can see it."

"You need to take a yoga class," he wrote back, making her cringe. She had forgotten how she first met Bart, in the basement of a church where he was doing the downward dog position while packed like a giant pot roast into stretchy pants that were two sizes too small for his large body. "You're way too stressed out. You need to stop worrying about the little things."

"LOL," she typed. "Actually, Dr. Tinley pays me to do exactly that!"

Bart wrote back right away. "Why are you so stuck on old Tinley, anyway? He treats you like a slave, from what I can see."

Why, indeed? Parker clicked out of Twitter, not bothering to answer Bart. Dr. Tinley's eyelids were fluttering to half-mast while Dylan kept talking. If his eyes stayed shut for more than ten seconds, she would have to walk to the edge of the stage and snap a series of flash photographs—one of her tricks for keeping him awake during public appearances. He had been so much fun, at first—younger when they started working together; less vulnerable to fatigue and flashes of anger at the end of a long day. Still, she loved his subtle cologne, his healing hands whenever they took flight to explain some arcane point of science, and the way he opened doors for her and told her, every now and then, that she was the best. Of course, as she watched his eyelids drooping, she didn't need a shrink to tell her she had never stopped longing for her father's attention.

Onstage, Dylan had begun to sweat under the lights and he kept trying to straighten his impossibly wrinkled linen jacket.

Parker felt a vibration where her hand was wrapped around her phone. Seeing Arden's text message caught her off guard, nearly causing her to laugh out loud. Arden must have found Parker's note, with the phone number at the bottom, after all. *She had found it, she had found it.*

"There's a hearing on Silver Park," Arden's message said. "Adjacent property owners were supposed to be notified. Eleven-thirty in the county building, room 24."

Parker's breath felt like a cork, stuck in her throat. It was already ten-thirty. She would have to deal with post-press conference interviews before heading all the way downtown. Dylan finished his video flyover and Van der Griff started droning on about his facility. Parker managed to stifle a giggle as he tossed around terms like "state-of-the-art" and "cutting-edge" and "world-class."

Finally, mercifully, it was over. One of the reporters stood up and stretched, yawning. A single hand rose when Dr. Tinley asked for questions from the audience—a softball query about how Dylan could distinguish certain types of destruction from others. Bart's question was easy, too. Something about next steps, which Parker conveyed through a handheld microphone.

"Any other questions?" Dr. Tinley glared at the audience, clearly furious, daring them to speak up. Someone's chair creaked. "With that, I'll thank our sponsor, Charles Van der Griff of the Healing Voices Foundation, and our audience for being here today."

A few weak claps, and that was it. The event hadn't been nearly as bad as Parker feared it would be. Reporters sprinted for the exit doors.

Never before had she seen Dr. Tinley's lower teeth. Normally, he kept them tucked carefully behind his lip. As he barreled toward her, red-faced, his lower teeth were uncapped and dingy-looking, twisted as the Great Wall of China and overlapping in spots. "That was terrible," he hissed, pulling her into a corner. "Charles looks furious. I thought you said we'd have reporters here."

A fine mist of his spit cooled the side of her neck. "Actually, I told you I needed at least another week to promote this event. I also told you and Charles we should hold it downtown, where the reporters actually work. You completely dismissed my advice. Even so, you had a decent turnout, all things considered. I had the Associated Press covering it remotely, which means you'll have plenty of pickup tomorrow. I promise you, that reporter didn't log on because of the news value of this event. He logged on because he's a friend of mine. I called in a favor."

Dylan was beside her, touching her arm. "Everything okay?"

"I'm surprised at you, Parky," Dr. Tinley whispered.

Parker's face tingled. "I understand," she said, but she didn't.

"Charles is so disappointed, he says you'll have to set up some radio interviews for him before he'll give us the rest of the money. You need to make it rain."

"No, sir. No more rain. Sorry. My magic wand's broken."

"This isn't optional, Parky. You've really let me down. You've made mistakes."

I'm not the only one, she thought. His sugary eyes sagged. A sweaty musk overwhelmed his lemony cologne. Parker thought about the dead weight of her father's hand as she let go of it, the stiffness of the hospital sheet under her fingers. The air-conditioner had hummed, pushing a floral stench over the bed. On the windowsill, a single helium balloon had tapped the glass. In her mind, Parker opened the window and pulled the ribbon to let it fly, absolving him, and herself, at last.

"I love you, sir," she said, "but I can't do this job anymore. I quit."

"Oh, Parky." He wagged his head back and forth in a slow, deliberate way.

She unhooked the laptop and picked up her satchel. "My name is Parker." The auditorium doors slammed behind her.

In the parking lot, Dylan caught up with her and reached for her hand. After all those years, his eyes were still as green as when they had first met, but he looked scared—not cocky and strutting the way she had seen him on TV. "Listen, screw him," he said. "Who is he, anyway, the Sultan of Brunei? You did an amazing job, a better job than they deserved, blind-folded and with both hands tied behind your back."

Parker kissed his cheek, quickly, before she had time to think about it, and she pressed her mouth against his ear, whispering. "Good luck, old friend."

His lips brushed the edge of her jaw as she pulled away, knowing she would never see him again.

CITY IN A FOREST

20.
ARDEN COLLIER

Arden moved back to the microphone and planted her feet far enough apart to keep her knees from knocking. When Esther hunched over her elbows, grinning with one side of her mouth, Arden didn't blink.

"Ms. Arden Collier," Esther said, checking her watch, "I'm quite confident that we've given you more than ample notice regarding the multiple ways in which your property remains in violation of county regulations. You've had every conceivable opportunity to make things right."

"Respectfully, ma'am, I disagree." Thundering unexpectedly through the microphone, Arden's words made several onlookers jump. The TV cameraman slid in front of her, zooming in on Arden's face. She ignored him, keeping her jaw locked.

Esther tipped her head back so that her nostrils seemed to take over her face. "I see," she said on an exhale. "Well, then, why don't you tell us why you've chosen to ignore all the citations we've sent in response to complaints from your neighbors? While you're at it, please share with us why you're resisting Mr. Caldwell's exceptionally generous offer, which would benefit you as well as every other citizen in the county."

The language part of Arden's brain felt paralyzed by the fear that was seeping down her spinal cord. She sucked wind and started talking, not quite sure what was going to come out of her mouth. "My grandfather's park is for everyone. It's true, it's private property now, owned by Parker Gozer, but it's also open to the public if anyone wants to visit. The covenant says it has to remain accessible to the entire community *unto perpetuity.*" She loved those last two words—all the lovely, rhythmic vowels signifying the weight and seriousness of her grandfather's gift to the neighborhood. She hit them hard, whenever she said them out loud. *Unto perpetuity.* "My grandfather and Parker's father set it up that way because they wanted to preserve Silver Park for future generations. Buddy's development would change all of that."

"We did an environmental assessment," Esther said, clipping every word. "The impacts would be negligible."

The microphone smelled of stale spit when Arden leaned over it, wrapping her mouth around its foam cover. "I don't see how that could possibly be true. The lake is full of bream and catfish and turtles. There are walnut, dogwood, and pine trees—even an old chestnut tree, believe it or not."

At the end of the table, Vincent made a huffing noise. He started leafing back through his papers with his forehead bunched up like a tangle of yarn. "That's impossible," he said. "Chestnuts went extinct years ago. Fungal blight."

"There are still a few left around the country. There's one in Silver Park. Maybe your environmental assessment missed it."

"I highly doubt that. It's probably a hybrid."

"It's just a stump, but it sprouts leaves, every spring."

Esther tipped her head sideways until her neck cracked.

Arden straightened her back, turned her head, and smiled into the glare of the TV light. She glanced over her shoulder at Maura Levine, who was perched on the edge of her bench. "My neighbors and I love that lake, and as you heard from these other folks, the community's historic. It's a living piece of history right here, in the middle of Atlanta."

Esther pinched the bridge of her nose and peered at Arden, heavy-lidded, through her fingers. "We'll take another look at at the environmental assessment. You have my word on that. As for the historic designation, I took a drive back in there, and quite frankly, I couldn't for the life of me figure out why that was ever approved. First, there was your blighted property, and I also saw a number of dilapidated old clapboard dwellings that can only be described as shanties."

Arden let out a noise like a cat with its tail caught in a door. "Excuse me, but I resent you calling our homes—"

"Let me finish, please," Esther said, holding up both hands. Her rosy cheeks brightened, pulsing bronze under the TV light. "I even saw an outhouse by one of the dwellings back in there, and a number of wells. Now, I grew up in Birmingham during segregation. Nobody needs to lecture me on the importance of African-American history, but you can't tell me those citizens don't want to save some money on their taxes next year. The revenue from development could make that possible. Maybe then they would be able to undertake a few improvements—indoor plumbing, perhaps, and running water. The children in those homes need to break out of the cycle of poverty. I'd like to hear your thoughts on exactly why you think development would be such a bad thing for your community."

A freezing shudder wracked Arden's shoulders and her mind went blank. Through the microphone, her breath sounded uneven. She remembered her grandfather's face—*Mr. John Collier*—with his bright eyes in perpetual motion and his cheeks wrinkled all the way around perfectly white dentures whenever he smiled. She had learned her family's history in bits and pieces, each of them like shiny, colored beads sliding down a trembling thread he let her hold, as a child. She had trailed endlessly behind him, hoping he might turn, winking, and hand her a hunk of red licorice twisted in wax paper.

For the camera, Arden channeled his smile, letting his warmth infuse her whole face. She bent her neck over the microphone, once more, ready to lift up his life story an inch at a time as if it might be a precious piece of jewelry, out of the box at last. "Silver Park was founded by John and Hannah Collier—my grandparents. The story of Silver Park is their story. The only way to tell it properly is from the beginning."

"All right," Esther said, sighing heavily. "We'll hear you out, Ms. Collier, but let's skip the advent of fire and the first stone tools in the cave, shall we? Keep it relevant."

Taking a deep breath, Arden began. "They grew up in Collins Knob, Tennessee. They set off for Crockett County when they were both eighteen." Her voice hummed with stage fright. She was trying to remember everything her grandfather had ever told her about his honeymoon. *"Three days on a bow-legged mule and the house was only half-built when we got there."*

"Interesting," Vincent said, leaning forward on his elbows. "Please continue."

Esther cut her eyes at him.

"My grandmother Hannah was already pregnant," Arden said, louder than before. "My grandfather had been promised work as a sharecropper. Their first house in Tennessee had a fireplace with four sides—four rooms on each side, but they could stick their hands through the holes in the floorboards."

Esther's breath heaved and rolled around the room, undulating against the wood paneling and the bumpy ceiling tiles. "I just told you not to start with the advent of fire, and what did you go and do?"

"That was 1937. My grandmother gave birth two days after they got to Crockett County. My grandfather managed to kill a wild hog and they ate every bit of it all winter, salted and smoked. She nursed her baby— my mother—by the fire and they got by, that first year. When their first crop came in, she carried the baby into the fields with her."

Arden took a moment to survey the room. The reporter was watching her through slightly softened eyes. Maura Levine stared into space with her lips set in a hard, flat line, looking like she might cry. Buddy was perched stiffly on the end of the bench with a furious expression, as if his spinal cord might shatter at any moment. Arden remembered the damp room in Foster Gozer's basement where Buddy was living when she visited Parker once—the dust and mold and dead flies fossilized on the windowsill. A shudder rippled across the back of Arden's neck. In her mind, she said a word of thanks for Aunt Wilma, who had kept her safe. *Her hands had wings.*

At the back of the room, the door opened and Parker appeared, all dressed up, looking as fearful as ever. She nodded at Arden and hurried to the back of the room.

"I'm begging you to fast forward," Esther said. "Begging."

Arden pictured her grandfather, propped on the end of his broom, fading into the shadows of memory. *"Cotton looks pretty, but when you pick it, you feel those thorns. White clouds, Lord, hiding razors."* She thought about Joel, too, waving goodbye. She was ready to let him go, finally, to stop clinging to what used to be. She shifted her weight, opening both hands as she spoke. The old sorrow rolled off her fingertips, vanishing. Her words sounded more rhythmic and deliberate. It was a story she had heard many times.

"From that first crop," she said, "they bought beans and rice for the next winter and fabric for the baby's coat, but they couldn't grow more than they ate. After that, the boll weevil chewed through everything they had planted."

"Yes, I've read about that," Esther said, shaking her head. "It was hard back then."

Arden opened her mouth again, but she wasn't sure where to take the story next. She thought about the terrifying picture of a boll weevil she had seen at Parker's house—a close-up photograph on a magazine cover. Foster Gozer kept old copies of *National Georgraphic* in the same corner hutch with his wife's collection of tiny silver spoons from all the places she had traveled—Mexico, Canada, England, Austria, France. Arden thought about racism, poverty, the luck of the draw, the Gozer family's incredible good fortune, and how hard her own grandparents had worked.

"It was a horrible time to be a sharecropper," she said after a pause. "They might have made it, but the government paid my grandfather's boss to do a third less planting. Grandma Hannah had another baby—a son. When the boss died, they had nothing, and nobody, their fourth year in Crockett County."

Behind her, Buddy's impatient sigh stretched into a groan.

When Esther opened her mouth, Arden cut her off. She locked her knees, imagining her grandmother leaning back in a creaky homemade rocking chair, nursing her son in a weak, orange circle of firelight while he coughed and shook and cried from hunger. Near the end of her grandfather's story the first time she heard it, Arden had slipped the licorice back into her pocket, too scared and ashamed to eat it anymore. She could hear his voice in her head:

"Her milk was gone. She fed the last of the rice and a jar of canned apples to our little girl—your mama. I rode the mule five miles to our neighbor's house, asked for any little scrap they could spare—a few hunks of fatback. Lord, the wind was howling sideways. I couldn't feel a thing in my hands, my feet, my face. When I got back, my son was dead. He was as gentle as a dove and not much bigger, lying there in Hannah's arms. She sang him the prettiest song. She said he'd remember her that way, in heaven."

Outside the courthouse, the constant hum of traffic escalated, punctuated by horns. There was a jolting crash of metal on metal, slamming doors, and voices screaming.

"Their infant son starved to death," Arden said.

Esther had gone motionless and quiet. The room itself was silent above the distant, muffled cacophony of an accident below the windows and the fatal collision of history.

"In the middle of the night," Arden said, continuing, "they hopped a train, without tickets, and they moved to Atlanta. His sister, my Great Aunt Wilma, was already here."

On the fly, Arden decided to skip the part about Wilma's husband George being a cradle-robber who made piles of money off his illegal moonshine factory.

"When Aunt Wilma's husband died, the probate court assigned his property to my grandfather, not his sister," Arden said. "She had gone blind and he was taking care of her at the time. He built a house that I'm still living in now. Built that place with his own hands. He helped other families build their homes, too. This was back when white farmers were moving into the textile mills. The sharecropping system had fallen apart. Poor black families were rushing into the cities, desperate for work."

For the first time, Esther's smile gave off a glimmer of light, flickering but warm. "That's a very moving story," she said, suddenly twisting her smile into a frown. "How does it end? Or should I say, does it ever end? If so, when?"

Arden took a breath and kept going. "My grandfather worked for many years as a janitor. In his spare time, he built the Mount Zion Baptist Church first, then the Silver Park School during the days of segregation, and a little store where neighbors bartered with each other. Near the end of his life, he went to work for Foster Gozer, who was—"

"I think we all know who Foster Gozer was," Esther said. "He built half the city some years back. Bulldozed half the trees, too. Did you know that Atlanta was the fastest-growing urban settlement on the planet in the 1970s?"

Vincent piped up. "Really?"

"True story," Esther said.

Ignoring them, Arden went on. "Foster Gozer talked my grandfather into setting up a park, which was a good thing, but unfortunately, he also talked him into deeding the land over to the Gozer family. Silver Park is still my grandfather's legacy, no matter what. He loved it and he wanted to keep it pristine."

Finally, Arden stopped, spent.

Esther grimaced like she might be experiencing indigestion. She clicked her pen once, twice, three times, until she had created an entire Morse-code alphabet of irritation. Chandler the Clerk adjusted his colorful glasses.

Turning, Arden looked for Parker, who was leaning against the back wall. A sad, hopeful smile twitched on her lips. Arden thought about her Aunt Wilma's expression in a long-ago photograph—an eager, fearful girl wearing the same apologetic kind of smile, ready to clean the Gozer family's house, chase after Parker, or drink moonshine steeped in lead car parts if her husband gave it to her. *That's what good girls do.*

Arden froze, remembering her grandfather's warning about the shed on the far side of the lake. "One more thing," she said. "That property's got lead contamination from an old distillery. I'll want to see the soil tests. The public's got a right to know."

"Oh, Jesus," Buddy said and he banged his fist against the bench.

"Order," the deputy said.

Esther's uplifted face fell, muscle by muscle, until she was scowling with her mouth, her eyes, her nose, her once-buoyant cheeks, and her eyebrows. She turned toward Vincent in his creased polo shirt. "Did we, or did we not do a lead test?"

Again, Vincent rifled through his file folder. "I—I'm not sure," he said. "Lead is one of those things you test for if you have a reason to believe it might be there, but I'm not aware of any documented industry on that site, and I—"

"Madam Chairwoman," Parker shouted, hauling herself upright. "I can verify Ms. Collier's statement. Mr. Caldwell told me he'd need to pave over an area of lead contamination on his building site."

"And who might you be?" Esther said. Her tone suggested she didn't want to know.

"My name is Parker Gozer."

The historical society representatives leaned their heads together, whispering. The cameraman stepped over a chair to reach Parker's side.

"Mr. Caldwell," Esther said. Her glowing red cheeks looked like they might start smoking. Light leapt into her eyes, flashing. "Is this true?"

Buddy narrowed his eyes. His lower lip puckered up. "They're lying," he said, staring straight ahead. "This is a ridiculous waste of time. Honestly, ma'am, both of these women have a history of this type of thing, instability and so on."

Arden felt sure she could kill him if they weren't in public. "My uncle had a whole series of stills back in there," she said. "He used radiators to make moonshine. Lead salts leached into the alcohol. A bunch of people got sick. He died. My aunt went blind."

"That's exactly what Mr. Caldwell told me," Parker said, "about the radiators. I would also like to review the soil tests."

An ominous rush of murmuring erupted at the back of the room.

"Brownfield," someone said in a hushed tone. Arden thought it might have been Maura Levine's voice.

"Superfund site," someone else said.

The TV camera was still rolling. "Ms. Collier and Ms. Gozer are both adjacent property owners. The county recognizes that they have rights," Esther said. "We'll be happy to provide everyone with all of the information we have so far, and we will request lead testing, which seems to be needed."

"Move to adjourn," Vincent said.

"So moved," Esther said, banging her gavel.

One more time, Buddy glared at Arden, blurry-eyed, and he shook his head, looking disgusted. He turned toward the clerk's desk. She wondered if it was the last time she would have to set eyes on his sorry ass. She hoped so, but she doubted it. He would most likely keep popping back up for the rest of her life, like a zombie that never really dies, no matter how many times you knock it down or poke a stick in its heart. Her fight with him surely wasn't over, not by a long shot.

The reporter pulled out a business card. "This is a great story," she said. Her solid, old-fashioned-sounding name, printed in thick black letters, surprised Arden: *Constance Presley.* "I've been investigating Caldwell's shady business deals for months now. Call me, okay? Keep me posted."

"I will," Arden said.

Parker was still smiling in a hesitant way at the back of the room, waiting, as Arden made her way toward the door. The space between them shrank until Parker looked larger than life. "I got here as quickly as I could," she said when the gap between them was small enough for Parker to leap forward, arms outreached for a hug, which Arden dreaded more than a steaming pile of liver and onions. "That was wonderful testimony you gave. Very moving. I loved it."

Arden crossed her arms and stepped back, out of reach.

Parker's peach-colored cheeks twitched and glowed. Her perfectly straight teeth were clenched into a weird sort of grimace. Her jaw pulsed. "Thanks for letting me know about the hearing."

"You're an adjacent land owner. You've got rights." *And I needed all the witnesses I could round up,* Arden thought.

"Let me help you with all this," Parker said. She reached out, but stopped herself, thank God, before latching on. "I know a good law firm. They worked for my father."

Under Arden's collar, a wave of heat was gaining strength. "I don't want your help."

"I can't blame you, but I want to be your friend, if you'll let me. We both love that park. I don't want anything bad to happen to it, or to you."

With her chin lifted, Arden inhaled, held it an extra second, and let it go. "My grandfather never should have given that land away. Your old man tricked him. White men always know how to trade beads for land. I realize it wasn't your fault, but that's how it worked out."

Parker's face turned rusty-looking. "Dad wanted to protect Silver Park. It was wrong, what he did—"

"Yeah, it was."

"—but I think he meant well. Near the end of his life, he tried to make amends for bulldozing so many trees all over Atlanta, so he talked your grandfather into protecting most of the park."

"Poor Daddy." Arden tightened the cross of her arms so she wouldn't be tempted to flail them around. "He felt entitled to feel better about himself."

"He didn't think about what it would do to your family. It was an injustice, and I'm sorry. That land belongs to you, but it's locked down."

"You're telling me things I already know."

Parker pressed her shaky hands together, as if she wanted to pray over her chewed-up fingernails. "I can't change what happened in the past, but I can hire a lawyer for you now."

"As I said, I don't need your help." Arden turned to leave. The sudden absence of adrenaline had left her feeling tired. "I don't live on your plantation."

It would have been the best exit line ever, but Parker hurled another one at Arden's back. The words made a dent right between Arden's shoulder blades, forcing her to stop. "I miss you," was what Parker said. "You were my best friend."

All the breath rushed out of Arden. Her head dropped. She spoke without making eye contact because she didn't want to see Parker's face all scrunched up from trying not to cry. "Let's give it some time," Arden said, nearly whispering. "We're going to be okay."

21.
PARKER GOZER

The front door of Parker's house clicked behind her, ringing in her ears.

Who was she kidding?

She didn't want out of her marriage—did she? No way could she break Joie's heart. Joie loved her Daddy. Parker was disoriented by the confrontation with Buddy and the great speckled horror of her history. Good grief, it had been disturbing. Anyone would lose their bearings. She only needed to breathe, relax—try to give herself a break for once, the way Jolene was always telling her to do. She needed to sleep for three days and wake up refreshed, ready to be a good parent again. Every working mother in America was performing the same plate-spinning, foot-stomping, harmonica-playing, juggling act as Parker, every single day.

At Joie's bedroom door, Parker was overwhelmed by her daughter's scent—a mixture of strawberry shampoo, the clean clothes folded on the dresser, and the sweaty athletic socks that nearly tripped Parker as she moved across the darkened room. At the narrow four-poster bed, her chest tightened. She pulled the blue dolphin blanket and the pink sheet all the way off the bed, but Joie wasn't in it.

A clock hummed on the vanity, not quite two in the morning. The shadows of prancing horses, crescent moons, and stars were spinning in a slow procession around the walls, circling an illuminated cylinder that washed the room with a flickering blue light. Joie had forgotten to turn off her night light again. Parker's head ached. A week's worth of adrenaline disappeared and she keeled over, pressed her face into Joie's pillow, and inhaled.

Where is my baby?

As a newborn, Joie had the eyes of a cartoon alien, bottomless and wide open, many nights by the sliding glass door in their first home. Not the best of neighborhoods. Next door, three kids had played kickball, smoking cigarettes in the alley after midnight while their parents screamed at each other. *"Where's the money, Jane? Huh, Jane? Answer me."* Silence came closer to dawn, most days. Nauseous from sleep-deprivation, the softness of Joie's tiny hands and her cheeks huffing in and out returned Parker to the world, keeping them glued together. In those early days of motherhood, the long fingers of a maple tree tapped the glass while Parker nursed her baby, breathing in synchrony, alone in the Martian stillness.

Love, always.

Parker and Beamer had worked long hours over many years to buy a better home in a safer neighborhood, to get her family out of there.

She flinched, lurching back to the present, when Beamer clicked a lamp on the vanity. It lit up Joie's collection of hair accessories and the underside of his jaw, leaving the rest of the room in darkness. He leaned against the door and crossed his arms. The shadowy, high-stepping horses changed shape, distorting as they rolled across the hardness of his face. "She's at a sleepover," he said.

Parker pushed off the pillow, lifting her head to look at him in his plaid boxer shorts. Her chin felt weirdly heavy. His gaze was flat, indifferent. He stared at a point between her eyes. "Hi, honey," she said, groggy.

"I thought it might be a good idea for her to spend some time with her friends tonight. Seems like we need to talk."

Blinking, Parker struggled to focus. "A sleepover? At Jolene's house?"

He smirked and shook his head. "No, I think we may have worn out that welcome for a while. Jolene's been chauffeuring Joie around all week, you know."

Every time the horses hit his cheek, she heard a gear grind inside the spinning cylinder. "Where's the sleepover?"

"Rosie's house."

Did he smile for a split-second, victorious, or did she imagine it? She pictured Joie's strange teammate in her pink princess skirt with the ruffled white hem and her black patent-leather shoes that made her look six years old instead of fourteen. Parker saw the stained golf sweater that Rosie's father was always wearing. "Howie? I'm surprised you let her spend the night with Howie. You know what a strange guy he is. Doesn't he make you uncomfortable?"

"Well," Beamer said, scratching his bare chest, "I'm pretty sure she's on a sleepover with Rosie, not Howie. The whole lacrosse team's over there. I talked to the Mom and everything. The Mom's there."

He looked so old and round-shouldered, slumped against the door, barely recognizable as the boy from Inman Park who played the guitar beside a red lamp. "You know what I mean."

Beamer sighed. "Yeah, I know how you are."

A long silence, punctuated by the groaning night light, stretched between them. He uncrossed his arms, watching her as if she might be an intruder who had slipped through an open window. She had mostly forgotten, until that moment, being perched on a lumpy green couch, back aching, explaining the statute of limitations to her husband the first year they were married. A cat had howled in the alley while she waited for her new husband to say something—anything. His baritone filled every corner of the cramped room, finally, pressing against the walls, ominous. "Let it go," he said. She told him she might never have another chance to hold Buddy accountable. *The legal window of opportunity is closing."* It was what her father's lawyer had said. Beamer wouldn't meet her gaze. "Drop it," he said again. "You don't need the stress. You're trying to have a baby. We can't go through all that."

Parker pushed off Joie's bed, stood up, and nearly lost her balance. Her eyes were fixed on the pattern of the rug—a series of overlapping orange and red circles. Beamer was breathing in time with the humming clock. She headed for the door, moving fast in case he got any ideas about touching her while she was angry with him. He almost never touched her anymore. But still. "I'll pick her up from Rosie's house," she said when they were a foot apart. "What time did you tell them we would be there?"

"I didn't, but we obviously can't pick her up right now. It's the middle of the night."

Parker's body went rigid. "Oh, yeah. Right. I'm so tired. I'm going to lie down and try to sleep for a while."

Without warning, he reached for her. His grip was tentative, almost tender. She stared down at his hand on her arm. "We need to talk," he said again. "Don't you think?"

Around and around in a circle, she thought. They had done all that, talked it to death with a string of counselors over the years, and on their own after they got sick of role-playing exercises in rooms ripe with incense. Inside Joie's room, the horses kept spinning and spinning. Parker knew what she wanted to do, and it wasn't because she was tired or angry or going crazy, although she was all of those things, at that moment. In the darkest corners of her mind, she had known for months, maybe even for years. It occurred to her how much easier it would be if Beamer had been a wife beater or a mean drunk, an Internet porn addict or a gambler. He was a mostly great guy, a loving father, somebody she would like if she met him on the street. "I can't," she said. *Can't what? Try anymore.* "I'm exhausted."

"I'll make a pot of coffee." He released her arm but shifted his feet so he was blocking her escape. "Please, honey."

"You're not hearing me." She felt trapped in the doorway. His warm, soapy smell, familiar and sweet as the feel of their sheets, made her want to cry. "You never hear me. I could be dropping dead, which I am."

"I've been awake every night this week, worrying about you down there." His voice surged, rising a half-note. His chest pumped up and down. "I deserve to understand what's been going on."

Parker knew he was talking about Dylan, and he was right—she needed to level with Beamer. She opened her mouth, thinking she would ask him to sit down first. He cut her off.

"You barely called me," he said. "You were gone a week and I practically never heard from you. It was like Joie and I didn't exist for you anymore."

Her knotted hands felt heavy, as if they were pulling her shoulders to the floor. If she had to tell him one more time to turn on his phone, she might scream. "I was working."

The lines in his forehead deepened and expanded. His lips were pulled back from his teeth. "I guess I don't understand your priorities. This was Joie's last week of school. Why didn't you just tell your boss no when he asked you to travel?"

Her lungs deflated, all at once. A sudden heat seared her chest, her cheeks and her neck. Her eyes strained in their sockets, inflamed. "I quit my job." The look on his face, contracting in horror, gave her a brief, sadistic thrill. "I guess you could say I've set new priorities for myself."

He stepped back with his hands on the back of his neck. "What?" His mouth was hanging open. Parker thought about the smelly fish tank in Buddy's office.

Edging by him, she slipped through the door. "I couldn't do it anymore," she said with her back to him. "I told you it was killing me. The commute alone makes me want to pluck myself bald, not to mention all the travel and being away from Joie all the time. I've told you a million times."

"Wait." His feet pounded after her, down the blue hallway full of their family photos. The frames flickered by like a silent movie: Joie and Beamer smiling on a roller-coaster. Joie seeming to fly through the air in her lacrosse uniform. Beamer pushing her on a green bicycle with training wheels. Joie posing with Beamer, every year since kindergarten and on her first day of school. Except for their wedding portrait, Parker wasn't in any of the shots. She had taken all of them. "We won't be able to pay our bills," he said.

Parker walked into their bedroom and moved to the far side of it. "That's ridiculous. Of course, we will."

"No, we won't, not living right outside D.C., we won't. The mortgage alone will crush us. What were you thinking? What about Joie's college fund? Are you having a nervous breakdown?"

She stared at him, shaking her head, mute. Her tongue felt numb, incapable of shaping words. *Not anymore, I'm not.* "I'm sorry, sweetheart," she said. "We've been going through the motions like robots for a long time now. You know that. I don't want to live like this anymore."

"Honey." He was hovering over her, hands outstretched.

Parker tossed a duffel bag onto the bed, shocked by what she was doing, not recognizing her hands as they moved through a drawer. *I want out, I want out, I want out.* The empty fruit bowl on their dresser smelled of citrus. She remembered the sticky fragrance on his fingers the first day she met Beamer, in high school. He had peeled an orange for her, nervously cradling the sections on a corner of his dusty bomber jacket. A single bead of sweat quivered in the wispy fuzz above his lip. His dimpled smile had been so unlike Buddy's face whenever he had a hangover and wiry veins sprouted like red chigger bugs under his skin. Behind them, Sid had been playing the banjo, boots thumping against the rickety steps to their classroom in a time and place that felt like it must have been on another planet.

Beamer's unshaven jaw, stubbly and elongated by the strain of his frown, began to pulsate on one side. "Think about what you're doing," he said. "Come on. You're just tired. You're depressed. We can make some changes."

Parker piled shoes, stockings, underwear, pants, and blouses into the duffel. Her suitcase was still parked in the foyer, unpacked, but it was full of dirty clothes. She wanted to start over.

Oh, Joie. Will you ever forgive me?

"Stop and think," Beamer said as Parker zipped the bag shut. "You're going to break your daughter's heart."

Picturing Joie's sweet, smooth face, Parker stopped. The bag's padded strap felt soft but unbearably heavy, slicing into her shoulder. The day her father left, Parker was thirteen. She had spent the whole day sitting motionless next to a bay window, waiting for him to reappear with his suitcase. He never did. "Not fair," she said.

Beamer took hold of her shoulders, panting. "Look, I love you." His eyes were saturated. "If I've made mistakes, I'm sorry. I'll try harder. We can go back to that counselor we saw the last time. Please don't do this to our family."

The pain choked her, wracked her shoulders, made her feel as though she was floating disconnected above the room, herself, the two of them. "I've made more mistakes than you," she said. "You don't know yet, but I've made a big mistake."

He sat on the side of their bed, shoulders curling while her heart broke, again and again in waves. "With Dylan."

"Yes." She didn't move. "Nothing really happened. He couldn't—we didn't, but we almost did. I'm burning with shame and I'm sorry, but I have to ask myself why I would have put myself in that position in the first place. It's because something was already broken here."

Beamer shook his head, back and forth. He whispered into his hands. "You know what? I don't care. I forgive you. As long as it's over and it never happens again. I don't want our family to break apart. What is it that you want from me? Whatever it is, I'll do it."

She sat beside him and thought about it, trying to slow her breathing. The spinning light groaned. "I want you to hear me. Listen when I tell you I'm over my limit."

Beamer reached for her hand. The corners of his eyes sagged. "I will. I get it. I love you."

"I don't want to live here anymore. I want a simpler life, for both of us, for Joie. I want to go home, back to Atlanta. This isn't where we belong."

He looked away, around the room, but he didn't let go of her hand. After a long pause, during which Parker held her breath, he said, "There's a lot of construction work down there. We would make a big profit, selling this place, even with what we owe on it. What would you do in Atlanta?"

Parker laughed. She couldn't stop her tears, or her grin. "Everything," she said. "Anything. Something with my hands. I'd volunteer with Trees Atlanta. I could reconnect with our old friends. I know plenty of people who would hire me to do freelance writing. Mostly, I wouldn't drive my car three hours back and forth to work every day."

"Good luck with that. Traffic's pretty awful in Atlanta, too, you know."

"I'd try to stay out of it. It would be a better life for Joie."

Beamer was smiling, back to his funny old guitar-playing, zipline-making self. "Where would we live, exactly?"

Parker stared at him and they said in unison, "Inman Park."

In her husband's embrace, she felt the breeze off the waterfall in Silver Park. She heard birdsongs under the cool shadow of the thickest oak tree she had ever seen, in Arden's side yard. She pictured the spot by the blue-green lake where her father had taken her for a picnic once, so many years before.

22.

JARED ASTOR

Jared was sweating through his undershirt. He was unprepared for the meeting.

Like a meerkat on high alert, his assistant Sarah had been standing on the second-floor landing of his gallery that morning, watching as he hiked up the steps to his office. Before he had even caught his breath, she thrust a slip of paper at him and whispered in his ear. He stared at the name, which she had underlined three times. "Mrs. Vera Van der Griff of VMS Designs would like to see you right away at her home." There was an address.

Thirty minutes later, Vera's wrought-iron gate breezed open for Jared's chauffeured sedan. He stepped onto polished brick pavers, clutching an Italian leather briefcase full of photographs—professional shots of his most prized acquisitions, still unsold. He was especially eager to show Vera a series of origami-like sculptures by an emerging Japanese-American artist. At the request of a particular New York City dealer, Jared had agreed to promote the work. Despite a series of showings, he had so far been unsuccessful in moving the pieces. He had tens of thousands of dollars tied up in them.

Enormous double doors, framed by two massive white columns, gave way before Jared reached them. A housekeeper, slender and delicately curved in a sky-blue uniform with a pleated skirt, stepped over the doorsill. Jared smiled as expansively as his nerves and his damp underarms would allow, tipping his head as she waved him into the cavernous foyer. She asked him to wait. As soon as she disappeared, he repositioned his feet on the glossy stone tiles, bracing himself. His face, reflected by the floor, looked tense and sweat-polished.

As she floated into the room, Vera was trailed by several yards of diaphanous lilac-colored fabric that fluttered from the waistband of her tight black trousers. She didn't exactly return his smile, but her smooth, pulled skin lifted slightly at either side of her mouth as she greeted him, murmuring her thanks. Her face gave off a bright light, the color of amber rum. Her neck was a darker brown, below her jaw where the makeup ended too abruptly. A heavy floral scent drifted toward him when she leaned forward, lowering her eyelashes. He mimicked a kiss, careful not to let his lips make actual contact with the gummy lacquer on her cheek.

"Oh, my dear, you're as lovely as ever," he said. "How have you been? I was thrilled to hear from you, and it's a wonderful coincidence because you were on my mind just the other day. I was at an exhibition for a brilliant new artist with a very different style, and I—"

"What sort of style?" Vera asked the question without waiting for an answer. Gesturing for him to follow, she walked down a wide hallway lined with photographs.

Jared hustled to catch up with her. Twice, he nearly became entangled in the gauzy fabric tails that flapped in her wake. "He's a charismatic young man, Japanese-American, moved here with his parents and studied at—"

"I've got no interest in Japanese-influenced work or European work or anything reflecting life in wealthy industrialized regions." She entered a small room lined with shelves crammed full of leather-bound books, framed botanical illustrations, and small figurines carved from pale green jade and brilliant blue lapis lazuli. *Chilean,* Jared thought. On the room's far side, a bay window overlooked her garden. Immediately, he spotted the pair of painted bronze *dikenga* figures Vera had purchased years earlier. Arden Collier's work. The figures were on display beside a pond stocked with orange and black-speckled koi fish. "I don't want to see work that makes me think of my own life. I want to be transported. The most interesting work, in my opinion, reflects life in places like Africa and South America."

Jared fingered the zipper on his briefcase, waiting as Vera arranged herself on a pink, crescent-shaped cushion by the window. "Last time we met, I recall being very impressed by the eclectic range of your collection and also your knowledge of each piece," he said, taking a seat after she had done so. "I remember that you particularly appreciated fine examples of sculpture. The artist I mentioned is experimenting with shapes that evoke both origami and the twists and turns his family's life took after they relocated to the United States. There's quite a bit of buzz about him at the moment. You might want to take a look simply in order to—"

"Yes, yes, I get it," she said, clearly attempting to scowl despite cosmetic injections that had left the upper third of her face nearly motionless. "This is someone you're promoting at the moment. I do understand how the business works, Mr. Astor. I'll be glad to take a look in a moment, but first I need your help with another matter."

He claimed a chair covered by a textured fabric that had been dyed orange, brown, and green. His stomach lurched; he mourned the digestion of his breakfast—English sausage on a buttered croissant with an excess of hot sauce and a side of roasted potatoes. Perhaps the housekeeper would appear soon with refreshments—say, a soothing cucumber sandwich on bread relieved of its crusts, or a splash of sparkling wine in a glass of freshly squeezed orange juice. As Vera waited for his reply, he felt out of kilter, unbalanced by her cryptic manner, or his ever-present hunger, or both. "Of course, I would do anything to be of service," he said. "That's what friends are for."

"Let's not kid ourselves." She said it without blinking. "This is business."

On the wall to her left, she had displayed a flowery, cross-stitched version of an African proverb: *If you want to go fast, go alone. If you want to go far, go together.* The kumbaya-style platitude caused him to stifle a sour belch. "I'm listening."

Vera glanced at a tangle of flower-studded vines in her garden, pointing with her chin at Arden Collier's bronze figures. "You remember the artist who created those pieces?"

He pictured Arden's gray braids and the way her sagging breasts had popped without warning through the malfunctioning blouse, in his office. "Why, yes, of course. I was delighted when you took an interest in those figures. Frankly, I was surprised when you declined to look at other work."

"You didn't want to show me more of Arden Collier's work. You kept trying to steer me away from it. I couldn't understand why. I know what I like and what I don't like. I found you presumptuous and annoying."

Like a punctured tire, a sudden surge of air burst involuntarily from

Jared's lungs. *Oh, you imperious witch,* he thought. Arden had begun to show signs of instability soon after her one and only major museum exhibit. He dropped her like the wrong end of a snake after she missed a series of deadlines, disrupting his entire exhibition calendar and leaving him on the hook. Shifting his weight, Jared eyeballed the briefcase, wondering whether he should go ahead and crack it open, to hell with Vera Van der Griff. He decided against it. He needed her money. "I didn't realize you felt that way," he said, measuring his words. "I'm very sorry to hear it. Perhaps we should start over. How can I help?"

Vera handed him a business card. "Call my friend Maura Levine."

"I know the name. Head of the historical society, I believe?"

"No." She prolonged the vowel in a sarcastic fashion. "That would be me. Maura stepped down last year, but she remains active, as my deputy."

"I see." Jared was feeling more confused by the second. Hunger had made him light-headed. Where was that housekeeper with a tray of tomato and basil crostini?

"We're fighting an ill-advised plan to build a high-rise in Silver Park. Maura read our statement at a county hearing yesterday. The hearing was unscheduled; it popped up rather suddenly. We had very little time to alert the news media, as we normally do. Fortunately, someone else seems to have contacted one of the local television stations. The news coverage was helpful."

"Silver Park."

"Correct. Arden Collier lives there." Vera inspected her fingernails, which were trimmed short and painted a glossy pink. "She spoke at great length and quite eloquently during the hearing about her family's struggles, leading up to her current situation. I found it deeply moving. Are you still in touch with her?"

Jared leaned back, feeling disoriented. "She came to see me this week, in fact."

Vera flashed her perfectly straight, white dental veneers. "Did she?"

"She wanted me to fund a new project she has in mind. She told me all about it."

"And you said—?"

An orange cat had slipped into the room. It rubbed one side of its body against Jared's pants, turned, and did it again. Long bits of fur clung to the dark fabric of his suit. He fought the urge to shove the creature away from his leg. "It didn't sound promising. She's been recycling the same material for at least a decade. Now she's talking about a project

178

based on memories of her family or something along those lines. I'm sure you understand why overly autobiographical art is usually disappointing."

Vera reached for the cat, which began to purr as soon as she rubbed its head. "What a patriarchal, condescending thing to say. Where do you think most artists find the emotional content for their work?"

Jared was regretting his decision to visit Vera Van der Griff. She seemed unhinged, and more importantly, she clearly was not interested in the work he needed to sell. He tried to picture the final few grains of his patience, tumbling through the glass timer in his head. Again and as always, he felt hungry. "Yes, obviously it all comes from someplace, but what she was describing to me sounded more like navel-gazing."

"You turned her away?"

"Not exactly. I gave her a deadline to produce three new pieces for my review."

"And when would that be?"

"Next Tuesday."

Vera snorted and lowered the cat gently to the floor. "You turned her away. You can't possibly give an artist a deadline like that and expect her to deliver anything well-formed."

"As I just told you, I gave her—"

"Stop." Like a traffic cop, Vera Van der Griff flashed a palm at him. Her tone made him think of the signaling horns on a cruise ship. "The details of your conversation with her don't really matter. This is what you're going to do for me now. You're going to get Arden Collier on the phone today and begin planning a major exhibition with her. Then you're going to call a few of your media friends to interview her. I'll be happy to offer commentary as well. The publicity will make it much more difficult for the county to seize her family's estate under eminent domain law. If the county can't commandeer her property, the developer won't be able to bring water and sewer lines to his site. That will prevent him from building a high-rise in Silver Park. The property on the other side of him is protected by historic designation."

Heat crept unpleasantly under Jared's skin, intensifying as it rocketed into his fingertips. The beds of his fingernails felt hot and bloated. He didn't have to take this. Who did she think she was? He hadn't seen a dime of her money in years. Why in the hell would Silver Park be his problem? It had nothing to do with his gallery, his business, or the art collection he had curated over many years. His hands were shaking as he reached for his briefcase. "I'll be leaving now."

"I'm ready to look at that sculpture," Vera said, sitting on the edge of her cushion, alert. "If I like it, I'll buy all of it. I'll even throw a party for the artist so that my friends and business contacts can meet him. I'll spare no expense."

Jared hesitated before hauling the briefcase slowly onto his lap, where he opened it without taking his eyes off her. He didn't trust Vera Van der Griff. He had worked with her type before. A newly rich woman who was probably bipolar or alcoholic or both. He didn't care, so long as she could sign her name to a check. "I don't understand. What changed your mind?"

"I want you to call her today," Vera said. "This is important to the historical society and to me personally. I'd like to hear from you after you've spoken with her."

"Arden Collier."

"Yes."

"Do I understand you correctly? *Quid pro quo?*"

"Those are my terms. Correct."

In Jared's mind, a five-digit number kept clicking higher and higher as he leafed through the plastic-encased photographs in his portfolio. By the time he found what he wanted to show her, the price tag had tripled and it had six digits instead of five. He slipped the first image from its translucent sleeve and handed it to her with his biggest smile. "I'll do it," he said.

"I have your word?" She placed the photo on the table without glancing at it.

"You do indeed. Yes, ma'am."

Vera closed her eyes, smiling as her hands fluttered to her throat. "Excellent. Please tell her, from me, that she's going to be okay now."

"I'll do that."

"Arden Collier's going to be huge—famous and fabulous. I'll see to that."

Her plan was fine with Jared Astor because he going to be richer than he had been when he first walked through Vera Van der Griff's door.

23.
PARKER GOZER

Parker's car purred to life the day after her Big Talk with Beamer and their decision to move back to Atlanta. A warm wind, tumbling through the open windows, lifted her hair, making her feel lighter as she moved closer to the sports field where she would be reunited with her daughter, at last. It had been a long night and day, an endless week, but it was over. She had missed Joie, who called early that morning, begging to stay with friends until the end-of-year party for her lacrosse team.

On her way to the game, the mostly empty, late-afternoon streets surprised Parker. She was soothed by the blank, wide-open flatness of the asphalt, the rhythmic thumping of her tires, and the knowledge that she would be with Joie soon.

She grabbed the team's dinner order from a pizza joint and kept rolling, nearly swooning from the smell of pies stacked in boxes on the back seat. She reached the school in eight more minutes—twelve ahead of the schedule Jolene had sent via email. Circling the red-brick school building, she cruised into the parking lot by the sports field, found a spot, and rolled to a stop.

The team wasn't there yet. A mother goose was picking her way across the sports turf. She waddled with brutal efficiency, as if she might be late for a conference call or a two-hour sale at the mall. A dozen gray fuzzballs ran to catch up with her, legs wind-milling, with the stumps of their unformed wings askew. Three other groups of geese stuck close to the mother and her babies. Farther off, Parker recognized another goose she had seen before—an injured female with a missing wing. She was pecking near the field's perimeter, alone. Coach Billie had waged a losing battle against the geese and their many curling piles of soft-served poop on the field. The geese scattered whenever the coach blew into her whistle, but they always returned just as quickly.

There was no sign of Howie's huge Econoline van or Jolene's SUV.

A lime-green Volkswagen beetle idled in one corner of the lot, near the concession stand where they would eat pizza and hand out awards to the players, after the game. A blue station wagon backed sideways across two spaces. A tan-colored Lexus circled the lot. These were the parents of Joie's teammates, parking in formation. Two girls—Number Fourteen's sisters—burst from the back seat of the Lexus. Their long, beaded braids flew behind them as they raced onto the field. Parker thought about Arden's braids and how they had whipped behind her when she ran through the woods near her house, as a kid. A sweet, pinching pain rippled through Parker's chest at the thought of moving home, closer to her old friend. In time, maybe she and Arden could patch up their friendship.

The geese jumped and fluttered, squawking. More than anything, Parker wanted to call Arden, to let her know they were moving back to Atlanta. She peered over the hood of her pollen-coated car at the narrow lane where Howie's van should appear at any moment, carrying Joie and her teammates. On the field, the mother goose raced after a stray baby, rounding her up. The injured goose lifted her head, flapping her single wing, and continued to peck the field.

Across the field, Parker made out the shape of a sedan as it came to a stop. She climbed out of her car and stepped onto the curb. The sedan's back door opened. A man's silhouette took shape, tiny in the distance, growing larger, headed her way. She wobbled, balancing on the lip of concrete that separated a thin patch of grass from the team's bus lane. The pointy toes of her shoes dangled over freshly tarred asphalt.

The shadow looked, for all the world, like Dylan, but it couldn't be Dylan—could it? Behind her eyes, the athletic field tipped sideways. Her stomach shrieked. Maybe he had run his location-tracker software to find her. She pictured him bragging, between tequila shots, about how he could find anyone, anywhere, anytime. *Nothing's private anymore. We're all completely exposed. Get used to it.* Dread coiled itself around her throat. She wished him no ill will, but she never wanted to see him again. Turning her head left and right, she searched the landscape for a place to run, to hide.

In her hand, the Tinley-issued smartphone vibrated. She would have to return the phone and her work laptop as soon as possible. Jolene's name flashed on the phone's screen. *"With Howie and the girls,"* the message said. *"Almost there. You've got some explaining to do!"*

Parker ignored the message and went back to squinting at the turf. She was at least a year overdue for an eye exam. Distant objects refused to pop into focus. The man's frame was looming larger, slowly moving toward her in blurry shades of cream and khaki. He was carrying—what? A box? No, it looked more like a satchel. Parker swallowed, gulping for air, eyes locked on the approaching figure.

A thought much worse than Dylan came to mind. What if Buddy had tracked her down? He owned guns. Parker knew that. He used to make a point of telling her about his love for them. She could almost see the man's face and the shape of his hair. But no, it wasn't Buddy's rust-colored hair, thank God.

She knew it made no sense, but whoever it was, now that he was within a few hundred yards of her, he was a dead ringer for Parker's father. Stepping off the curb, she began walking toward him in a straight line, yet without rushing because he was right there. *Her father.* He wasn't driving away from her, red brake lights glowing. He wasn't disappearing through a cotton field at sunrise. He wasn't retreating into sleep right after dinner. He hadn't died too soon. He was right there. Parker didn't have to run after him. He was with her and he had always been there, watching over her.

Joie would surely cry whenever Parker worked up the nerve to explain why they were leaving D.C. Joie would miss her friends terribly for a while. She would need to make new friends, play with a new lacrosse team, and go to a new school. Would she be damaged by the move? Parker knew it would be best for Joie in the long run, but the short-term consequences ripped at her heart. Her ribcage throbbed. As she moved toward the field, she was vaguely aware of cars passing behind her, a swirl of exhaust fumes, and children's laughter.

The blurry man on the field lifted his satchel. Once Parker was closer to him, it looked more like a musical instrument. A black bell. A banjo like the one her teacher Sid used to play. She was confused and squinting. He hoisted the object above his head. Without warning, the sky seemed to crack open from the sharp blast of an air gun.

The field erupted in a chorus of flapping wings. The mother bird briefly took flight, squawking, while her babies hopped and squeaked and scattered. Only the injured mother bird stayed put at the far end of the field. The air gun sounded again. Parker's hands flew to her ears. She closed her eyes, recoiling at the membrane-stabbing noise and the realization that she was watching a park employee in his ivory-colored uniform, scaring birds off the sports field.

Not Dylan.

Not Buddy.

Not her father.

Behind her, a car horn honked. Parker turned, wide-eyed, feeling foolish. The lack of sleep and travel and stress had caught up with her. Jolene waved to Parker from the open window of her SUV. Girls were climbing out of Howie's van like it was a clown car. Number Two, Number Ten, Number Sixteen—one after another—all of the girls were streaking toward the turf. The man with the air gun let loose another blast. The baby geese ran, heading in different directions. Parker moved toward the group of girls, not sure yet whether Joie was in the squealing pack, or still in the van.

As the girls ran, they turned into a mass of black shorts and bare, skinny arms, shifting one way and then the other, changing course in unison. In the distance, their soft, high-pitched exclamations blended together, reminding Parker of the whispered sounds of sleep, or near-sleep, the prayers we chant—*she's going to be okay, she's going to be okay*—the words left behind by memories stamped too deeply to be forgotten—*love, always*—even in dreams, or the throes of dementia, the final edges of life before death.

She remembered Sid's face in hospice, Wilma's milky eyes. Mr. John Collier's incessant smile. The weight of her father's hand in hers. Joie's voice, straight and pure, rang out, calling for Parker—ecstatic, fleeting. The girlish whispers and the movement of birds and people seemed to converge, culminating in one word, a single gesture: Joie lifting both hands like a pair of hearts with wings, shouting for her mother, over and over. Behind her, the lone bird ran with its still-strong wing aloft, broken, healed but flightless, moving forward.

24.

BUDDY CALDWELL

Inside the county government building, Buddy's brain buzzed with his most recent dose of pain medication, along with Ken's words: *"Fix it."* Buddy flipped through a mangled copy of *County Planner* magazine, scanned newspapers arranged in blue plastic bins, and checked the time again. At least the head of the planning committee had agreed to see him. He took that as a good sign. He was ready to show her why they needed to complete the Silver Park project. She had kept him waiting almost an hour, but nobody had asked him to leave yet. His back ached from sitting still too long.

The clerk summoned Buddy into Esther Fielding's office, finally. He shook her hand, took a seat, and thanked her three times for meeting with him. A broken overhead light, combined with the blinding effect of a ridiculously large desk lamp, cast a pattern of long shadows across the ragged burgundy carpet and the chipped veneer of her desk.

"That hearing was a train wreck," she said before he had finished picking his pants out of his crotch. "I don't like surprises, especially not with reporters in the room."

Reaching into his pocket, Buddy fingered the envelope Ken had given to him. "Yeah, the liberal news media can be kind of predictable. So much fake news nowadays."

Esther leaned back in her chair and crossed her eyes, mocking him. "What?"

"It's going to blow over," Buddy said. He leaned toward her, trying to smile. "This project's going to generate so much money for the county, you're going to be a hero once it's all said and done."

Out the window, where Esther was looking instead of listening to Buddy, the thin leaves of a willow oak shuddered against the onslaught of a hard rain—the kind that had converged mid-afternoon, rocket-fueled by the heat of an Atlanta summer. Her face, illuminated by the window, turned slowly back toward him, icy. "What is it that you want?"

He sat back, trying to look taller. "I want to talk about next steps."

Her eyes got big over a lop-sided smile. "Are you kidding me? You're project's dead in the water. There's lead contamination, for one thing. Lead contamination that you apparently knew about but didn't disclose, which made me look like a fool in that hearing. Also, the number of variances you've requested is prompting unwanted attention. It's never a good idea to mess around with the historical society. Game over."

He pictured Arden's smug, bloated face at the microphone and Parker at the back of the hearing room in her fancy, pretentious suit. A furious surge of blood started pin-balling around his brain. Why were chicks constantly getting in his way? He should've killed them both when he had the chance, drowned them like unwanted puppies when they were little. If he could go back in time, he would have left Atlanta years earlier. He could have moved out west to put as much distance as possible between himself and the Gozers, especially Parker. Now he couldn't afford to move anywhere. He was stuck. "It's lead from a moonshine still," he said. "It's going to be trace amounts, very easy to remediate—not a big deal. I don't have to tell you, there's actually some federal money to help with that kind of thing nowadays."

"Trace amounts or not," Esther said, picking at her cuticles as if Buddy weren't even in the room, "the public relations problem is huge. You've got the historic nature of the neighborhood and a long-time homeowner who has been paying her taxes and doesn't want to move. The commissioner's up for reelection, and he—"

"We can work on the public relations thing," Buddy said, waving one hand in the air. "What you said at the hearing was brilliant. You were exactly right. Why would anybody want to miss out on basic improvements like indoor plumbing? We would need for you to be vocal on this, but with your support—"

"My support?"

"Yes, your support would be essential."

"What do you mean?" She gripped the edge of her desk with both hands. "You think because I'm a woman of color, I'll be the poster child for your project? I resent that assumption, and frankly, I don't know why my research director was pushing this one at me so hard. I'm very disappointed in Vincent right now. He failed to mention quite a few things I should have known before that hearing."

Buddy was losing her. He could tell by the red wave rising up her neck, flushing her cheeks. He reached into his jacket and got a grip on Ken's envelope. "Vincent's a forward-thinking person. He has the county's best interests at heart, and I know you do, too."

She didn't move or say anything when he slid the envelope across the desk at her.

"Your investment in all this—the county's investment—is going to be considerable," he said, "and I'd like to offset that in some small way, to help prevent any burden on the administrative functions of your office."

Her hands moved with precision as she opened the envelope, looked inside, and handed it back to him. It all happened so fast, after that. Her words came out in a deadly, low rumble. "I don't ever want to see you again. This project file is closed. Your ordinance waivers are hereby rescinded. Get out of my office." Pressing a button on her phone, she summoned the clerk. "Chandler, please show Mr. Caldwell the door and get Vincent in here now."

Outside, Buddy lit one cigarette, then another. He drove as far north as his old car would take him on the small amount of gas he had left in the tank. Near a tiny airport where two-seater planes hummed over the runway, he pulled off the road. He vaguely recalled Parker being ten or eleven, rambling on and on at him about picking blackberries there once, before the field got all paved over. She was the original tree hugger, always whining about cigarette butts on the side of the road, turtles squashed by cars, and seabirds choked to death by plastic six-pack rings. He wondered why he was even thinking about her, as if he gave two shits about her.

His breath was coming hard and fast at the thought of having to call Ken with the news about Esther killing their project. As he thought through what he needed to say, and what Ken was likely to say in reply, Buddy realized he didn't need to make the call, after all. His partnership with Ken was over, either way. He could send the guy a letter and wait for Ken's lawyer to ask for money. Meanwhile, he figured Ken's competitor, Cedar Point Associates, would want to hear from him. They might not be able to revive the Silver Park deal with the county, but he was pretty sure they would be willing to give it a shot, with all their cash. They would definitely want to know what Buddy knew about Ken's business. Buddy propped one elbow on his open car window and he dialed the number.

25.
PARKER GOZER

The man on the other end of the phone line sounded so formally cordial, enunciating every vowel and consonant, Parker felt as though she might be listening to a phonograph record from the 1940s—a beautiful melody from an earlier time. Introducing himself as Philip Smith III, he explained his connection to Arden's grandfather, the Mount Zion Baptist Church of Silver Park, where both men had served as deacons for many years, and his status as a retired attorney at law. He had spoken with Arden about her situation. He was aware of the news coverage regarding her situation.

Parker had been packing boxes in her townhouse outside of D.C. when the phone rang. A call on the old landline phone usually meant telemarketers. Parker was eager to get her books packed for the Big Move. She walked to a window, where she could keep an eye on Joie, who was kicking a ball around the garden, and she said hello while exhaling loudly. After his lengthy introduction, Philip Smith III continued speaking in a measured way, thick with subordinating clauses, about an addendum to her Silver Park deed.

Parker reached for a pen and paper.

"Perhaps it's not my place to intercede," he said, "and please be assured that I fully respect your position, whatever that may be, but this has weighed on my mind, in case you may be unaware of the implications of Addendum Fourteen of your property deed."

"I understand," Parker said, although she didn't have a clue what he meant. She wrote down, *Addendum?*

"Ultimately, I concluded it was my duty to inform you of Addendum Fourteen, given that I'm now the only living party to the circumstances that resulted in Silver Park's protected status."

Outside, Joie ran at the ball and kicked it as hard as she could against the side of the house. *Whomp.* Her feelings about the Big Move had been mixed, to say the least. She didn't want to leave her best friend—there were tears—but she was excited about living near the silvery waterfall and the blue-green lake surrounded by curling honeysuckle vines she liked to nibble, for their sweetness. Parker had promised Joie she could invite D.C. friends to visit Atlanta, anytime, and they could go shopping at Lenox Square mall. "Pardon me, sir," Parker said. "Are you calling on Arden's behalf? Is she suing me or something?"

"No, no, nothing of that nature," Philip Smith III said. "I didn't feel compelled to tell Arden that I would be calling you. The poor girl has had enough on her mind lately. As I said, I simply felt that you should have all the facts before you. Very few people read every word of a detailed legal document. I've personally seen the documents associated with Silver Park—John Collier sought my advice before signing them— and I must say, they are uniquely opaque."

Whomp. Again, the ball hit the house. Parker rapped on the window and she shook her head, mouthing, "Stop." Joie pitched the ball into the hosta plants. "You're right about that," Parker said. "My Dad's lawyer explained everything to me, but that was three days after the funeral. All I understood was that I can't develop it or sell it or give the property away. There's a trust fund that can't be used for anything other than upkeep of the property."

Smith let out a sigh. "Yes, but shortly before John died, he grew worried about the permanency of the encumbrances on the property. He spoke with your father. A fourteenth addendum was written and fully executed. I was a witness to the signing. I managed to find a copy of the document in my archives. I don't know why I kept it. I served only as John's witness, not as his lawyer, but it seemed important at the time."

Parker held her breath. "What does the addendum say?"

After a discreet flushing of his throat, Smith began to read. "Whereas Mr. Foster Gozer, having purchased outright from Mr. John Roberts Collier the real property known as Silver Park, and having established said parcel as a protected, public-access wildnerness, for all intents and purposes, now wishes to stipulate, through this amendment, special circumstances under which ownership and rights may be returned to descendants of Mr. Collier."

Turning away from the window, Parker sat down. "There's a

loophole."

"That would be the lay-language term for it, yes."

Thank you, Dad, she thought.

Her pen hovered over the paper. "What are the special circumstances?"

"The language specifies economic hardship as a primary condition. If a descendant faces true economic hardship, the deed can be transferred to that individual."

Parker shook her head, confused. "Arden definitely has an economic hardship. Why didn't I know about this before?"

"In the event that the property is transferred to descendants," Smith continued, "all protections on the property would become null and void."

"Arden could have her family's land back," Parker said. She was speaking so loudly, Beamer poked his head in the door, looking worried. Parker waved him off. "She could sell five acres, pay off her debts, and fix up her house without hurting the park. That would make things easier on her, and the park would still exist. There's plenty of land there."

"There's one more stipulation."

"What is it?"

"The property owner must agree to the transfer. Even if descendants are experiencing hardship, the land will remain under your ownership until such time that you choose to dispose of it under the terms of Addendum Fourteen. The law cannot compel you to implement Amendment Fourteen unless it is your desire to do so."

Briefly, Parker envisioned a gas station, greasy asphalt, and a convenience store by the waterfall. She pictured candy wrappers and cigarette butts in the lake and the forest stripped of its trees—but no, Arden would never let that happen. She loved her grandfather's estate. She would be a good caretaker of his legacy.

"Yes," Parker said, jumping to her feet. "Silver Park doesn't rightfully belong to me. It never did. It belongs to the Collier family, to Arden. I want to turn the deed over to her under the economic hardship clause as soon as possible. How can we make that happen? Who do I need to call? Where do I sign?"

His instructions came at her in a blur, but she did her best to write them all down, word for word. He gave her a name, a phone number, a time, and a place. She thanked him and sat in stunned silence, breathing hard and periodically laughing out loud.

"Are you okay?" Her husband, wearing black jeans and a T shirt, was leaning against the door frame, looking both amused and concerned. "You're not cracking up or anything like that, are you?"

"I can give Arden her property back. There's a loophole."

"So I heard." Smiling, he crossed his arms, which caused his biceps to bulge. While he waited for new construction jobs to happen, Beamer had been killing time by lifting weights on their back deck for hours at a time. Under his shirtsleeve, Parker spied a translucent nicotine patch—part of his strategy to stop sneaking cigarettes. "You were talking kind of loud. Pretty sure the neighbors heard you."

"Oh, sorry." Parker smoothed her hair, hoping she didn't look like a crazy person. "Isn't it wonderful? I can finally make things right with Arden."

"Absolutely." Beamer massaged his arm muscles as he spoke. Parker had a sneaking suspicion he was showing off for her benefit. She loved him for it. "Kind of sad if the park goes away, but it's been a lot of stress for you, keeping up with that place. It's not like we get anything out of it."

He stretched his back so that his shirt rode up, briefly, exposing his flat stomach. Yes, he was deliberately putting on a show, clearly attempting to drive her insane. "Where's Joie?"

"She was feeling kind of sad, so I sent her over to Jolene's house, to play with Anne Marie." He placed his hands on his waist and flexed his pectoral muscles—left, right, and left again. Parker stifled a laugh. "Hope that was okay, honey."

"For sure, it was a good call," Parker mumbled without taking her eyes off his torso. "She's worried about missing her little bestie, but I'm going to make sure they have plenty of visits together after we move."

"*Winter, spring, summer or fall,*" Beamer crooned, doing his best rendition of James Taylor singing about steadfast friends, "*hey now, all you've got to do is call.*"

As always, his lovely, deep voice turned her into an overheated bowl of Jello salad. In the doorway, Beamer was grinning, victorious, well aware of his effect on her. Parker raised her arm and pretended to inspect an imaginary wristwatch. "Oh, look at that," she said. "Did you know it's time for Sadie Hawkins Day?"

He rubbed his palms up and down his puffed-out chest. "Is that the day when all the girls get to chase after the boys they like?"

"Yep."

Beamer opened his arms. "Baby, you don't have to chase me. I want you."

"I noticed."

"Do you want to chase me anyway?"

Parker smiled, meaning yes.

"Ready," he said, "set, and—go!"

Laughing, he turned and ran in super slow motion down the hallway, toward their bedroom. He was singing the theme song from "Chariots of Fire," the movie about Olympic runners in the 1920s. Parker walked behind him, enjoying the view. Their waterbed quaked when he fell on it and opened his arms. His kiss transported her to the forests of their childhood, full of promise, new growth, and adventure.

26.
ARDEN COLLIER

As she pulled the truck alongside her house, Arden pictured the two boxes, waiting for her in the hallway, where she had left them. She had spent the day carting six loads of old clothes to the dump. Her house remained stuffed with at least fifty times that much junk, but at least she had managed to clear enough room for Jared to sit down during his next visit. Already, he had stopped by three times after telling her about Vera Van der Griff's amazing offer. The news had caused Arden to choke on one of the dainty, fruit-filled pastries he had mailed to her house before calling with the good news.

Inside her house, the kitchen sink was finally empty, although it didn't look that way to Arden; it looked ready for her to fill a teapot under the faucet, rinse spinach, or mix plaster for the next piece she wanted to cast for her new series, *Her Hands Had Wings.* Jared had taken to calling the show, "Triple-H-W," for short. Her show had its own acronym. She liked that. A stream of water sputtered brown at first, turning clear and sweet and warm, rushing through her fingers. Her hands were dusty from stuffing plastic trash bags full of clothes all morning. Enjoying the warmth, she let the water roll over her skin. She slipped a bar of soap between her palms until they were white with a flowery lather. With a yellow towel, she dried her hands.

She wasn't eager for what would come next.

It's time, she thought. *Time to take back what's mine.*

The boxes, frayed at the corners, had been shedding bits of cardboard for at least a year, and when she lifted them, two gleaming rectangles appeared on the floor like a pair of crime-scene silhouettes. She pushed her hands through the perforated handles on each box and half-dragged, half-carried them down the hallway, through the kitchen, onto the back deck. Thick plastic windows offered a blurry glimpse of what was inside each box: Her embalmed wedding dress and Joel's faded black tuxedo, complete with his red bow-tie and cummerbund. Her plan was to drive the boxes out to her favorite thrift store in Chamblee. She was sure they would find a good home with some young couple who couldn't afford brand new wedding clothes from a boutique.

As she wiped the dust off the boxes, she remembered Joel's face, tinted pink, gold, and blue from the light streaming through a stained-glass window at the front of the church where they were married. She could barely breathe inside the dress, which had a tight satin bodice covered with hundreds of white beads. The train had dragged heavily behind her, yet she felt almost weightless, as though they were flying together, defying gravity, pessimism, and death by being there, in that moment.

Arden's hips hurt. She sat down on the porch step and put one hand over her face. All the dollar-store toys, three-for-one skirts, and collectible pottery hadn't moved into the house overnight. Arden had brought in each piece like individual grains of sand, as Joel had spent longer and longer afternoons and evenings at the school. Finally, he had stopped coming home altogether, and Arden knew, without asking him. She had seen him with the pretty science teacher, the one who wore pearls and navy-blue skirts that were always clean and pressed. She was the kind of wife Joel needed, not a heavy-footed, paint-covered woman constantly moving through a dark cloud of fear and bad habits. Arden didn't fight it. She let him go, asking for nothing.

Tires crackled over gravel, out front, and by the time Arden had stepped around the side of the house to see whether it might be Jared paying her another visit, Jackson Bennett was already out of his truck, flexing his knees—kicking them out, one at a time. Even before he saw her, he was smiling, swiveling his gray head all around to look at the trees, her house, and his pointy boots, which were shined to a high gloss, the color of maple syrup. He was wearing a pale blue dress shirt, which he had left open at the neck, a pair of neatly pressed blue jeans, and a belt braided together from three strips of leather in different colors: Lavender, turquoise, and amber.

Arden's chest fluttered. Her hands flew to her face. She shoved a wild strand of hair behind her ears, licked her lips, and rubbed her cheeks to bring some color into them.

"There you are," he said when he was standing close enough for her to smell his laundry detergent. He didn't seem shy about having his big, smiling teeth right up in her face. "I hope you don't mind me stopping by like this, unannounced. Ha ha haah."

Arden smiled and ducked her chin, resisting the urge to step away from him. "I'm glad to see you, I guess, unless your brother's going to give me another summons."

His cheeks turned a darker shade of red, and she was sorry she mentioned the sad business that had brought them back together, after so many years. She knew William Bennett had only been doing his job. "I wish he didn't have to do that to you." Looking down, Jackson shifted his weight. "But my visit's got nothing to do with all that. I came on personal business this time."

She waited a beat for him to explain what he meant. When the silence expanded between them, she said, "Thank you again for your help with my old truck. I've been driving all over the place now. I feel like I've been set free."

He inhaled deeply. "Ha ha haah. It makes me happy to hear you say that."

"I even went on I-285 the other day, just to say I'd done it."

"I wondered if you might go out with me." He blurted it out so quickly, Arden's smile wobbled uncertainly around her teeth for a second. "Maybe we could get dinner or see a movie. We could do both. I like art, too. I'd be glad to go to a show, or just take a walk, whatever you want to do. You could tell me."

Arden put one hand on her chest and laughed until he did, too. It didn't take long. "Yes."

"Ha ha haah. Really?"

"Why not? My aunt's not here to stop us. Come and get me Saturday night about six. We'll figure out a plan together. See what kind of trouble we can get into."

She let him give her a brief, chaste hug. Clapping his hands together, he nodded and jumped back into his truck. Arden watched him go. She waited for the dust cloud behind his truck to fall onto the road. Finally, she turned and walked slowly back to the job she had left unfinished on her back porch.

Her hands felt dry from too much washing. A trace of blood

appeared on her cracked knuckles when she sat down and flexed her fingers. She rubbed the spot, holding her hands together, and closed her eyes, breathing. The idea came to her fully formed. She didn't have time to think as she tore the tape off both boxes, unfolded the flaps, and tugged the starched fabric from their plastic inner casings. She was on her knees, ripping her wedding dress into thin, white strips, but the bodice wouldn't pull apart in her hands. She finished deconstructing the skirt and the sleeves. She ran to the kitchen for scissors, to finish the job.

When her wedding dress was lying in a heap of fabric remnants, she started on Joel's tuxedo, too, and she began braiding the strips together—two white pieces intertwined with a single black or red one, back and forth, over and over. The sketchpad, beside her now, was filled with all her ideas for sculptures.

That morning, she had added a new one—a centerpiece to everything she had been designing for a week. Something had been missing, though. The central figure, a woman, sat amid the wings Arden had been constructing from casts of her own hands. Scratching the charcoal pencil against the paper, she added streamers of fabric. They radiated from the crown of the figure's head and all around her face, safe-keepers of her memories, love, and hope.

ACKNOWLEDGMENTS

I walked this path for some years before it turned green. Many teachers offered encouragement, instruction, and feedback. Those close to my heart have included Lauren Groff, Fred Leebron, Barbara Jones, and Michael Kobre of the Queens University of Charlotte M.F.A. program. I'm also deeply grateful to my teachers Connie May Fowler and Laura van den Berg.

Many friends read early drafts without defriending me, or offered insights to the publishing process, especially Atlanta author Jessica Handler as well as Kim Sheeter, Mickey Dubrow, Liza Nash Taylor, Dr. Heidi Moore, Brad Windhauser, Michaela Jarvis, Carol Longacre, Gerry Landers, Mary Manley, and Bethea Dowling. To Carrie, Katie, Maggie, Jonathan, Dad and Darsa, Teresa and kiddos, Bart, Melinda, Mary Lou, Linda, and everyone else in my family—thank you for supporting me. I remain indebted to the late Caroline I. Roberts, my mother, for applauding all of my writing efforts—the good, the bad, and the ugly.

Although this fictional work explores broad issues related to absent fathers and the impact this loss can have over generations, I must emphasize that my real-life Dad has always been there for me, without fail, and I love him dearly.

Similarly, I have been lucky enough to work with long-term supervisors who became my friends and mentors. The fictitious boss in this novel needed to have a key (annoying) character flaw in order to drive the plot forward. No one should confuse him with my exceptionally kind real-life supervisors over the years.

Gratitude always to Anne Botteri, Alan Leshner, the late Steve Sigur, the entire Paideia School crew (too many dear ones to name), and my friends with AAAS.

To my neighbors and the wonderful staff in Atlanta's 870 Inman building as well as the Ponce Harbour, Southpoint, and Eastwind communities of Ponce Inlet, and to my colleagues at Embry-Riddle Aeronautical University—thanks for the warm welcome.

Michele Amato, my love, offered unwavering support and opportunities for laughter.

My daughter Caroline, light of my life, called me brave. That meant the world.

NOTE FROM THE AUTHOR

Word-of-mouth is crucial for any author to succeed. If you enjoyed the book, please leave a review online—anywhere you are able. Even if it's just a sentence or two. It would make all the difference and would be very much appreciated.

Thanks!
Ginger

ABOUT THE AUTHOR

Ginger Pinholster earned her M.F.A. from Queens University of Charlotte, studying with Lauren Groff and Fred Leebron. At Eckerd College, her teachers included Florida's Poet Laureate Peter Meinke. Her work has appeared in *The Northern Virginia Review, Eckerd Review, Atticus Review, Blackheart Magazine, Crab Fat Magazine, Gravel,* and *Dying Dahlia Review,* and in the book *Boomtown: Explosive Writing from Ten Years of the Queens University of Charlotte MFA Program.* Raised in Atlanta, Georgia, Ginger now works in Daytona Beach, Florida. She also volunteers with the Volusia-Flagler Turtle Patrol.

Thank you so much for reading one of our **Women's Fiction** novels.

If you enjoyed the experience, please check out our recommended title for your next great read!

The Apple of My Eye by Mary Ellen Bramwell

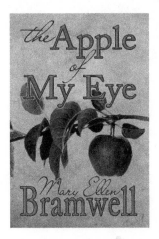

"A mature love story with an intense plot. This book has something important to say." -William O. Shakespeare, Professor of English, Brigham Young University

CPSIA information can be obtained
at www.ICGtesting.com
Printed in the USA
LVHW040122080520
655210LV00004B/1069

9 781684 333189